LONE STAR JUSTICE

LONE STAR JUSTICE

Wayne M. Hoy

AuthorHouse™ LLC
1663 Liberty Drive
Bloomington, IN 47403
www.authorhouse.com
Phone: 1-800-839-8640

© 2014 Wayne M. Hoy. All rights reserved.

No part of this book may be reproduced, stored in a retrieval system, or transmitted by any means without the written permission of the author.

Published by AuthorHouse 03/10/2014

ISBN: 978-1-4918-7211-6 (sc)
ISBN: 978-1-4918-7192-8 (hc)
ISBN: 978-1-4918-7195-9 (e)

Library of Congress Control Number: 2014904591

Any people depicted in stock imagery provided by Thinkstock are models, and such images are being used for illustrative purposes only.
Certain stock imagery © Thinkstock.

This book is printed on acid-free paper.

Because of the dynamic nature of the Internet, any web addresses or links contained in this book may have changed since publication and may no longer be valid. The views expressed in this work are solely those of the author and do not necessarily reflect the views of the publisher, and the publisher hereby disclaims any responsibility for them.

To my son-in-law, Mike, who kept after me to write a western…well Mike, here it is.

★

CHAPTER ONE

Hannah Lea Gibson knew she should have waited for Ted Stoes to assist her from the buckboard instead of acting like she was out on roundup wearing overalls and boots and not attired in a low-necked sleeveless evening gown. But she hadn't and now as she looked down at the long ragged rip in the skirt of her new gown, readily visible in the glare of lamplight through the open door, she cursed under her breath. She couldn't go into the dance like this; her stocking-clad leg exposed all the way to her rose-bud ornamented garter midway up her right thigh. There was nothing for it, she'd have to return home and change to another gown. The dance would be half over by the time they got back, and she had been waiting for this evening for weeks. Why was she forever doing foolish things? And how many times had her uncle cautioned her to think before she flew madly into something? She emitted another curse, this time a little louder not caring who might hear.

"What's wrong?" Stoes asked advancing from around the rear of the buckboard.

"This!" she heatedly exclaimed impulsively twisting her hips toward him. His eyes sped to the expanse of shapely stocking-clad leg revealed through the large gap in the material.

"Whew-ee," Stoes whistled staring.

She'd known Ted Stoes since they were kids. His mother, Anita was her uncle's housekeeper, so she hadn't given it a thought showing him her ripped skirt, but the heated look in his eyes that was altogether new, brought a fiery blush to her cheeks. She quickly turned her back as she gathered the torn edges of her skirt together.

"How'd yu do that?" he said breath uneven.

"Getting out of this stupid buckboard," she replied stiltedly. "We have to go back home so I can change."

Without a word he held out his hand and taking hold of it she placed one slippered foot on the hub and swishing her skirt out of the way of the wheel settled in the seat staring straight ahead chin in the air. Not a word was said as the buggy bounced along on the darkened road her hand holding the ripped edges of her skirt together. Arriving at the ranch Stoes drew the horses up before the porch and quickly jumped to the ground. Hannah waited for him to assist her this time.

"I won't be long. Do you want to come in?"

"Nix. I'll stay with the team," he replied.

Without another word Hannah hurried up the porch steps and into the house. Hastening down the hall to her bedroom she became aware of loud voices coming from her uncle's office. The door was closed, but she recognized her Cousin Edward's voice. She halted in the hallway her stomach churning as it always did when the two argued. How cruel and nasty Edward's tongue could be if he didn't get his way. She crept closer to the door debating if she should go in. Perhaps she could placate Edward, so he wouldn't say such spiteful and hurtful things to his father, but she dreaded facing Edward and his obnoxious tongue. She tried to listen. She suspected it was about money to make good his gambling debts. It never changed. She didn't want to hear more. Biting her lower lip she continued on to her room. At her bedroom door she paused glancing at the closed door at the far end of the hall. She could use Anita's help changing. She half turned in that direction before she remembered that her uncle's housekeeper had gone to stay the night in town with her sister. Well, she would just have to change to another gown by herself. Hopefully nothing needed ironing. She lit the lamp on her bedside table and quickly wiggled out of her torn gown and tossed the ruined garment on the bed. Opening her closet she stood for a moment staring. Then with a sigh she began rummaging through the collection of dresses finally selecting one from last season. She held it out running an appraising eye over the garment before shrugging her approval. It would have to do. Moments later she was hurrying down the hall. She halted before her uncle's office listening for a moment but there was no sound from within. The door was slightly ajar. She knocked softly on the door as she pushed it inward.

Her uncle sat at his desk gazing at something before him. She slowly crossed the room toward him. When she was only feet away she softly called his name. He looked up an almost vacant look in his eyes as though his mind was miles away. She was struck suddenly by how old he looked. Had he always looked that way and she just hadn't noticed; had been too occupied with herself. She blinked seeing him in her mind's eye as she had known him when she had first came to the ranch as a six year old; pioneer and rancher, huge of frame and broad of face, hard and scarred and grizzled, with big eyes of blue fire. A powerful man, afraid of nothing or anyone.

"Is something wrong?" she asked.

He stared his eyes focusing on her.

"Oh, it's yu, child. I thought yu was at the dance," he said after a moment's hesitation.

"Clumsy me," she sighed rolling her eyes skyward. "I tore my dress and had to come home to change. Ted's waiting out front for me. I better run."

"Ah-huh," he nodded, keen deep blue eyes searching her face. "Hannah child, are yu sweet on Ted?"

"Uncle Bob! Gracious no!" she chortled in genuine denial.

"Wal, I reckon I'm glad," he said.

She glanced down at his desk curious as to what had held his attention so deeply. He noticed her look and slowly closed the small blue leather-bound book lying open before him. She hadn't recalled seeing it before.

"You don't have to worry, Uncle Bob, I'm not going to leave you anytime soon," she replied with a dazzling smile. She longed above all things to be good, loyal, loving, helpful, to show her gratitude for the home and the affection that had been bestowed upon a penniless orphan. She stepped around the desk to give him a quick peck on his cheek.

His eyes lit up his weathered face. "I reckon that's shore comfortin'," he said. For a moment his bright blue eyes searched hers. "Wal, I reckon yu ought te get a move on. Yu go an' have a good time."

"All right, Uncle Bob," she replied squeezing his hand. At the door she paused and peered back at him. "Don't wait up for me," she said and hurried out into the hall and down the porch steps to where Ted Stoes waited beside the buckboard.

Ted handed her up and then climbed in himself. Slapping the reins they started off. Hannah leaned back on the seat hands in her lap and closed her eyes unable to get her uncle's words out of her mind. Damn her cousin Ed for causing her uncle such worry. An instant later they flew open as Ted's hand closed over hers. She flashed him a questioning look but made no attempt to pull away as she considered his action. In all the time she had known him she never entertained the slightest romantic notion toward him. Oh, she wasn't blind to the way he had begun looking at her lately, and he hadn't been the only one. Few voiced their thoughts; however, for it was just as common to find her in overalls and boots as it was in dresses, perhaps even more so.

Hannah looked askance at him to find him staring boldly at her. She was suddenly conscious of an unfamiliar sense of uncertainty seeing him differently from any other time in the years they had known each other. He had been ten and she six when she had come to live with her uncle following the death of her parents. She had to admit he had matured into a handsome young man; tall, slim, round-limbed, with the small hips of a rider, and square, though not broad shoulders. But they had not always gotten along. In fact they fought as much as they played together in those early years. It was actually funny she thought how they used to fight like cat and dog. She suddenly remembered the time he pushed her into the old mud-hole, and how she had laid in wait for him behind the house and hit him with a rotten cabbage. But somehow in the last few years they seemed to have grown out of that remaining cautiously sociable toward each other. She wished it would have been the same with her cousin. Edward had always been mean and selfish, and had never changed. She avoided him as much as possible.

Suddenly Stoes reined the buckboard in among a stand of cottonwoods.

"What are you doing?" she demanded as he quickly wrapped the reins around the brake handle and turned toward her.

"Hannah, I've fallen in love with yu." he declared, hotly.

"Oh, you couldn't have!" she cried, incredulously.

"Don't yu know I always was moony over you—when we were kids," he said. "And now—gosh, you've grown up—so pretty and sweet—such a—a healthy, blooming girl . . . ."

Hannah stared at him remembering how, as a boy, he had always taken a quick, passionate longing for things he must and would have. Suddenly he lunged for her, mouth seeking hers. And before she could react she found herself flat upon her back upon the seat, his weight upon her. She managed to twist her head to the side avoiding his kiss.

"Are you mad?!" she screamed. "Get off me!"

"Hannah, I'm off my head over yu," he panted raring back to stare down at her.

Gritting her teeth and taking a deep breath she swung a roundhouse right smacking him a solid blow on his jaw with her closed fist. His head jerked back, and he uttered a curse, but the blow seemed to sober him and he slowly straightened. Hannah sat up scooting to the far side of the seat.

"If you ever try that again Ted Stoes I'll—I'll—shoot your leg off!" she panted eyes blue shards.

He drew himself up. In the dark she couldn't make out his features clearly but knew his jaw was clinched. Silently he unwound the reins and slapped the team into motion. Neither spoke. Arriving at the dance Ted silently helped her down. She made her way into the dance without waiting for him.

Refusing to allow the incident to put a damper on the rest of the evening, Hannah danced every dance. To her relief she saw little of Ted the remainder of the night. Later as she danced a waltz with Sunset Smith one of her uncle's riders she spied Ted talking earnestly to another cowboy. They stood by the wall back away from the crowd. The cowboy was a stranger to her. He was quite handsome; tall with a clean square-cut chin and sun-bronzed face and the slim hips of a rider. He was hatless, his hair almost reddish in the candlelight. She wondered who he was and if he would ask her to dance. She hoped he would.

Like most cowboys, Sunset took his dancing serious, doing little talking, concentrating on his steps anxious, she supposed, of not squashing her thinly slippered toes with his booted feet. Hannah searched for the stranger as they whirled past the next turn around the dance floor, but both he and Ted Stoes had disappeared. She never saw either of them again that night.

She got a ride home with Bud Jackson, one of Eula Mae's cowboys. It must have been close to three in the morning when she reached the ranch house, nearly exhausted but having thoroughly enjoyed herself despite the troubling incident with Ted Stoes. Opening the front door she stepped into the hall. She glanced at her uncle's office and noticed a glimmer of light from under the door. He must have waited up for her. Suddenly the unease she had felt at his odd comments earlier returned, and she was sorry she had not stayed to question him. But she had been anxious to return to the dance, and then there had been Ted's unsettling declarations that she definitely wished to forget. She decided to go tell her uncle she was home.

There was no answer to her knock. She opened the door and stepped into the room. It was late he might have fallen asleep at his desk she thought smiling to herself. But he was not at his desk. She walked farther into the room and that's when she saw him lying on the floor his feet and ankles protruding from behind his desk. She rushed to his side, and saw the blood . . . and the gun, lying near his right hand.

"Uncle Bob!" she gasped trembling hand pressed over his heart. "Oh God!" she cried knowing he was dead.

She suddenly had an eerie feeling that she wasn't alone; that she was being watched. She tossed a frantic glance around the room eyes searching the dark shadows where the light from the lamp on her uncle's desk failed to reach. As she did so she reached and picked up her uncle's gun. Her gaze happened upon the door to the large safe where her uncle kept cash and his important papers. It was standing wide open. Slowly the significance dawned upon her. Her gaze flitted back to the shadows in the far corner of the room, eyes narrowing trying to pierce the gloom. For a terrifying instant she thought she could make out the dark outline of a head and shoulders—! The sound of footsteps in the hall abruptly seized her attention.

"What the hell?!" she heard someone exclaim and whirling about she stared up into the face of her cousin Edward. Behind him stood his drinking and gambling partner, George Gans.

"Edward," she gasped.

For an instant Edward seemed stunned as his eyes flitted from her to his father's body, then his gaze darkened.

"Murderer!" he shouted catching her wrist in an iron grip. He twisted the gun from her hand. She thought he was going to strike her with it.

"Edward, I didn't—" she sobbed.

"Shut up! Just shut up!" he screamed.

Shocked speechless she knelt there, mouth agape feeling suddenly more dead than alive.

"What're you goin' to do with her?" Gans demanded.

"Lock her in the storeroom," Edward ordered, "Keep her there while I go for the sheriff."

Hannah made no resistance as George Gans jerked her to her feet. Twisting an arm behind her back he propelled her out into the hall. He shoved her before him into the kitchen. There was no light in the room only that from the moon slanted through the window. The door to the storeroom—more like a pantry—was to the side of the large cooking range. Still holding her arm he jerked the door open and shoved her inside and slammed the door. She staggered, bumping hard against a shelf. It was pitch black inside the small room. She heard the key turn in the lock then the only sound was the loud thump of her heart and her sobbing-panting breath.

Hannah placed both hands on the door and pressed her head upon the hard wood heart racing, feeling cold all over. She could think of only one thing. No one would believe her innocent . . . she would be sent to prison . . . Oh, God, maybe even executed! Hanged! A long ago memory flashed before her eyes. She must have been ten at the time. Her uncle had told her to stay put in camp, but she had disobeyed. She had followed the men . . . and saw him! A man swinging by his neck at the end of a lariat rope from a tall cottonwood. He was kicking in a horribly grotesque manner. She had fled back to camp sick at her stomach the sight forever etched in her mind. She had never told her uncle what she had seen and he never talked about the incident, but she had instinctively known the man was a rustler. Panic welled in her now as she saw again the man's distorted face, eyes distended, mouth wide, tongue out—and her only thought was that she must escape, get away before Edward returned with the sheriff. If she could just reach her own room she could change out of her dress into her old riding outfit. Once she reached the stables . . . but it was hopeless, the door was locked.

Perhaps not so hopeless, she thought suddenly, finding her mind at once surprisingly lucid. The lock was typical of all the others in the house. It used a standard skeleton key which could be inserted into the lock from either side of the door. She ran her hand down the door locating the keyhole. If only George had left the key in the lock . . . She uttered a silent prayer as she felt around on one of the shelves until her hand came in contact with a cardboard box. She pulled it off the shelf and quickly removed the items inside. She tore the box down one seam, flattening it out. She stooped and slid the cardboard under the door leaving a handhold on her side. Then reaching up she pulled out a long hairpin, one of several holding her golden curls in place. Feeling in the dark she pushed the hairpin into the keyhole. It collided with the key still in the lock! She breathed a relieved sigh. She carefully pushed sensing the key move. Just a little more . . . She exhaled a pent-up breath upon hearing the soft clink as the key slipped from the lock and fell upon the piece of cardboard. Bending she slowly drew the cardboard back to her side of the door. She moved her fingers over the cardboard until they came in contact with the key. A moment later she heard the lock click as she turned the key and she slowly pushed open the door.

She crossed the moon-lit floor on tip-toes. Reaching the backdoor she let herself out. The moon was low on the horizon; dawn would be upon her soon. She didn't dare attempt to reach her room through the house for fear of running into George. She knew the area around the side of the house like the back of her hand and wasted no time reaching her bedroom window. There she halted. She had to get into her room in order to change out of her gown into overalls and boots. But she would have to climb through the window in her long dress; not an easy task. In fact it appeared hopeless. She needed something to stand on. Her only recourse was to go back to the kitchen and get Anita's step-stool. Holding her skirt up she hurried back the way she had come. She didn't know how long she had been in the storeroom fiddling with the key but it must have been some minutes. Edward couldn't possibly return with the sheriff though for at least an hour or more. She still had time. If only Gans didn't come to check on her. Once inside the kitchen it took only a moment to find the step-stool and return to her bedroom window. The window slid open easily and hiking her skirt up above her knees, she stepped up on the stool pulled and wiggled herself over the sill. She collapsed awkwardly onto the floor her skirts tangled about her legs. She struggled to her feet and quickly set about stripping off her dress. She didn't light a lamp but felt about in the dark finding her clothes aided by the moon's light. Hurriedly she donned her calf-length drawers, which she had shunned to wear under her gown, and pulled on her overalls. She slipped a shirt on over her camisole and buttoned it to the neck, then pulled on her boots. Grabbing two of her day dresses off the rack in her closet, not caring which ones they were, she crammed them in her little valise. She stuffed another pair of overalls and a shirt in the valise along with undergarments, stockings, a pair of shoes and her small walnut toiletry box, a comb and small hand mirror. The thought suddenly occurred to her that she couldn't get anywhere without money. She had not one cent to her name. She sat heavily upon her bed, shoulders slumping.

Her eyes happened upon the shadowy outline of her little jewelry case on top of her chest of drawers. It contained an assortment of necklaces and bracelets and rings, gifts through the years from her uncle. There was even some of her mother's jewelry. Of course; she could pawn or sell her jewelry to get needed cash. She stuffed the jewelry case into her valise. She would sort out the items later. Lastly she picked up a small volume of poems, a gift from her uncle that had meant more to her than almost all the others items. The valise bulged with the addition of the book of poems. And then she climbed back out the window and raced for the stables. It did not take her long to saddle her little mustang. She hooked the valise over the saddle horn and mounted. For a long agonizing moment she stared up at the house.

"Oh, Uncle Bob," she sobbed. "Forgive me!"

The thought of abandoning her uncle, leaving him lying cold and alone on the floor tore at her heart. He had been the father she had never really known. Now she had no one. She was alone. She swiped at her eyes with a gloved hand and setting spurs to her little mustang rode out of the yard.

Shadows were giving way up the slope as she rode to meet them. At the top she reined the mustang to a halt. All was silent. The valley had begun to brighten the rose and gold gradually lightening. Below, on the level floor of the valley, lay the rambling old ranch-house, with the cabins nestling around, and the corrals leading out to the soft hay-fields, misty and gray in the morning's early light. The air was cool. From far on the other side of the ridge she had ascended came the bawls of cattle. A wild sound pealed from beyond the slope, making the mustang jump. Hannah had heard it before.

"Rowdy, it's only a wolf," she soothed him.

The peal was loud, rather harsh at first, and then softened to a wild, lonely, haunting mourn echoing the pain in her heart.

★

CHAPTER TWO

Hannah Lea Gibson stepped outside the back door of the Owl Café leaving the door standing slightly ajar. She took a deep breath of the cool night air that swept up the alley from South Pacific Street ruffling the damp golden curls that had slipped from the coil on top of her head. She momentarily closed her eyes reveling in the breeze fanning her moist brow. She could hear muffled clanging of metal from behind her; the Mexican Javier cleaning the dirty pots and pans left over from the days cooking. She leaned her weary shoulders against the rough wall behind her. She was so tired, but she knew if she kept herself busy she would not have to think. And with luck she'd only have nightmares about being in this little town with little funds and no family, and not that other nightmare. That was no nightmare though, that was real. She was a wanted person now; wanted for murder; a murder that she didn't commit. How could anyone, especially Edward, think she could have done such a thing? She loved her uncle. He had been the father she never really remembered.

Memories came flooding back, washing over her and she gazed into the gathering twilight wonderingly. She had been only six years old when she came to live with her Uncle Robert Harlan. That had been thirteen years ago. Her memories of the day she arrived at her uncle's ranch were vivid, but before that, just vague flashes; of golden curls and blue eyes . . . her mother; and of a large man with a thick dark brown mustache. That would have been her father. Those memories were still alive because her uncle had made sure she knew that she had parents who had loved and cherished her. Yes, her uncle assured her, they would have returned, but something happened. Something terrible.

It was years later that she was told the full story. Before that only what a little girl of six could accept; that her parents were not coming back. Her father and mother had been on their way back from Austin when it happened . . .

Her father had business with the bank there her uncle had told her. It was to be a long ride in the buggy and he had decided to take Hannah's mother along to see the sights of the Capital while he conducted his business with the bank. Her mother, Uncle Bob's only sister, had never been to Austin and was excited at the prospect. On their return trip they had been intercepted by outlaws somehow alerted that her father was carrying a large sum of cash from the bank loan. Her father attempted to flee, but the horse had been shot and the buggy overturned in a wash, killing both her mother and father.

And so the years had passed, and the memories of her parents, and their tragic deaths faded, and Uncle Bob became the only father she would know. And now, sad and alone she struggled with the strange longing of her heart. She slumped onto a rickety chair beside the door and leaning her head back until it rested against the hard wall, let her memories consume her.

"*Old Bob is the best man ever.*" How many times had she heard people speak such of her uncle? "*Everybody in Bexar County and all over owes Bob something. There never was anything wrong with him except his crazy blindness about his son, Ed . . . the gambler and drunkard.*"

But she knew it wasn't crazy blindness. No, her uncle was well aware of his son's faults, he had shared his hurt and frustration with her on many occasions, recognizing in her what he found lacking in his own son. As a child she and her uncle were as close as any father and daughter. He taught her so many things, how to ride, to throw a lariat rope, to fish and hunt. She was a regular tomboy, always with torn overalls and skinned knee. She was hardly ever in a dress except to church. When older, she had even worked right alongside her uncle's riders, when he would let her, of course, with all the will and pleasure of youth, and the roses of health bloomed in her cheeks. Old Anita swore that the sun itself shone in her golden hair where the curls made waves and ripples, and the deep blue of the sky at sunset was reflected in her eyes. She suddenly thought of Ted Stoes; how on the night of the dance he had tried to make love to her. Ted had ridden for her uncle since he was old enough to saddle a horse, and she had to admit there wasn't a better bronc rider to be found. With his blue eyes, bolder perhaps from their prominence than from any direct gaze or fire, he was rather handsome. It seemed as though there had always been a repressed character about him though. There was something about him that always held her aloof, and it wasn't just the fights she had with him in her youth. His presence that night, his remembered words and actions, again stirred in her an unutterable spirit of protest. She smiled wistfully. Her flashes of fire came from her mother she was told, and she supposed looking back now she had been rather headstrong at times, and may have tested her uncle's patience on more than one occasion. It was in her early teens when the strange longing for a mother had surged up in her like a strong tide. She had so wanted someone to lean on, someone who knew and understood the mysterious yearnings of a young girl's heart. She breathed a deep sigh. Someone to help her now in this hour when all seemed lost—how she needed that!

The uncle, the only father she had known who she loved with all her heart was dead—murdered. An irrefutable fact. A sob caught in her throat. Everyone she had ever loved had been taken from her. She had no one; not one single soul who loved her. She was alone. She seemed to be growing old swiftly, her life slipping from her.

She got wearily to her feet and went back inside to her stuffy little room where she fell forlornly onto her narrow bed. But sleep would not come, not once she had stirred the memories to life. They whirled about in her head and would give her no rest. Her glum thoughts, slowly though, gave way to exhaustion, and sleep finally brought her relief . . . but not for long. The face of her uncle was there before her in her dreams. His eyes, discolored in death, glared accusingly at her, his hands reaching for her throat.

"No, I didn't do it!" she moaned as his hands, black talons, closed about her neck. She couldn't get enough air. Terrified, she thrashed wildly with her hands and feet coming suddenly awake. She was no longer dreaming, she really couldn't breathe. She was suffocating. There was something pressing down on her face. A pillow!

Her attacker momentarily loosened the pillow and she took a deep shuddering breath.

"Where is it?" the dark figure hissed. "Tell me or I'll finish the job!"

She had no idea what he was talking about so instead of answering, she screamed. The scream bounced off the wall echoing down the hall. A door crashed; the sound of footsteps in the hall and shouting, anxious voices apparently convinced her attacker to flee. Hannah threw off the pillow and swung her feet to the floor seeing as she did so the dark form of a man slipping through the open window across from her bed. She leaned against the wall to catch her breath as someone pounded on her door. She staggered to the door and flung it open.

"Hannah, what in the world—are you all right?" Mrs. Mullin demanded. She held a kerosene lamp in one hand. She was dressed, apparently she had not gotten ready for bed yet, which was fortunate for Hannah. Peering over the café owner's shoulder Hannah saw the Mexican Javier's wide eyes.

"Someone was in my room," Hannah squawked hand at her raw throat. "When I screamed he fled out the window."

Fright flowed like a chill through her and she shook. She hadn't seen her attacker, but she had felt him. Felt his strength, and known the threat was real.

Mrs. Mullin hurried to the window and looked out. "No sign of anyone," she muttered. "Are you sure you weren't dreaming?"

She had been dreaming all right, that terrible nightmare that had been haunting her ever since she fled San Antonio more than a month ago, but she only shook her head.

"Well, I'll talk to Marshall Cuter tomorrow, but I don't reckon that weasel will do much. You better shut and lock that window."

Hannah nodded, shutting the window and locking it. After the others had left, she lit a lamp and sank onto the bed, her head between her hands, and sighed. Someone had tried to kill her—no, only wanted to scare her, get her to tell him where . . . what? She had no idea what he was talking about, and that realization sent a cold wave of terror washing over her. Dragging in a breath, she held it, forced the chill from her skin, waited until the shivery tremors had died.

"*Where is it?*" the dark figure had demanded. A lump rose in her throat that would not go away, and she found it difficult to swallow.

She had been working at the small café now for nearly a month, spending her nights alone in her small room in the rear of the café that the café owner, Mrs. Mullin had provided for her, and working, always working. At night she soaked her tired feet, and cried. And each day she held her breath as she made eye contact with every new customer who entered the café, especially dusty hard-eyed riders or shallow-faced men in store-bought suits that might be a hired sheriff, or a Pinkerton detective, watching to see recognition in their eyes, and know her time had run out. But she was so tired of running and hiding. She was fully aware of the reputation of this little town of Las Vegas, New Mexico. "The hottest town in the country," the old-timers' enjoyed telling her as they sat drinking their morning coffee and passing the time with their harrowing tales of gunfights, murders and hangings. But they always added with a deliberate wink, that the town was not as rough and tough as it used to be three years ago back in 1879 when the railroad arrived. She wondered though what they would think if they knew of what she had been accused of, the reason she was here in this place waiting tables, alone, with no family.

Yes, she knew hardly a soul save for these regular customers who frequented the café, and then only by their first names. She very seldom ventured out and only then to the grocery a block away to order food items for the café. And she warily guarded her identity always watchful that she let nothing slip about herself. So, as far as she knew no one here knew anything about her past. There was only one inference she could make as to the dark figure. The man Edward must have sent to track her down had found her. Oh, how Edward must hate her. But why would he send someone to find her? What was it he wanted from her that he must think she possessed? *"Where is it?"* her attacker had demanded. She was at a loss to know what he was talking about. Maybe it was not anyone her cousin had sent; maybe it was someone else, someone looking for something she had? But that was silly. She had nothing of value. She had sold off her jewelry long ago, and the wages Mrs. Mullin paid her were barely enough to buy necessities.

Mrs. Mullin turned and walked down the hall mumbling to herself. The girl was really a sweet thing. She wondered again as she had numerous time these last few weeks what the girl was running away from. She never talked about her past despite the woman's gentle probing. It was sad. The girl couldn't be much over eighteen or nineteen and quite a pretty thing she was, and a hard worker too who minded her own business. Sometimes Mrs. Mullin would stop whatever she was doing and look at the girl, wondering at her beauty. And the café owner was not the only one. There was not a full grown man in the county who would not go many a mile to look upon her—with varying desires. But there was unknown quantity in the girl, sometimes she was all melting sweetness, and sometimes fire that flashed and was still. And then there was the anxious look in the girl's eyes each time a stranger entered the café. It was obvious the girl lived in fear of something in her past. Mrs. Mullin had had enough hard times in her own life so couldn't help having a soft spot in her heart for the girl.

Back in her room Hannah remade the bed and crawled under the sheets, but try as she might she only slept fitfully the remainder of the night.

Hannah Gibson had just placed steaming plates of food before two customers at a table against the far wall the next morning when the tall slender rider entered the café. Smiling at a teasing comment by one of the men at the table she turned to peer at the newcomer. Her smile slowly faded as her eyes met and held his tight-lipped, intense gaze. She knew. He had arrived at last. No, he wasn't the dark figure of two nights ago. That much she knew, and although she had never seen this man before, she knew Texans.

She required no second look at this strapping rider. It was evident in his eyes of clear gray, singularly direct, in the lithe easy way he stood, wide-shouldered, small-hipped. He had tawny hair, his boldly cut features handsome. He wore a black sombrero and vest, overalls tucked into high-top Mexican boots and large-roweled spurs. She guessed him about twenty-four. An ivory-handled Colt rested low on his right hip and she saw another gun butt protruding from a cross-draw holster high on his left side. She stood unmoving as he walked to an empty table in one corner and sat down facing the door, his eyes never leaving hers.

★

CHAPTER THREE

Texas Ranger Jack Lintell pulled a slender metal case from his vest pocket. With a jingle of spurs, he braced one booted foot against the backrest of the seat in front of him. The train would be pulling into Las Vegas, New Mexico within the next ten minutes, so the conductor said. Opening the case, as he had done countless times in the last five weeks, Jack Lintell gazed silently down at the photograph of a young woman. The photograph had been taken two years ago when Hannah Lea Gibson was seventeen years old, Texas Ranger Captain John McKenny had explained. He had added that he didn't think she would have changed that much; not enough that he wouldn't recognize her. Lintell agreed.

Taken in black and white the photograph had been painstakingly painted by hand. Intelligent eyes of the deepest blue stared with artless innocence back at him from a smooth oval face. A pronounced cleft in her slightly pointed chin added to her unpretentious charm. Her black silk-ruffled bonnet, set back on her head, unveiled a mass of curly golden bangs overhanging her delicate forehead. But it was the wood-sprite eyes that always drew his attention; that and the pink Cupid's-bow lips with their feigned allusion of worldliness. There was not the slightest suggestion in those lovely features that would cause one to remotely suspect she was a murderess. But then looks were obviously deceiving. From what he knew of the case, and the witnesses he had interviewed, there was little doubt. She had been caught with the smoking gun in her hand standing over the hapless victim; the girl's uncle no less. According to the victim's son and his companion, they had just rode up to the house when they heard a gunshot and hurrying inside found the suspect Hannah Gibson standing over the dead body. The victim's safe had been ransacked and a large sum of cash from a cattle sale was missing. It was a simple open and shut case. Caught in the act of robbing the old man she had shot him. That part was easy to surmise.

He remembered that day he was called into Captain John McKenny's office and told to have a seat.

"What yu know of a feller named Robert Harlan over Santone?"

"Not much. Word is he runs lots of cattle."

"Yep, that's common knowledge. Anything else?"

Lintell shook his head.

"Wal, he's been murdered; 'boot a week ago."

"Uh-huh," Lintell mused, waiting for his captain to continue.

"I want yu te go on down there and look things over.

Lintell nodded again. "What about Shardein the Town Marshal?"

"I reckon the killing's outside Phil's jurisdiction," McKenny replied, not taking his eyes off the papers in front of him. "And I ain't got much confidence in Sheriff Talbert. So the Rangers have authority. Report back te me in ten days. Any questions?"

That had been his introduction to the murder of Robert Harlan. The evidence though seemed pretty clear, the witnesses unwavering in their testimony. Only one snag in closing the case; the accused murderess had fled. For Lintell that was guilt enough.

"Wal, son," McKenny said, "I got an out-of-state warrant—"

"An out-of-state warrant for a female, Cap? Hells fire!"

The Captain continued as though Lintell had not spoken. "Yu know Lintell, I had te do some tough arguin' fer that warrant."

"Oh?" Lintell said, eyeing his captain quizzically.

"Yep. It seemed Ed Harlan, Harlan's son was fixin' te hire Joe Arment—"

"Who's Arment?"

"Bonny hunter," the Ranger Captain said curtly. "But I nixed the idea right off. Anyhow, I went te Major Jones an' got 'em te sign the warrant. I reckon that girl's goin' te get a fair trial. So, that's why I'm sendin' yu. Yu're the only one I trust te bring her back unharmed. Shore, Harlan might still go ahead with that bonny hunter deal though, so be on the watch."

"Hell, Cap," Lintell grunted shaking his head in frustration. "I should be in Big Bend country, tracking down them rustlers and horse thieves that's been causing all the disorder down there, not chasing after a sprite of a girl."

"Yu got sisters?"

"Shore I got sisters, four of 'em to be exact. What's that got to do with it?"

"Wal, then, I reckon I can count on yu to treat the gal right, like Texas womanhood ought te be treated, with respect, no matter what the allegations," he said as though that settled the matter. "Now, here's a picture of Miss Gibson."

Jack Lintell took the proffered photograph, stared down at the image for a long silent moment.

"Cap, she couldn't weigh more than a hundred pounds soaking wet. Hells fire!" he growled. Her description, he noted, indicated she was five foot one inch tall and weighed one hundred-ten pounds. "You shore are picky about this here girl."

"Wal, son, I am, and that's a fact. The girl's the only daughter of an old partner of mine back when I run a little spread over te Austin. Both Frank Gibson and his wife were killed in a robbery about thirteen years ago. So, yu're right, I got a hawse in this race."

Lintell nodded glancing down at the photograph. The girl was strikingly good looking, and he felt a strange sensation like his heart had skipped a beat. But no matter his Captain's feelings, he wordlessly chided himself; the girl was most probably guilty. She had shot poor Robert Harlan to death with his own pistol. Still, maybe she was justified. He didn't know this Harlan. But that was an issue that would be cleared up at the trial. In the meantime he wouldn't let himself be bamboozled into doing anything foolish regarding the girl.

"Well, I shore hope the trail ends here for the good," he muttered thoughts returning to the present, the clickety-clack of the train wheels thumping in his ears. It hadn't been difficult to track the woman—too many people, especially the male of the species, remembered her—but it had taken time keeping to her trail following from place to place. He knew he was close on her heels now; at least from what that teamster had told him in Las Cruces.

"Yep, can't miss that face," the man had chuckled. "A lost sister you say? Wal, ye'll find her workin' tables o'r the Owl Café in Las Vegas. It's a rite popular place since she started there. I make a point te stop in there every trip."

She was waitressing in a café, so she hadn't spent any of the seventy-five thousand she had apparently stolen from her uncle's safe, at least not that he could tell. She must have the money hidden somewhere. Hopefully he could find and recover that to.

The shrill screech of the train's whistle interrupted Lintell's thoughts and he straightened peering out the window. Smoke from the steam engine momentarily blocked his view of the station. Gazing out the window on his side he saw a large grassy plaza encircled by a white picket fence. A row of two-story buildings with porches across the front and balconies on top supported by heavy timbers lined each side and to the south of the plaza. Several men stood about a heavy freight wagon curiously watching the newly arrived train. Beside the wagon standing hipshot were two saddled horses and farther down the street was a black-topped buggy.

Stepping down from the train with pack-roll in hand, Lintell walked back toward the rear cars. He waited while the door to a boxcar was rolled back and a stout wood ramp put in place. Lintell had removed his badge placing it in his pocket with his identification, and had made no comment as to what his business was, yet he felt eyes following him, intent, knowing gazes. He had the look of a lawman.

"Howdy, Colonel," he called after climbing up the ramp into the train car. He patted the neck of a tall strawberry roan with three white socks and a blaze face tethered with a short halter rope in the front of the car. The horse was a magnificent animal, clean-limbed and heavy-chested with the head of a racer. "Reckon you survived the ride fine ole boy."

The horse neighed, head nodding up and down as though in answer. Leading the horse down the ramp, Lintell stepped easily into the saddle and started off toward Bridge Street which crossed the Gallinas River to West Las Vegas, the old part of town, where he was told he would find the Owl Café. Turning down a dusty street of brick and frame buildings with high weather-beaten signs he saw on the far corner a group of cowboys in dusty trail outfits. Saddled horses were hitched to a rail; buckboards and wagons showed farther down the street; Mexicans in colorful garb sat in front of a saloon with painted windows on the opposite side of the street. Lintell was subjected to hard-eyed stares from several cowboys as he rode past reining up before the small café on the far corner fronted by a large glass window that looked out upon the street.

He had been wrong, Lintell thought, as he took a seat at a corner table, she had changed. She was much prettier than her picture. What he saw was a graceful sprite of a girl with golden curls piled high on her head and tied with a yellow ribbon to match the cheerful color of her dress, somewhat hidden, however, beneath a large white apron. Her moves were willowy and flowing. Her face was exquisite with a serious straight nose, that little cleft chin, and deep blue eyes that at the moment were regarding him defiantly. She walked slowly toward him.

He watched her all the while telling himself that this was going to be a lot more awkward than he had even imagined when he reluctantly agreed to take the assignment. He was supposed to take her all the way back to San Antonio, Texas, three days, handcuffed beside him in the rail coach! Handcuffed! This slip of a girl! How was that going to look? Hells fire!

"What do you want, Mister?" she asked. There was a hint of a drawl and a bit of breathlessness in her soft and slightly contralto voice.

"A steak two inches thick, hash browns, and a cup of coffee would be fine," he answered. It took an effort to remove his gaze from her eyes. They were large, and either their deep blue color or their expression gave them a singular, haunting beauty.

"You know what I mean! What do you want from me?" she demanded.

"Your name Hannah Lea Gibson?" he asked in order to hide his surprise at her directness.

"You know it is!"

"Yes, ma'am," he nodded. The girl had spunk that was for sure. "I'm a Texas Ranger. My name's Jack Lintell. "I've a warrant for your arrest for the murder of Robert Harlan. I'm taking you back to Texas to stand trial."

"Show me your identification."

He grinned then, but reached into his pocket. She stared at the round silver badge with a five-point star in the center that he produced with the words 'Texas' across the top and 'Rangers' across the bottom of the circle. She recognized its authenticity immediately, remembering her uncle's old friend and partner—she had called him, Uncle John, tall and proud, a true Texas Ranger. She slowly nodded.

"I didn't kill him!"

"Why did you run?" he drawled, leaning back in his chair.

"Because—" She suddenly took a deep breath, her gaze shifting to peer out the large front window. She blinked several times; lips compressed, but said nothing more. She could not guess why this man should make her feel strangely uncertain of the ground she stood on or how it could cause a constraint she had to fight herself to hide.

Lintell followed her down the hall where she paused before the last door and turned to look at him. He could almost read her shifting thoughts on her expressive face. She didn't want him in her room.

"Pack what clothes you'll need, Miss Gibson. There's a train leaving this afternoon. We'll be on it."

She nodded, as though resigned to her fate, and opened the door only to halt, hands going to her mouth.

"Oh!" she cried.

Lintell peered around the door jamb. The mattress was half off the bed frame, the blankets tossed haphazardly on the floor. All of the drawers in the small chest of drawers were pulled out and their contents dumped on the floor. Even the one picture frame was askew.

"Not a very neat housekeeper, are you?" he drawled.

"I didn't leave it looking like this, you big galoot! Somebody's ransacked my room," she exclaimed angrily, casting accusing eyes upon him.

"Ump-umm, don't look at me," he denied.

She knew it hadn't been him. It had to have been that mysterious dark figure, the one searching for something she had no idea of. Could it get any worse, she sighed to herself. Well, this Texas Ranger was going to relieve her of this particular problem, she smiled grimly. She wouldn't be around to be hassled by whoever it was looking for whatever he thought she had that she knew nothing about, and didn't want to know anyhow.

Someone had obviously rummaged through the girl's room. It didn't take a scientist to figure that. Looking for what? The seventy-five thousand dollars the girl had stolen from her uncle? That was the first possibility that came to Lintell's mind. But who around here knew about the money? Remembering Captain McKenny's remark, Joe Arment . . . the bounty hunter leaped to the forefront of Lintell's thoughts. Lintell felt a prickle of unease. It boded well for him to keep a watchful eye out. This whole situation regarding this girl was becoming downright peculiar, he decided. What had seemed a day ago to be routine was now giving him cause to rethink.

Hannah set about, for all practical purposes, to pack a small valise with what little clothes she had, but all the while her mind whirled. Completing the task under his watchful gaze, she set the satchel on the bed and turned, peering at him with the most doleful expression she could contrive.

"May I say goodbye to Mrs. Mullin?" she asked, tears glistening like pearls on her long dark lashes.

Hells fire, what was he going to say? He followed her as she went to find Mrs. Mullin and stood at the door just out of earshot while she spoke to the woman who cast him a steely glance.

"It's a sad day when the law has to harass a poor innocent imp of a girl," the woman sniffed, loud enough for him to hear.

Lintell made no comment.

Mrs. Mullin gazed down at the girl. "Do you need anything, honey, money, whatever?"

"Thank you, Mrs. Mullin, that's very thoughtful of you, but I'm afraid I'm under that ranger's charge now."

"Humph!" Mrs. Mullin snorted.

"You've been very kind taking me in and all. I'll miss you," Hannah sighed kissing the older woman on her cheek.

"*Señorita*," the Mexican Javier whispered, "What is happening? Thees man, he takes you away?"

"Yes, Javier . . . They think I did something terrible back in Texas. Oh, I cannot face going back. I'm afraid they are going to—to hang me, and I am innocent," she whispered in return.

"*Señorita*, Javier will help you," he said voice low, furtive black eyes watching the ranger.

"How?" she gasped.

"Do not worry, *Señorita,* Javier know how to fool thees Texas Ranger. I have done ees many times."

"Javier—!"

"Shh!" he hissed. "*Escuchar*, listen. I have thees cousin, he live in Juarez . . ."

Javier talked; Hannah listened, not saying a word.

★

CHAPTER FOUR

They were the only people in the lobby of the train station. The man at the ticket counter related that the east bound train to El Paso via Las Cruses would be leaving in half an hour. Lintell led Hannah to a seat at the back of the four rows of chairs lined up in the center of the small lobby. She sat holding the small valise on her lap, head bowed. He took the seat beside hers. The big ivory-handled gun on his hip bumped with a solid thud against the arm rest as he slid into his seat. She glanced quickly down at the gun butt nearly brushing her hip and shivered. She looked up to see him watching her.

"You all right?" he asked.

"May I have a cup of coffee?" she said by way of answer.

"Shore, but I reckon you'll have to come with me," he drawled.

She rose and walked beside him. She was exceedingly relieved that he had not handcuffed her as she had at first feared. That certainly would have rendered Javier's plan useless. But that omission had told her much. He was a Texan, what her uncle's old friend John McKenny called the old breed, and for a moment considered rethinking the whole thing that Javier suggested. But then she mentally shook her head. She must go ahead with the plan, and this first part depended solely on her. Adventure just happened to be her forte. She could do this. She darted a look about the lobby. It was still empty. It was too soon. She had hoped there would be people in the lobby. That was the first part of the plan, her part. Without it falling into place the rest would be worthless.

Hannah stood silently beside the ranger at the little lunch counter located in one corner of the lobby feeling rather conspicuous.

"You hungry?" he asked turning to peer at her.

"Just coffee," she answered quietly still anxious about her next move.

He ordered two coffees and gave the girl behind the counter a dollar bill. She was no more than fifteen and smiled coyly at Lintell as she handed him two steaming cups.

"It's hot," she warned with a bright smile, "Don't you-all burn yourselves."

Hannah sat her valise down at her feet and took the cup in both hands just as the outside door opened and two men and a woman entered. One, an older man, was dressed like a cattleman the other, younger, wore a well-tailored business suit. The woman was attired elegantly in a long brown skirt and white blouse with matching brown cuffs and collar. She appeared to be the same age as the younger man. Her light brown hair was arranged in a neat coiffure upon which was perched a stylish bonnet in matching brown. Hannah thought her very attractive, and it was obvious that the woman shared that opinion, chin uplifted haughtily as though completely bored with the whole goings-on.

Here was the opportunity Hannah had been waiting for, but she suddenly found herself hesitant. What if it didn't work . . . or what if it worked too well, then she would be on her own again. But this time in a wild, lonesome country fraught with all sort of dangers from maundering Mescalero Apaches to Mexican desperadoes, or perhaps worst, getting lost and dying a slow death of thirst. She had little choice she decided. She pretended to take a sip from the cup all the while aware of one of the two men approaching behind her. She waited until she sensed he was almost upon her and then she turned gritting her teeth in anticipation of the feel of hot coffee soaking into her skin.

"Oh!" she cried as she collided with the man letting the coffee cup upturn splashing its hot contents onto her dress.

"What the—!" the young man in the well-tailored business suit exclaimed, backing a step and then hands shooting out to steady her. "Ma'am, I'm terribly sorry! It was clumsy of me. Are you injured?"

"Oh, dear!" she moaned, brushing at the dark brown stain spreading over the front of the gown. There was no need to pretend as the hot liquid reached her skin. She knew she would have a huge red mark on her stomach.

"Oh, no, sir. It was entirely my fault. I wasn't looking where I was going. But, oh goodness, I think my dress is ruined," she moaned, face a bright red.

She looked imploringly at Lintell who was staring at the front of her wet gown which clung to her like another layer of skin.

"You're burnt. We'll get you to a doctor," he said seeing the pained expression on her face. He reached to take her arm.

"No, I'm all right. I'll just get out of this dress. I have extra clothes in my bag. Is there somewhere I can change?"

"Are you shore you're all right?" he asked. The concern in his voice took her by surprise.

"Yes, positive," she replied giving him a dazzling smile.

"Ma'am," the girl behind the counter called, "The station master's office is down that hall. He's not in today. You can use that."

Lintell nodded, reaching to retrieve her valise and walking her down the hall. For a wild moment she thought he was going into the room with her, but he stopped before the door and handed her the valise.

"Thank you. I'll be as quick as I can," she murmured, and disappeared into the room closing the door firmly behind her.

The well-dressed man was waiting for Lintell when he reached the end of the hall.

"I take it that the young lady is with you?" he said.

"Yep, you could say that," Lintell drawled in his slow easy voice.

"Well, I hope you don't take offence," he said, nodded in the direction of the woman, "but my companion suggested that it would be proper to offer to pay for the damage to the young lady's gown."

"That's right decent of you, mister, but it shore seemed like an accident."

The man gave a slight bow. "Nevertheless, perhaps you would appraise her."

"Shore," Lintell acknowledged.

Lintell took a seat where he could watch the door to the office. He stretched out his booted feet with a jingle of spurs, crossed one over the other to wait. This was not going to be easy he thought remembering the way her wet gown clung to her. He thought her beautiful before, but when she smiled at him the whole room seemed to light up. The idea occurred to him that perhaps he ought to hire a matronly woman to accompany them, just for propriety sake. From under the brim of his black sombrero he regarded the young man in the fancy suit, recalling the way he had gawked at the girl. He didn't have the cut of a westerner, he decided. He peered down the hall at the closed door. Women were the very devil, he thought closing his eyes. But he didn't sleep. He was very aware of what went on around him. After some time he opened one eye regarding the door at the end of the hall.

"She shore is taking her time," he muttered under his breath. He thought of his sisters and gave a frustrated sigh remembering how they primped and fretted with their hair and gowns. Memories now stirred within him, memories of home where he had not been for several years. He knew from his mother's letters though that Sue, his oldest sister had married and both Amy and Alice were engaged.

"Probably married by now," he soliloquized, "Dog-gone, I'll shore make it a point to visit when this escapade is over. At least Molly—what was she now, sixteen—was still at home. But I bet she has a beau, or two or three."

"Train departs in ten minutes. All them that's going better get aboard," the man behind the ticket counter called out.

Lintell glanced at the big clock on the wall, and then at the closed door at the end of the hall. He got to his feet and made his way down the narrow hall and knocked on the door.

"Better hurry ma'am, train's leaving in ten minutes," he called loudly.

There was no answer. Suddenly the hair on the nape of his neck stood up. He knocked again louder. No answer. He tried the door latch. It was locked.

"Hells fire!" he cursed and with quick steps, spurs jingling, he sprinted out the side door and around the back of the station, cursing himself a fool as he went. He spied the open window and knew even before he peered inside that he had been bamboozled. The gown she had been wearing lay over a chair but she and her little valise was nowhere to be seen. Hells fire, he had let her pretty face hoodwink him. He never even checked to see if the room had a window. He shore must be getting soft in the head.

"Damn if I won't turn her over my knee when I catch up with her!" he growled.

But then his lawmen's instincts took over. He searched the ground below the window and saw tiny booted tracks leading away. She must have changed into a riding outfit. Damn! Why hadn't he noticed? Perhaps a dozen yards or so he saw where a horse had been tied to a tree. Obviously it had been there for some time as the horse had stomped its feet impatiently. Lintell stooped to study the tracks closely looking for any mark that he could identify in the future. On what would have been the off side front hoof he found what he was looking for. Whoever had shoed the horse had used an egg bar shoe, probably to correct some problem with the hoof. The shoe's oval shape would be easy to follow—provided she kept the same horse. He struck off at a walk following the tracks which he soon discovered circled the train station and headed toward town. Lintell hurried back to the station. He needed to get his horse out of the boxcar before the train got underway.

After a heated argument with the train's conductor, which nearly resulted in physical blows, the ramp was put up to the boxcar and Lintell led the big roam off the train. But by this time the girl had nearly a two hour head start. Thankfully her horse's tracks with the egg bar shoe were not difficult to follow. Lintell rode to the rear of the station where he had left off. It wasn't long, however, before he lost the trail going through town when it became overrun with other horse tracks. As he rode along Lintell cursed under his breath.

"Damn if I'll ever be sympathetic toward a female prisoner again—God forbid I ever have to! McKenny, I should smile you're going to hear about this!"

The sun had set some time ago and twilight's shadows made picking up the girl's trail too difficult to even attempt. He would have to wait and start in the morning at first light. Question remained; where was she headed? He would sort out which direction she had gone in the morning. Fortunately that egg bar shoe would be easy to trail, and she wouldn't have gotten far in the dark. She would have to stop for the night. He couldn't help but be concerned for her wellbeing. Any number of things could happen to a girl alone in this wild country, and none of them were good.

He rode over to the Owl Café. It was packed with the supper crowd. He stepped through the door and spied the owner Mrs. Mullin. She apparently saw him at the same moment. Her features registered outright surprise. It was obvious she knew nothing of the girl's escape. She hurried toward him.

"What are you doing here, and where is Hannah?" she demanded arms akimbo.

"I was about to ask you that same question," he drawled.

She tilted her head to the side, eyed him suspiciously. "What has happened?"

"Well, ma'am, I'm afraid she shore pulled a good one over on me—"

"She escaped!"

"I reckon, ma'am. Somebody had a horse tied out behind the train station waiting for her—"

"Don't you look at me young man," she scolded.

"Shore, I reckon you're innocent. Where is your Mexican?"

"Javier? You don't think—"

"Where is he?"

"In the back, cleaning pots and pans," she replied uneasily.

The Mexican's eyes were as large as saucers when Lintell appeared in the doorway.

"*Señor*!" he gulped nervously.

"Greaser, I shore got a bone to pick with you!" Lintell growled.

"*Señor*, I no speak English good."

"You *comprende,* poky, Greaser—jail?"

"*Si, Señor*! *Me comprende*!"

"Well, did you leave that horse behind the train station for Miss Gibson?"

The Mexican shook his head. "I know nothing, *Señor*," his shifty black eyes avoiding Lintell's.

Lintell shook his head, growling under his breath. Somehow he had expected that answer. He would get nothing from the Greaser.

Jack Lintell was up at dawn. He ate a hurried breakfast at the tiny café. Mrs. Mullin waited on him, taking his order without a single comment other than, "What would you like?" Finishing the meal he stopped at the general store for supplies and extra canteens. He didn't know where the next water would be found. Leaving there he soon was off intent on picking up the trail left by Hannah Lea Gibson's horse with the egg bar shoe on its right front hoof. Two hours later, having circled nearly half way around the town, Lintell came across the tracks he was searching for, plain as could be, headed almost due south.

The early morning sun showed gold and red upon the snow-tipped ramparts of the Sangre de Cristo Mountains when Lintell set out on the girl's trail. From the look of the tracks, she had been moving at a fast clip, making up ground, he figured, as speedy as she could in the growing darkness.

"Dog-gone," he muttered, "She shore was a chancy thing, riding high-speed in the dark in this rough country. But then, she would have figured I was quick on her trail. Well, I shore would have been if I had of took her more seriously. I shore won't make that mistake in the future," he grunted.

He figured he had traveled ten miles or so when he noticed she had slowed her horse to a trot. Before him a long gulf yawned wide and shallow, a yellow-green sea of desert grass and sage. A smoky haze hung over the valley on this warm June day. It was a lonely land, and the girl was all alone in it, and for some reason that thought disturbed him. Maybe it was because she was such a tiny thing, an easy prey for any number of predators from Indians and desperados to wild beasts.

An hour's ride up the slow incline brought Lintell into a zone of cedars. Their gray-sheathed trunks, fragrant with massed green foliage brought a welcome coolness. Once among the trees, Lintell drew rein. Ever since he had left Las Vegas he had this feeling that he was being watched. He peered back along his trail, but saw nothing out of the ordinary. No riders, not one single creature moving. He continued to watch his trail for several minutes, then nudged the roan on. He did not, however, dismiss the feeling. After four years chasing wanted outlaws he had honed his instinct for sensing danger to a fine edge.

Shortly he came upon the place near a rugged creek where she had stopped and spent the remainder of the night. He could see why. It was dim and cool among the trees. Previously, back in the open valley he had seen where the girl's horse had run into a mesquite bush and had to back off before going on around the bush. The girl had been asleep in the saddle. Now, in the trees where it was darker still she had halted rather than continue on and risk getting turned around. He marveled at her spirit, but then she was Western, a Texas girl, no less. He swung from his saddle and surveyed the ground. He saw where she had fed her horse oats, and laid out her bedroll for a few hours' sleep.

"Well, I'll be!" he snorted, "She shore hadn't been toting all that stuff around in her little bag. That Greaser shore set her up good. Horse, grain, bedroll; I wonder what else."

Lintell stepped into the saddle and started off. Down through the trees he spotted a herd of maybe fifty cows being driven by three dusty cowboys. He reined his horse in that direction.

"Howdy," one of the riders greeted as Lintell drew near.

"Howdy, yourself," returned Lintell genially.

The cowboy's sharp-eyed gaze looked Lintell over, but he said nothing waiting for Lintell to start the conversation.

"Any riders cross your trail?" Lintell asked casually.

"Nope," the cowboy answered.

"Say, where would I find the nearest water? I'm shore running low."

"Yu headed south?"

"Yep."

"Wal, thar's a fine spring at Encino, aboot ten mile south of here. Yu can't miss them big cottonwoods, but if'n yu ain't got business that ways, I'd shore head back in the other direction."

"How's that?"

"Yu ain't heard then. Word is Old Nana left his camp, on his way te join Victorio."

"Who's Old Nana?"

"Wal, I knowed yu was a stranger round here. Old Nana's a Mescalero Apache war chief. He attacked a wagon outfit two days ago and escaped with their mules after killin' all but three of the outfitters. Nobody knows where he's headed next. Boss wants all the cattle moved in closer te the ranch."

"I reckon that's sound advice, seeing how things are, but my business can't wait. See you boys," he said, and with a wave of his hand, bade the riders good-by. He spurred his horse into a trot.

"That little idiot!" he cursed when he reached the point where he had left off the girl's trail, "She's riding right into a bunch of bloody savages! Well, it'd serve the little fool right if that Apache scalps her." Hah! Who was he kidding? The little sprite was now his responsibility. He touched spurs to the roan prodding the horse into a ground-covering lope. He figured the girl was near four hours ahead of him. He'd have to get a move on if he was to catch up with her before nightfall.

Lintell rode on. The zone of cedars fell behind and a red, sun-baked, hoof-marked hollow glared up at him. He drew rein and stared down at the much-trampled ground. The small herd the cowboys had been driving had passed this way. The trail he had been following had been obliterated under those sharp hooves, and night was coming on. Even now the setting sun cast long shadows out across the mesquite and sage cloaked range. If he didn't pick up her horse's tracks quickly it would be too dark and he'd have to make camp. And she would have to spend another night alone in this wild country.

★

CHAPTER FIVE

Hannah Lea Gibson slid with a sigh from her lame and weary horse. The sun was setting. A cool breeze blew across the open range bringing with it the tangy smell of sage and cedar. Hannah sat upon the ground physically drained. She had hoped to reach Encino where she would replenish her canteen with fresh water from the spring her friend Javier told her about. She unbuttoned her old baggy coat and took off the black floppy brimmed sombrero she wore and tossed it aside. She needed to secure more food too. She peered up at her horse. They had come upon no water all day, at least none fit to drink. At the last camp the water was bad and her horse refused to drink. That could be the reason he turned up lame. She knew the animal was in a bad way.

Twilight was stealing down, night would soon follow. She debated going on. She darn sure would, she thought, if she had any idea how far away this Encino was. She lay back on the ground, stared up at the darkening sky and evaluated her progress so far. All had gone well as could be expected up to this point. She had encountered no one on the trail save three cowboys driving a small herd of steers. She had heard the bawling of cattle long before she saw them and so had made it across the hollow and up into another patch of cedars before they came into sight. She didn't want to draw any attention to herself if it could be avoided. The boy's disguise she had adopted would not undergo close scrutiny. Thoughts of the ranger suddenly popped into her head. What was his name? Jack . . . yes, Jack Lintell. She smiled.

"I bet he could strangle me over the trick we played on him!" she murmured aloud. 'Well,' she thought, 'he'd just have to go back to Texas and tell them . . . tell them what? That she made a fool of him?'

That certainly wouldn't go over very well on his account, and she suddenly felt a twinge of compassion for the man. But then the notion occurred to her that maybe he wouldn't give up! No, there was no way he could still be on her trail. She had made it a point to ride through town where her horse's tracks would be trampled over by the heavy town traffic. No, he wouldn't be able to identify her horse's tracks from any others she smiled smugly. The only thing she had to worry about besides getting lost, wild animals, Indians and desperados, was finding Encino and, water . . . and a bath! Oh, a hot bath, a soft bed, and a full belly would feel like heaven right now. She fished out the crude map Javier had left for her. Water holes were marked as well as towns and other landmarks. She would have no trouble finding her way. Javier must have traveled this route many times, she guessed to know the terrain so well.

Hannah unsaddled and hobbled the bay, then unrolled her tarp under a low-branched cedar. She bit off a chunk of beef jerky and took the last swallow from her canteen. Finishing the jerky she stretched out on the blankets trying not to think of how thirsty she was. The night darkened, the air cooled and with it the staccato cry of coyotes. At home in San Antonio she had always loved to listen to their cries, often dreaming of a life on her own. She hadn't quite thought of it happening in such a manner though.

She pulled her blanket up over her shoulders. The soft feel of wool, the hard ground, the smell of cedar, the twinkling of a star through the cedar branches, the moan of rising wind, the lonesome coyote bark, and silence. A tear slipped from under her closed eyelid and coursed slowly down her cheek.

Hannah woke with a start, almost as if someone had walked over her grave. She lay still listening, trying to get her bearings. She stared up through the cedar branches at the gray sky beyond. Dawn. Even though she was stiff from lying on the hard ground she didn't want to rise and start her day. She had never been so tired. There was coolness in the air that made her shiver. Then she heard the sound. The thump of hooves. It was her bay coming into camp, she sighed. No, there was more than one horse . . . several! She rolled over on her stomach, peering with keen-eyed alertness under the cedar branches at a number of dark shapes perhaps a hundred feet away, moving slowly in a line one after the other. Who were they? —Indians! The thought sent a cold shiver down her spine. Her heart was pounding. If they discover her . . . Oh, God, she didn't want to think of what would happen to her. She mustn't make a sound. Suddenly she thought of her horse grazing a short distance away. She stopped breathing . . . if he neighed!

The bay must have wandered down the opposite slope in search of grass she suddenly realized, with a slow outlet of breath. The dark riders slowly disappeared down the incline swallowed up in the gray mist, the thump of hoofs gradually fading and dying. She waited a long while before pulling on her boots and coat. She plopped the old black sombrero on her head and snatching the bridle from where she had left it hanging over the saddle horn, she went in search of her horse. She intended to get as far away from those dark riders, whoever they were, as she possibly could, though she just knew they were Apaches.

Emerging from the cedars she saw the bay partway down the slight grassy incline. The horse was lying down. That was not a good sign. Her heart sank. But then the horse got to its feet as she drew nearer. She slipped the bridle over the horse's head and fastened the throat latch. Then she removed the hobbles and led the animal back to her camp site.

"I'm so sorry, Moses, I know you must be thirsty, but if it's any consolation, so am I," she said as she patted the bay's neck.

Hannah had named the bay Moses because, she decided, he was going to lead her to freedom. If both of them lived that long, she sighed, spreading the horse blanket over the animal's back. She grunted as she swung the heavy saddle up and fastened the cinch. She tied her bedroll behind the cantle and hooked the small valise over the saddle horn before mounting. Dawn was giving way to daylight with a ruddy tinge in the eastern sky when Hannah rode down through the cedars. Some hours later the scenery began to change, the juniper became thicker and taller, the terrain hillier. Suddenly a building was visible through the trees. Encino! At last!

A small stone house with a low flat roof sat back against the trees and Hannah could hear the soothing sound of flowing water from beyond. Her throat hurt with just the thought of swallowing. The bay picked up his gait. When she grew near the house a man short in stature stepped out of the door. He watched her, a friendly expression on his face. He was older, maybe in his sixties, Hannah thought, his face was ruddy from sun and wind. He had a round belly protruding over his belt, which seemed even more prodigious because of his short build.

"Howdy, son," he called.

"Hello. Is this Encino?"

Encino's 'bout two miles west of here. This is Willy Spring."

"Well, I shore smell water. Is it all right if I fill my canteen, and water my horse?" she asked, affecting her best Texas drawl.

"Shore, son, spring's off yonder where yu see them tall cottonwoods," the man said. "Where yu headed?"

"I reckon, south."

"Ah-huh," he grunted, looking her over casually. "Wal, go on and help yurself te the water. When yore done come on in. I reckon yu could wrap yoreself around some hot vittles, couldn't yu?"

"I reckon I shore could," she grinned, at once taking a liking to the old man.

It was cool under the Cottonwoods. Hannah stepped from the saddle and led the bay to the water. As the horse eagerly drank she knelt and filled her canteen. She pushed the old sombrero back off her forehead revealing soft golden curls matted against her sweaty forehead. The water was cold and refreshing as she drank from the canteen. She didn't care that some spilled around the corners of her mouth to drip off her chin onto the front of her shirt and down the smooth valley between her breasts soaking her shirt. Oh, it was heaven, she sighed. She undid her bandana and dipped it in the water wetting the back of her neck. She debated for a moment ducking her head in the water but vanity prevailed.

She knew better than to drink too much all at once, and so made herself stop. She pulled her hat back down over her forehead, and taking up the reins of the bay started walking back to the house where she had met the old man. She tied the horse to a post and slipped a nosebag with the last of the oats up over the bay's ears. She then went to the door and knocked. She heard footsteps and shortly the door opened. Hannah was taken by surprise to be greeted by a homely woman wearing a clean but worn dress.

"Did you wash your hands, young man," the woman scolded cheerily.

"No—ma'am," Hannah said feeling her face reddening.

"Well, come on in. You can use the pan there by the pump," she smiled.

The smell of food caused Hannah's stomach to rumble audibly as she stepped through the doorway.

"My name's Eva McNew," the woman continued, "that short dumpy fellow there is my husband, Albert."

Hannah halted just inside the door awash with sudden relief.

"Mrs. McNew, I guess I ought to tell you . . . I'm not a—boy."

And she pulled the old sombrero off her head. Curls, bright and golden, spilled down around her pink cheeks. Hannah held the sombrero before her in both hands, head bowed, embarrassed at both their open-mouth scrutiny.

"My word!" the woman exclaimed. "You're a girl! And I'll say a pretty thing too. I saw you out the window when you rode up and I said to myself that sure is a handsome boy, near as pretty as a girl. And I sure was right about that," she said nodding her gray head wisely. "How old are you child?"

"Why, I reckon she can't be more'an ten or twelve," her husband interjected.

"I'm nineteen."

"Land sakes," the woman gasped. "Now, you tell me, what's a pretty little girl like you doing in this wild country, and alone?

It's a long story," Hannah said softly, tears glistening in her eyes.

"Oh, dear, oh, dear! Of course. You come sit down. You can tell us all about it," Mrs. McNew said kindly, ushering her to a worn cushioned chair near the window.

Sometime later Hannah sat at the table, a plate of food in front of her, her story told.

"Young lady, don't yu think yu ought te go back an' clear yur name. Yu can't run forever," Albert McNew said.

"I just can't, sir."

"What about this ranger that's come after yu? I reckon he's still on yore trail," McNew said.

"Surely not. He couldn't have picked up my trail out of Las Vegas."

"Don't count on it," he grunted. "Yu ought te know Texans, especially Texas Rangers."

Yes, she thought, she knew, and she felt a tremor of disquietude. Jack Lintell would sure have a score to settle with her, and he didn't look like a man that would give up easily. Well, she would still continue with her plan. She would be safe in Mexico. At Mrs. McNew's insistence, and with little argument on her part, she stayed the night.

Hannah was up early the next morning, shared breakfast with the McNew's. Neither made any attempt to dissuade her from continuing her reckless trek. Mrs. McNew hugged her tightly kissing her cheek as she handed her a sack.

"A little grub I packed for you," she explained. "Ain't much, but I can't have you go hungry."

"Thank you," Hannah whispered around the lump in her throat.

Hannah waved goodbye and rode off before she burst into tears. The sun had yet to top the ridge when she set off. The sun never appeared; instead low heavy clouds hung overhead and with it a wind cool and smelling of rain. Rain would be good, Hannah thought.

The rain started about midmorning and in moments, with no slicker, Hannah was soaked to the skin. The wind penetrating her wet garments set her to shivering.

"Be careful what you wish for," she muttered, teeth chattering.

The rain stopped around noon, though the sky still remained dark and dismal. Wet and cold Hannah stopped near a rock outcropping and ate part of the plentiful fare Mrs. McNew had put up for her. Shortly she was once more on her way. About mid-afternoon she came upon an old road, and rounding a bend she saw a grove of cottonwoods. Proceeding at a walk, eyes watchful, she suddenly spied a low red-roofed adobe building. Hannah saw three men loafing outside the front of the building. She pulled the floppy-brimmed sombrero lower on her forehead, heart pumping. There was no stopping now. They had spotted her. She would have to keep going, hopefully pass them uneventful.

The men, she saw, had the look of cowboys. They wore dusty garb, and they watched her approach with keen, hard-eyed stares. One leisurely got to his feet, rubbing his hands on the back of his overalls before stepping inside the building. Two horses were hitched to a rail in front and Hannah saw another tied back a ways from the building under the shade of a Cottonwood. She was abreast of the building when one of the men called out to her.

"Hay, there boy, what yu got in that bag?"

Hannah didn't answer. A man stepped out of the building, peered at Hannah. It wasn't the same one who had gone in a moment before. This man was big; in fact he was the biggest man Hannah had ever seen in her life. His massive shoulders sloped from a bull neck, and his hands looked like mallets. He stared hard at her and then said something to the others, but it was too low for her to hear. Suddenly a figure leaped from behind a tree and grabbed the bay's bridle.

"Let go of my horse!" Hannah cried.

"Here now boy, we just want te see what yu're packin' in the bag," the man laughed.

"It's only my—clothes," she snapped.

"Wal, now boy yu're kind of young. Yore pappy know where yu are?"

"Yes, and he'll shore come looking for you if you lay a hand on me."

Panicky now, Hannah kicked out with her foot, but the man caught her leg and jerking hard drug her out of the saddle. She hit the ground with a thud that send a shock of pain up her backbone, and in the process her sombrero slipped down over her eyes. She scrambled to her feet ignoring the pain and made to run. A rough hand clasped the collar of her coat. She twisted, struggling to get away. The buttons tore loose and the coat ripped from her shoulders. Her shirt fared no better. Buttons popped and creamy white flesh was laid bare.

"Ah'll be damn! A gurl!" the man choked, eyes staring as she frantically attempted to cover herself. He let go of her and backed away.

"Bring her in here," the big man ordered.

"Aw, Bull, she's just a kid," the man protested.

"Damn yu, I said bring her in here!"

At that moment a clatter of hoofs swept up on the scene like a storm before the wind. A dark-clad rider flung himself from the saddle even as the roan bound to a standstill hurling gravel before it. Two guns leaped into the rider's hands.

"Freeze—you!" pealed out Jack Lintell. "Hands up!"

"They're up," the cowboy said, laconically.

"Wh-where did you come from?" Hannah gasped staring at Lintell as she held her torn garments clutched tightly together.

"Never you mind," Lintell hissed his eyes seeming to take in the men and the house in one keen glance. "Get on your horse and ride off yonder!"

The man called Bull took a slanted step sideways, and Lintell saw the pistol at his side. With a snarl, Bull's hand came up. At that same instant flame shot forth from the pistol in Lintell's right hand. The man grunted. The massive fist clinching the pistol wavered. The Colt in Lintell's left hand spouted flame. Bull staggered backward then collapsed sliding down the rough siding of the house leaving a smear of blood in his wake.

"Who are yu?" one of the men asked, hands in the air.

"I reckon I'm the feller who ain't quite made up my mind not to shoot the bunch of you," Lintell drawled.

Hannah hurried to the bay and caught up the reins. She made a fumbling attempt to get her foot in the stirrup while trying to maintain her modesty and mount at the same time. She finally managed both, but she didn't ride far away.

"Hell, mister, that was Bull's idea goin' after the gurl," cried the man who had jerked Hannah from her horse. "I shore as hell thought he—she was a boy."

"Please," Hannah appealed. "I'm really not harmed. Let them go."

"And have them slip up behind me and bore me in the back? Ump-umm."

"Mister, we don't know who yu are. Yu let us ride out of here, an' yu'll never see the likes of us again," the same man exclaimed. The other two seconded him.

"I reckon it's your lucky day, gents," Lintell said backing to his horse and stepping into the saddle without holstering his Colts. "Move," he said flashing Hannah an icy look. Hannah never looked back as she nudged the bay into a lope, hearing the thud of hoofs behind her as he followed.

They rode at a steady clip. Lintell watched her. She sat stiffly in the saddle, back ramrod straight one hand clasping her coat closed. The little fool, he grumbled, riding off on this crazy stunt. A few moments more and he'd of been too late to save her. Hells fire, he wanted to shake her until her teeth rattled. They had ridden perhaps five miles before he came up beside her and grabbed the bay's reins and pulled both horses to a halt. She turned flashing blue eyes upon him,

"Thank you for getting me away from those men," she said stiltedly, and then she leaned forward and struck him a hard blow on his chin with her closed fist.

"Ow!" he cried for an instant seeing stars, "What the hell was that for?" he demanded rubbing his tender jaw.

"For everything!" she ejaculated.

Her eyes suddenly filled with tears. And in the next instant her shoulders were shaking with her deep wrenching sobs.

"Hells fire," he muttered.

★

CHAPTER SIX

Lintell dismounted and led both horses under the shade of a cedar. Hannah sat her horse, head bowed, one hand clinching the saddle horn, the other holding her torn garments together. Though her sobs had quieted tears still streamed down her cheeks. Lintell kicked at a tuft of grass. He hated it when a woman cried. It always left a man at a sorry disadvantage. He glanced up at her and then he remembered his vow never to let a pretty face bamboozle him again. But he suddenly became silent, aware of the expression of intolerable pain in her eyes. It was the look of a hunted fugitive—a creature fettered, tortured. It called to the depth of Lintell in a message that fired his pity.

"You got another outfit in your bag?" he asked.

She shook her head.

"Well, you can't go all the way to Texas holding your shirt and coat together with one hand."

Her eyes narrowed to blue shards.

"Yeah, well," he murmured. "I reckon we'll hit upon a town or a ranch hereabouts so we'll find something for you."

He didn't know just where they were. For four days they had been heading pretty much south. He didn't know this country. He swore under his breath. If it hadn't of been for her hair-brained scheme they would be in San Antonio now, or close to it. Well, one thing he did know; he was going to shoot his captain's leg off when he got back for getting him into this God forsaken mess in the first place.

"How come you were headed south? Where the heck were you going?"

"Mexico."

"Mexico!" Lintell was shouting now. "You were headed to Mexico; a girl all alone?!" He looked at her as though he now knew she was mad.

"I'd of been safe in Mexico. Javier has a cousin—"

"Hells fire!"

"It was a bad idea, huh?" Hannah said meekly.

"Bad idea; I should smile!" he growled.

"You don't need to shout," she said calmly.

"I'm not shouting!"

"You are too."

He took a deep breath, kicked at another tuft of grass with the toe of his boot. "If you're not the most—"

"Well, that's easy for you to say, you're not the one who's been arrested, hounded for something you never did. You've already made up your mind that I killed my uncle."

She was right, he conceded. He had made up his mind, even though he kept saying it was up to the court to decide, he had been certain of her guilt. He had never asked her for her side of the story he realized. He looked up at her.

"All right, why don't you tell me what happened? I'll listen," he said.

She peered at him with those deep blue eyes for a long moment. Then she stepped from her horse still holding her coat tight against her throat, and sat down under the cedar. She drew her knees up to her chin and wrapped her arms around her booted ankles. She stared off into the distance as though remembering.

"The evening before my uncle's murder I happened to overhear an argument between my uncle and cousin, Edward Harlan. I wasn't meant to hear the exchange you see. Everyone had gone to the dance at Eula Mae Casey's. Me too, so my cousin Edward must have thought he was alone in the house with my uncle since Anita, our housekeeper had gone to spend the night at her sister's in town. I had to return unexpectedly—" She looked up at him and blushed. "I—"

"Why?" he said.

"Why, what?"

"Why did you return unexpectedly?"

"It doesn't matter," she said casting him an annoyed glance.

"Oh?" he said, raising one eyebrow.

"Getting out of the buckboard at Eula Mae's my gown ripped. There was no way to repair it. I had to go home to change my gown," she said cheeks red. "There, are you satisfied?"

"Ah," he grinned.

"You made me lose my train of thought," she scowled.

"You returned home unexpectedly and happened to overhear your uncle and cousin arguing," he prompted.

"Exactly. Like always it was about money. This time I guess Uncle Bob had refused to pay off his latest gambling debts. I didn't stay to listen but went to my room and changed. Ted Stoes was waiting for me in the buggy—"

"Who's Ted Stoes?"

"An—acquaintance."

"More like a beau, huh?"

"That really isn't any of your business. Now, do you want me to tell you what happened or not?"

"Go on."

"We went back to the dance. When I returned home—it must have been close to three in the morning—"

"Who brought you home, Stoes?"

"Well, no. It happened to be Bud Jackson. He's one of Eula Mae's cowboys," she replied nose in the air.

"Did he see you into the house? Maybe he'd be a witness for you."

"No," she slowly answered a thoughtful expression on her face. "But there was something odd now that I think about it. Course it might be nothing—"

"What?"

"Well, when I opened the front door I distinctly heard a door click shut down the hall. I thought at the time maybe it was caused by a draft when I opened the front door since there was no one else in the house except Uncle Bob, and I could see light under the door to his office, so I supposed he was in there. Anita, our housekeeper, had gone into town to stay the night with her sister—"

"What about your cousin Edward?"

"No, he stays in the cabin by the bunkhouse. And another thing. Before Ed and George burst into the room I had this eerie feeling that I was not alone in the room."

"Oh?"

"Yes it was a strange feeling, like I was being watched. I could have sworn there was someone hiding in the shadows on the far side of the room."

"Hmm. Your cousin said he heard a gunshot as they were riding up to the house and hurried straight into the house and found you standing over his dad with his gun in your hand—"

"That's a lie—I mean about hearing a gunshot. I was in the house for several minutes before they came. There was no gunshot or I would have heard it."

"Hmm. Strange. Go on."

Well, since Uncle Bob was still awake, I went to tell him I was home. I knocked but there was no answer, so I opened the door and went in. He often works late and falls asleep at his desk, so I thought maybe he had done just that. He was not at his desk. I walked farther into the room and that's when I saw—" A sob caught in her throat.

He waited giving her a chance to compose herself. She looked at him a strange light in her celestial blue eyes.

"He was lying on the floor. I saw his feet and ankles protruding from behind his desk. I didn't know what had happened, a heart attack, I didn't know. I rushed to his side. That's when I saw the blood . . . and the gun. I picked it up. I was afraid; as I said I had this weird feeling that I wasn't alone in the room. That's when Edward and George Gans burst into the room—"

"What happened to the money?"

She stared at him. "What money?"

"The money that was taken from Harlan's safe."

"You haven't believed a thing I said—"

"I didn't say that."

"You didn't have to. It's all there in your eyes," she choked, tears welling up in her eyes.

"Don't start bawling again," he growled, silently accusing himself of being a softhearted weakling.

She gave him a caustic look as she wiped her nose with the palm of one hand.

"I reckon I'm just curious that's all. Unless that little bag you got hanging from your saddle is full of cash—then what happened to the seventy-five thousand dollars that was missing from your uncle's safe?"

She stared wide-eyed at him. "I don't know anything about missing money."

"Empty out your bag."

She got angrily to her feet and jerking the valise from the saddle horn threw it at him. He caught it in both hands, giving her a surly look. She arched her chin and stared defiantly back.

He opened the bag and peered inside. He had watched her pack and had a good idea what he would see. But then she could have hidden the money and retrieved it later after she escaped from him. If so, then she would have it here in her valise. He reached and pulled out a silky undergarment and held it up. Her eyes looked daggers as a blush crept up her cheeks. He grinned and rummaged about in the bag. It contained only clothing, a small walnut toiletry box with various bottles and fittings. The lids were silver plated. On the cover, the mother of pearl insert contained the initials *HLG*. The faint but pleasant scent of lavender met his nostrils. Lastly there was a comb, a small hand mirror, toothbrush, and a book of poems.

"Well, I reckon you're telling the truth about that. Besides, I'm trying to figure how you could have made off with all that cash when your cousin surprised you before you could get away."

"Obviously, because I couldn't have. I didn't rob my uncle, and I didn't kill him either," she replied stiltedly.

"So why did you run away?"

"I made a foolish mistake, alright? The same I imagine you'll say I made trying to escape from you, but at the time I was so devastated; shocked seeing Uncle Bob dead that I wasn't thinking straight. I thought I would never get a fair trial, as Edward and Gans' lies would send me to the gallows. That's all I could think of. They locked me in the storeroom while Edward went to summon the sheriff. I managed to escape and climbed in the window of my room—and I want you to know it wasn't easy wearing a formal gown," she interrupted herself.

She went on to explain how she arranged the cardboard under the door and pushed the key through unlocking the door from the inside.

“I gathered what clothes that would fit in my little valise and changing to overalls and shirt, put on this old coat and sombrero and climbed back out the window—”

“Well, I reckon I can understand why you ran away. It must have been a tough experience for a girl. And me showing up didn’t make things any easier. But that little scheme of yours to hide in Mexico—”

“That was Javier’s idea.”

“And a damn harebrained one at that! What would have happened to you had you fallen into the hands of outlaws or desperados?”

She gave an audible sigh. “I guess I’ve been foolish all around,” she admitted hesitantly.

Impulsively Lintell reached and squeezed her hand. The instant he yielded to this kindly act he regretted it, and hurriedly pulled his hand back as she responded with quick tears and warm soft flush vividly betraying what a stranger she had been to another’s sympathy. For a long moment neither spoke.

“Say,” he said breaking the silence, “Just where was that gun when you picked it up?”

“It was laying on the floor near his right hand.”

“Hmm, maybe your uncle shot himself—”

“I’ve thought a lot about that since that night,” she replied. “But it doesn’t make sense. Why would he do that when he told me earlier when I returned to change that there was something he had to do; some arrangement he was going to make regarding Edward and his latest problem. He did seem serious, but at the time I was anxious to return to the dance—”

“So he could have—”

"No, he would never do such a thing," she denied fiercely.

"Well, maybe your cousin and that Gans fellow wanted it to look like he did. And when you stumbled upon the scene they decided to set you up. Sort of like killing two birds with the one shot, so to speak. Say now, I'm thinking that your cousin just might have let you escape."

"Let me escape?!"

"Shore. It was pretty careless leaving the key in the lock," he replied. "Why take a chance on going to trial, or worse, having suspicion turned his way, when he could have you on the run where you'd be out of his hair."

"Oh, God, are you saying Edward kill—killed Uncle Bob; his own father!"

"I reckon it all makes sense, a hell of a lot more sense than you killing your uncle. From what I've heard your cousin Edward's a drunkard and a gambler. He needed quick cash to pay off gambling debts and according to you had a heated argument over money with your uncle the night he was murdered. I reckon that figures to be a powerful strong motive to me—"

"You believe me!" she exclaimed.

"Yeah, little lady with the bluest, saddest eyes I've ever seen, I believe your story."

"Oh!" she cried, impulsively throwing her arms about his neck. Then, aghast, she jerked back covering herself, face a bright red. She rested her chin on her knees, not looking at him.

"I shore wish though you'd have stayed put and not run away like you did. Then we could have had this conversation a long time ago."

"I see now that there were a lot of things that didn't add up. I should have stayed and faced the consequences."

"I reckon you can say that again."

"We have to go back. I want to clear my name," she said simply, her eyes seeking Lintell's face.

He nodded slowly, turning to look out over the sage cloaked valley carrying with him the impression of dark, melancholy eyes. Suddenly the cedar branch inches from his head exploded showering him with needles and bark. Simultaneously came the distant crack of a rifle. Lintell leaped upon Hannah pulling her with him to the ground.

"What—" she gasped staring up at him with wide fearful eyes.

"Somebody just took a pot shot at me." he growled gazing down at her face only inches from his noticing for the first time a sprinkling of tiny freckles across the bridge of her nose.

"You think it was one of those cowboys you let go?"

"Stay here and don't move!" he hissed, and ducking under the cedar branches reached his horse where he jerked the rifle from the saddle boot. That shot had narrowly missed! If he hadn't of turned his head at that moment . . .

He leveled his Winchester, but he could see nothing to shoot at. Lintell heard the crash of brush off to his left; a rider moving through the cedars. Angrily he leveled his Winchester and fired two quick shots into the midst of the cedar brush. He worked the lever of the rifle as fast as he could, firing three more times. He could hear the whine of the shots and cracking of branches. He waited with the rifle cocked. There were no answering shots.

Lintell made his way back to where Hannah lay peeking from behind the cedar. She stared at him face white, eyes big and tragic.

"That shot came from that bunch of cedars yonder. I'm going to slip around and come up on the backside," he said, "You stay hidden where you are."

"Like hob I will!" she retorted. "You just got through telling me how dangerous it was for me traveling alone, but then you'd leave me on my own here while you go looking for somebody who just tried to murder you! Did you happen to think what might happen to me if he kills you?"

He stared at her his mouth screwed to the side obviously reconsidering. His mind vied to be in two places simultaneously; to find the shooter, and to remain here and protect the girl. He pulled the big Colt from his left holster, handed it to her butt first.

"You know how to use this?"

She leaned forward, took the gun, holding it in both hands. "Of course, I know how to use it," she replied and a bright glow suddenly burned out the shadow in her eyes.

Lintell started off. If he had hit the shooter with one of his random shots that would've been pure luck. And if the man slipped around behind Lintell while he was trying to do the same to him, and accosted Hannah, hurt her, he would never forgive himself. Nearing the clump of cedars his rushing mind slowed and he reverted to the hard, steely, vigilant lawman.

When he arrived at the place after cautiously approaching, he saw where a horse had stood and booted tracks moving off a ways to where the shooter had squatted. Lintell saw that he had an excellent view of the cedar where he and Hannah had stopped and talked.

"Damn clear shot from here," he muttered. "It's just a miracle he missed."

His searching eye spied an empty 44.40 casing a few feet away where it had been ejected from the shooter's rifle. It was the same type cartridge he used in his Winchester Model 1873. He picked it up and put it in his pocket. The shooter had made a hurried departure Lintell noted. The tracks pointed north. Lintell racked his brain, but could not remember seeing one of those cowboys who had accosted Hannah with a saddle gun. He would bet that whoever shot at him was not one of them. Who then, Joe Arment the bounty hunter? Was he the person who has been following them? The one who ransacked Hannah's room? But what purpose would Arment have in killing a Texas Ranger?

Hannah was waiting for Lintell where he had left her. She gave an inaudible sigh, and sat down heavily on the ground, her big eyes, wide and dark, appeared to engulf him as he strode up to her.

"Looks like our shooter hightailed it," he said dropping to the ground beside her. He took the Colt from her lap and slid it into his holster. "But I got a hunch we ain't seen the last of him."

He gazed meditatively out over the vista of sage and cedar. "Ever since I left Las Vegas I've had a gut feeling that I was being watched," he remarked after a moment. He looked at her. She peered back at him, her large eyes studying him quizzically. "I reckon somebody's trailing us; somebody who wants me dead. I shore didn't reckon I had any enemies in these parts."

"I think I know who it is," she announced nervously. "It's the same person who tried to kill me and ransacked my room—"

"Someone tried to kill you?"

"Well, I don't guess he wanted to kill me, not until he found out where something was he was looking for—and it couldn't be the money because I didn't steal it," she replied and proceeded to tell him about the dark figure who had invaded her room.

"You mentioned that you thought someone was hiding in the room when you discovered your uncle's body. Maybe that someone is the same person. Maybe he thought you saw him; recognized him."

"But I didn't!"

"What if he thought you did?" he insisted. "That could account for him trying to kill you—"

"But he wasn't trying to kill me—" she protested.

"Perhaps, not until he got what he wanted."

"Oh," she gasped.

"And if that's the case then the murderer doesn't have the money either. But on the other hand if it's not the stolen cash he's looking for, then what is it?" Lintell asked. "And where the heck *is* the missing cash?

"I don't know," she moaned, "And it frightens me to think Edward is involved."

★

CHAPTER SEVEN

Like most buildings in this part of the country this one was constructed of stone. A trail wound under a cedar-covered slope and through a clump of tall cottonwoods. In a rounded curve a wide bench jutted out, and here among the scattered cedar and gnarled old cottonwoods stood the low-roofed house, its flat odd shaped yellow stones a colorful vista against the green and brown setting. Farther back under the slope was a rambling jumble of cabins roofed with red earth. A ragged mustang stood haltered by a leather lariat to a hitching rail. The two riders were still a ways from the house when dogs set up a series of howls and barks. A woman ambled out of the open door. She wore a dirty gingham dress and turned a round pleasant face toward the approaching riders.

A rugged man in the prime of life stepped out the door and walked a few paces from the building where he stood watching Lintell and Hannah's slow advance. As they grew closer, Lintell saw the man give the woman a resounding slap on the backside and heard the hearty words, "Get the hell back inside." The man had a big voice, a big frame and a big hand. His boldly cut features were not unhandsome, but gave the impression that he might not be overly pleasant.

Riding into the yard Lintell saw that the man's eyes were a shade between green and hazel. Lintell had the intuition that he was a heavy drinker. Half-dozen hounds continued with a discordant racket from a pen a short distance from the house until a sharp curse from the man hushed them. At that moment a second man emerged from the house to disclose a swarthy face with eyes like bright beads and a tight-lipped mouth and hard jaw. Lintell realized they had fallen into bad company, which wouldn't have bothered him much had he been alone, but having the young woman with him put him in an entirely new and tense situation not at all to his liking.

"Howdy," Lintell drawled.

The big man said nothing, his sharp eyes moving from Lintell to Hannah who sat her horse slightly behind Lintell. Watching him closely, Lintell had the notion the man had not recognized Hannah for the girl she was.

"Say, me and my pard lost our outfit someways back," Lintell said in a cool easy drawl.

"Yu don't say."

"Where's the next town where a feller can buy a good pack mule and some supplies?"

"Which way yu headed?"

"I reckon south."

The man shook his head. "I reckon the next settlement would be Guadalupe," he said.

"How far to Guadalupe?"

"'Bout sixty mile, as the crow flies," he answered slowly.

"Ah-huh," Lintell acknowledged.

"Wal, that shore is a fine hoss yu got there," the man said with a zest of appreciation not lost upon Lintell. "What yu call him?"

"Colonel. Named after an old friend of mine."

"Colonel, huh? Not such a bad name. How long yu had 'em?"

"About four years. He's mine."

"Would yu sell 'em?"

"I reckon not. Have you ever loved a horse?" Lintell queried easily.

"That's the only love I ever had," rejoined the big man which brought a loud guffaw from the smaller man with the beady eyes.

"The boy looks plumb tuckered out," he said peering up at Hannah. "Why don't yu step down an' come in. I'll tell the cook te add two more fer supper."

"That shore is a kind offer, but I reckon there's still plenty of daylight left. We'll just mosey on," returned Lintell.

"Yu shore yu don't want te sell that hoss? I'll give yu a hundred, an' my hoss te boot," the big man said with the articulacy of a born horse-trader. And it also bore a note that grated on Lintell.

"Thanks, but I don't reckon I'll sell," Lintell drawled. "Come on boy," he said giving Hannah a nod.

"Wal, if'n yu've made up yore mind, 'bout five mile on this trail thar's a rite fine spring. Good water an' a tolerable place te camp fer the night."

"Much obliged," Lintell replied, and started off.

Hannah followed and after a short distance she nudged her horse up alongside his.

"Are we going to stop at that spring he mentioned?" she asked wearily.

"And get bushwhacked? That hombre shore wanted my horse Colonial awful bad. And I figure he wouldn't be opposed to shooting me in the back to get him."

"Oh," she sighed.

He glanced at her. She peered back at him and he could see the dark circles of fatigue about her eyes, the result of the strain of the past few days.

"Tired, huh?"

"Yes, as a matter of fact . . . and hungry too," she answered.

"We'll stop at that spring and fill our canteens and then keep on for a while. I'm kinda leery that hombre and his crony just might trail us."

Cedars and brush grew densely as they rode along. At the spring after satisfying their thirst they filled their canteens then continued on. Sunset caught them at the base of a slope. Lintell took to the thickest part of the cedars and mounted the hill. Hannah, clinging wearily to the saddle, followed after him. Emerging on top, to the right of the summit, he searched the rolling rangeland they had just traversed with binoculars for a long time. Seemingly satisfied, he then turned his eyes to the left down the slope where a stand of cottonwoods stood.

"Can you hold on a little longer? We'll camp in them cottonwoods."

Arriving at the spot, Lintell swung down from his saddle and reaching a hand helped Hannah. She was thankful for the leather ties

Lintell had cut for her to fasten her coat together modestly as she slid into his arms, too exhausted to think beyond that. Limping to one of the cottonwoods she sank to the ground her back to the tree.

"Rest," Lintell said, "I'll see if I can rustle up a couple of cottontail rabbits for supper after I see to the horses."

It was dry, lonely, silent, wild there under the cottonwoods; the sun had gone down red and gold in the west when Lintell returned. Hannah was kneeling by the tree, eyes wide and fearful.

"I—heard two shots," she said slowly getting to her feet.

"How many did you suppose I'd need?" was Lintell's drawling retort as he held up the two rabbits.

She came slowly toward him. "I thought—never mind. Can I help?"

"Ever skinned a rabbit?"

"Of course. I grew up on a ranch, remember?"

"Is that a fact," he grinned. "Well, you take care of a fire and I'll skin these fellers. We'll have broiled rabbit in a jiffy."

She quickly set about building a fire and soon smoke, smelling like burning leaves, wafted up. Lintell spit each rabbit on a sharp stick and handing one to Hannah they held them over the hot coals, turning them round and round. Darkness had settled down by the time they had the rabbits broiled a delicious brown.

"A little salt and pepper and now we're all set," he said squatting on his haunches in the manner of cowboys.

Hannah bit into the rabbit, too tired and hungry to worry about her appearance which she imagined must be frightful; a week without a bath, wearing the same trail-stained clothes. And this would be her first night on the trail with him sleeping in the open.

Hannah took one intuitive glance at his now impassive face and then went on eating.

Lintell drug Hannah's saddle up under the limb of a cottonwood and spread her blankets on the grass.

"It'll be a pretty warm night. I don't think you'll need more than one blanket over you," he said peering back at her.

She didn't move watching him spread his blankets opposite the fire. He took off his gun belt and laid it next to his head. After removing his boots and sombrero he stretched out on the blanket his head resting on his saddle and closed his eyes. Even though she felt drained Hannah fought sleep remaining there by the fire watching the flickering flames. Silence seemed a fitting thing. The fire burned down and presently the blackness and the lonely night surrounded her. Not far distant came the forlorn bark of a coyote. Finally, with a sigh, she went to her blankets. A constant sighing droned through the trees, a mournful, whispering sound that sent the shivers down Hannah's spine, made her think sadly of all the tragedies she had ever known.

She woke suddenly feeling the pressure of a hand over her mouth.

"Shh," hissed a whispered voice.

She screamed, but her cry was muffled by his hand. She struck out with her fist, she heard a stifled yell.

"Ow! Damn it," Lintell, snarled, face close to her ear, "It's me. Stop it! You're gonna tip them off!"

His words registered, and she suddenly stopped her struggles and lay staring up at him, a dark silhouette against the light of the moon.

"They're after our horses," he whispered. "Stay here and be quiet, I'm going after them."

She nodded, and he removed his hand putting one finger gently against her lips as he did so.

"Shh," he hissed again, and thrust a pistol into her hand. "Just in case," he whispered and was gone as silent as an Indian.

She sat up pushing the blanket aside and quickly pulled on her boots. Like hob she would stay here! There were at least two horse thieves, probably more. She was not about to let him face them all by himself. She had watched him slip off to her right, and so, holding the heavy Colt in both hands, she very quietly glided off, eyes searching the dark shadows. She thought she heard a noise like the stomp of a horse's hoof off to her left and crept that way, anxiously holding her breath. The thought suddenly struck her that she couldn't shoot a man. Goodness gracious what was she doing? The moonlight cast dark strange shadows that loomed up before her abruptly. Unexpectedly a large dark shape appeared before her perhaps four feet away. She uttered a tiny gasp. Conceivably that is what alerted the man, or it could have been the twig that snapped beneath her foot. In any event the figure whirled and she heard the metallic click of a gun hammer, then a startled cry and a muted curse.

"Damn it, woman, I told you to stay in camp," came Lintell's angry voice.

A gruff bellow sounded from Hannah's right, then a scuffing noise followed by a burst of red flame and the loud boom of a pistol. Hannah heard the sickening rend of a bullet striking flesh. It shocked and horrified her to see Lintell go down as if he had been hit by a club. Paralyzed with fear Hannah saw Lintell's gun flame red from low on the ground and the instant boom deafened her. Again his gun crashed and someone let out a terrified scream. Lintell was on his feet smoking gun leveled. There was more scuffing noise, painful curses and then the sound of horse's hoofs moving rapidly away.

"Jack, you're shot! Oh, my God—oh, how terrible!" Hannah gasped rushing to his side, reaching for him. Her hand encountered the rich warm feel of blood.

"You're damn right I'm shot," Lintell snorted. "I reckon they're gone, and they didn't get our horses."

"Oh, Jack is it very bad?" queried Hannah, her hands trembling as they felt the warm, soapy blood. "Come, can you walk? I'll build up the fire so I can see."

When they reached the camp site, Lintell slumped to the ground one hand holding his shoulder. Hannah quickly replenished the fire throwing several thick branches on the coals. Once the flames brightened, Hannah pulled Lintell's shirt wide open and down over his shoulder.

"Hurts like hell. But I can't see for the blood," Lintell grunted twisting his head in an effort to see. "I can move my arm . . . feel my collarbone," he said. "Ah, I guess it's all right. I think the bullet went clear through."

"It sure did, Jack," Hannah said with quavering voice.

"I reckon that's good. Then all I have to worry about is blood poisoning. Can you heat some water and wash them holes clean and then tie them up?" he asked weakly.

"Hold still and keep quiet," she ordered.

She examined the wounds, front and back. "I fear the bullet has carried some of the cloth from your shirt into the wound."

She hurried to her valise and rummaging through pulled out her walnut toiletry box. Opening the box she found her tweezers.

"This is going to hurt like sixty. I've done it more than once for Uncle Bob."

With trembling hands Hannah went to work with her tweezers pulling threads of his shirt out of the bleeding hole. Satisfied that she had retrieved all the cloth from the wound she proceeded to wash them and using a clean scarf from her bag, tore and folded it into pads and pressed them over the holes. Taking Lintell's bandana she tied them on tight.

"Oh, Jack, say you're not seriously hurting," implored Hannah.

"Well, I reckon—I'll be all—right," he murmured, head hanging low on his breast. "I—better lay—down," he whispered presently and he eased back on his blankets. "You'll have to—stand night guard."

Soon afterward Hannah realized the incredible fact that she, little Hannah Lea Gibson, was alone in a lonely place with a wounded Texas Ranger, who twisted fitfully in his sleep. Hannah felt that sleep was far indeed from her. She paced to and fro; she added a little wood to the fire. The blaze shone on Lintell's lean dark face, stern in the set rigidity of pain. After a while she rose, brave enough to go in search of their horses. She still had his pistol which she stuffed in her coat pocket, its heavy weight causing the garment to sag noticeably on one side, but it made her feel much safer. She found both horses and led them back into camp where she tied them. She then hovered over Lintell like a mother over her infant, and listened to the night sounds. Coyotes yelped with their keen, sharp, wild notes. From the grass and from the sage thickets, from all around, rose the low, incessant chorus of insects. Hannah solemnly visualized herself alone here in this place with grave responsibility forced upon her, cast upon her own resources of strength and endurance.

In this solitary place the profound realities of life fell with crushing force upon Hannah's dreams, upon all she believed in. From that midnight hour she realized there would be a tense strife between things as they were and things which she dreamed of. The fire burned down to a bed of ruddy coals. At length in the silent darkness before dawn Hannah went to her blankets and composed herself to rest if not sleep.

The night wind had stirred the cottonwood leaves and soon from all around Lintell came rustlings and stealthy sounds. Through half-closed eyelids he could see Hannah's little dark form huddled before the fire. He knew she was watching over him. She got up to pace to and fro, adding wood to the fire, and then came near bending over him as though listening for his breathing. He kept his eyes closed pretending sleep. Shortly she left the circle of fire light and some moments later he heard the thump of hoofs as she brought the horses close and tied them. After a while she went to her bed and he tried to sleep. But the dull ache persisted. From time to time he took a swallow of water from his canteen. These movements caused him acute pain, but when it subsided he suffered only the dull throbbing ache in head and shoulder.

He accepted it, for it wasn't the first time he had been shot. The pain he could deal with; it was only when it interfered with his pondering of his problem. He knew that in the morning he was due for a rough time on horseback, but they couldn't stay here. He knew that the fevers would come and he would be useless. How would the girl manage? She had no one at the moment; no one but him. Some late hour in the night relief from his mental struggle came, if not the physical stress. He had made up his mind about Hannah Lea Gibson.

★

CHAPTER EIGHT

Sunrise was gilding the eastern sky when Hannah suddenly came awake. She had slept longer than she had intended. She rose quickly throwing off her blanket and hurried to where Lintell lay, head resting on his saddle. She knelt beside him, stared down at his impassive face. He lay so still. She put a hand tentatively upon his chest, sliding it beneath his blanket, and through his open shirt to touch his bare chest.

"Oh, Jack, don't you dare be dead!" she cried pressing her ear convulsively upon his breast.

A hand entangled in her golden curls, tugging her head up. She peered down into his keen gray eyes.

"Jack, you're alive!"

"Shore I am. But I reckon you shore are getting rite familiar with my name, Miss Gibson."

"I don't know what you mean," she said.

"You shore been calling me Jack a lot recently."

"I don't seem to recall," she retorted, chin in the air. "Have I?"

He grinned. "I see you brought the horses in."

"Yes, last night. I was afraid those thieves might come back. Are you hungry?"

"I reckon I could eat."

"I'll heat up a can of beans and make some coffee and biscuits. They'll be ready in a jiffy," she said getting swiftly to her feet. "Then I'll feed the horses."

Lintell set up when Hannah brought him his food on a tin plate and managed to slowly feed himself with his right hand. She looked worn and it was obvious that she had spent a stressed, sleepless night. Presently she finished eating and went to feed the horses slipping a nose bag of oats on each animal.

"I reckon we ought to get on the road," he said when she returned.

"Can you ride?" she asked concerned.

"I'll manage. We need to put some distance between us and this place; in case them horse thieves decide to come back."

"Well, if you've finished your breakfast, I'll saddle the horses."

"I'll help."

"You will not! I can saddle the horses. I was born on—"

"A ranch. I know, but I reckon you're just a sprite—"

"All right, be stubborn then, and start your wound bleeding again," she said giving him a fleeting flash of eyes.

He sat there and watched her, marveling at her strength as she heaved the heavy saddles up on the backs of the horses. For a little girl she certainly was strong. But he should have known, he thought, remembering her wicked right hand. He waited as she hurriedly washed the pans and packed the camp gear stowing it behind both their saddles, and then mounted. How efficient she was, her movements quick and sure. He pulled himself into the saddle making an effort to hide the grimace of pain as he did so. He wasn't sure how long he would be able to last feeling a wave of dizziness sweep over him. Lintell managed fairly well the first hour, especially on the level ground, but when they reached the steep and rough ascents he had to hold on to the pommel.

Lintell led the way and as the days before, Hannah fell in behind. She didn't protest because in this manner she could keep an eye on him. She was worried. They should have remained in their camp, and she should have washed and cleaned the wounds again this morning. He had lost so much blood, and as she watched him her concerns were confirmed. By midmorning he was slumped far over and on one occasion she thought he was going to topple from the saddle. She rode up beside him.

"Jack, we have to stop," she implored.

He looked at her with feverish eyes and nodded.

"You're not going to fall are you?" she cried reaching to catch his horse's reins, and her words and spirited action implied singular apprehension.

"Not shore. I seem to be seeing two of you," he muttered, face ashen.

They must stop so he could lie down and she could clean and re-bandage his wounds, but where, not here in the open. She would have to push on. Hopefully they could find shelter in the zone of cedars which she judged to be maybe two miles distant. She pulled the map Javier had drawn for her out of her pocket and unfolded it.

Towns and waterholes were marked as well as landmarks she had recognized in passing, but there was nothing to indicate any ranch houses or any such places.

Hannah fell into a state in which there were no moments of relaxation. With wide eyes she kept a constant vigil, her gaze often sliding over her shoulder at Lintell and then back along their trail. Once she thought she saw a flash of color far behind and she stared for some minutes, but saw nothing further and decided it was just her over-active imagination.

She hadn't progressed far into the cedars when she noticed a dim long-unused trail leading off to her right and at the top of a slight rise she saw in the small clearing a flat-roofed stone house. She darted a glance at Lintell and saw that he was leaning far over his pommel, one hand entwined in his horse's mane. She was for a moment undecided, afraid of whom the occupants might be. But then on a second keener look she realized that the house was clearly abandoned. The glass was missing from the one window, leaving only the weathered and splintered sash. The worn and windswept door stood ajar. Weeds, knee high, surrounded the building. She nudged her horse up the incline leading Lintell's.

Hannah rode up to the door of the one room dwelling and slid from her horse. She glanced back at Lintell to be sure he was not about to fall and then pushed the door all the way open. It creaked on rusted hinges sending a shiver up her spine. She took a cautious step inside and peered around. Her heart leaped into her throat when a large scaly lizard darted across the floor and up the wall and out the window. A narrow bed frame absent its mattress, but possessing rusted springs was pushed against the far wall, and a small scarred table with two chairs sat in the middle of the floor. In the corner opposite the bed was a small, rusty metal stove. A stovepipe, once black but now heat-sheared and rusty like the stove, extended upward and out through the roof of the building. On the adjacent wall racks and shelves, which she imagined once contained various cans and sundry other foodstuffs, were now starkly empty and covered with dust as was the rest of the interior, but otherwise surprisingly clean and dry meaning, she thought, that the roof did not leak, which was good.

It seemed in the short interval that she was inside the sky had become overcast with dark clouds. Hannah was sure rain would be upon them by morning or maybe before, and she voiced a whispered prayer of thanks that they had discovered this shelter from the elements.

"Jack, I found a house. It's empty, and—and not so bad. Come inside and I'll see to the horses."

She reached up to him and he slid into her arms nearly carrying her to the ground. She could feel the heat of his burning fever through his shirt. With him leaning on her shoulder she was able to get him inside and seated on one of the chairs. She bit her lip worriedly. He needed a doctor. She found some kindling in a wood box near the stove and wadding up some old newspapers she found as a starter soon had a fire going. She put a pan of water on to heat, and then went to take care of the horses. Down the slope behind the house she discovered a small stream and led the horses there after which she hobbled them. There was plenty of grass for them to eat. On her way back up to the house she spied a small lean-to on the side of the building. She peered inside and saw a barn lantern hanging on a nail. She took it down and shaking it heard a sloshing sound. And when she unscrewed the cap discovered there was still kerosene inside. She looked about and saw a tall greasy can on a shelf. It was half full of kerosene. She carried both inside. Lintell was slumped in the chair.

"Let me look at your wounds," she said as calmly as she could, and began to unbutton his shirt. She pulled it off his shoulder and down off his arm. His muscular chest was pale and burning to the touch.

"This is going to hurt," she said. "The bandages are probably stuck to your wounds."

With unsteady hands she began to untie the bandana and then essayed to remove the blood-soaked pads. As she had predicted, the pads were crusted with blood and were stuck tight. She saturated the pads with warm water and pulled gently at them, but they wouldn't come loose. She tugged some more on the pads and she saw his jaw clinch.

"I'm hurting you aren't I?" she muttered.

"I'll—manage," he panted.

He peered up at her face but after one quick darting glance at him her eyes remained on the task at hand. Slowly the pads came unstuck.

"Ah," she sighed with obvious relief, "Finally."

She wet one of her scarves and with soap from her bag began gently to wash the wounds which were red and inflamed. She examined them closely; searching for any fragment of cloth she might have missed before but could see nothing foreign. She looked at the can of kerosene. She remembered her uncle pouring it on cuts, and once when she was seven or eight pouring it on her scrapped knee. It burned, but the cut healed with no infection.

"This'll hurt," she acknowledged, and slowly poured a few drops of kerosene over each of the wounds.

He flinched but did not make a sound. With trembling fingers, she reapplied the bandages.

"There, it's done," she breathed. "I'll fix the bed for you, and then you can lie down."

Taking his sharp long-bladed knife from the sheath in his boot she went outside and cut a load of cedar boughs. The light low down had shaded and rays of gold slanted through the cedars. Carrying the boughs back to the cabin she spread them on the bed springs and covered them with two blankets. After drinking deeply from the canteen Lintell gingerly stretched out on the bunk.

"I'll only lay here a little while," he murmured closing his eyes.

"Shore," she mimicked, unfastening his gun belt.

"Careful with those," he muttered as she hefted his gun belt.

She hung the belt over the bed post near his head without comment and then pulling off his boots laid a damp cloth on his forehead. He didn't seem quite as warm, she thought hopefully. As she set about kneading flour for biscuits she glanced around at the tiny cabin. She had hung a blanket over the open window, and the lantern's yellow light softened the harshness of the stone walls conveying a subtle pleasantness. She wondered what stories these walls could tell. Had the occupants here been happy or was there tragedy? Was that the reason the cabin was abandoned; some terrible and tragic event that had befallen them? Her eyes fell upon the dark form on the bed, and for a moment considered the way the light cast the shadow of his handsome profile onto the wall behind him making him seem larger than life.

Perhaps it was something about this little cabin, with its strong and secure stone walls; but it occurred to her that she was feeling easier. But then, she realized, it probably had more to do with thoughts of her uncle, the things he had taught her; to believe in herself, in family pride, that she was the granddaughter of Annabelle Clark of Virginia, and though she might be a tiny sprite of a girl, she had pluck; she was somebody. She suddenly had the most marvelous awareness that she could face whatever troubles fate decided to toss her way. She wished she could take a bath though. She really was finding it hard to stand herself under the circumstances.

Lintell ate little of the meager fare, again beans and biscuits and strong coffee. She had enjoyed cooking on the stove though. It was so much better than over an open flame. Afterwards, carrying the lantern, she went down to the stream and filled the canteens and washed the pans and forks. The horses were cropping grass nearby.

The black melancholy night seemed to envelop the cabin. The feeling of rain was more pronounced. She walked back up the incline toward the cabin leading the horses. With the advent of the storm she thought it best to shelter the animals under the lean-to.

Lintell had fallen into a fitful sleep and Hannah spread her blankets on the floor in one corner and after turning the wick down so the lantern emitted a soft yellow glow, stretched out on her bed. She placed the heavy Colt beside her in easy reach of her hand and tried to fall asleep, but she found herself listening for the sound of Lintell's breathing, aware of his restless twisting.

Finally she herself fell into a fitful sleep, harassed by strange dreams that became more and more morbid. Dark, frightening, faceless shadows closed in upon her where they finally merged into one in a ghastly climax which brought her suddenly awake. Only it wasn't a dream. It was real. But the dark shadow was not advancing upon her, but upon Lintell. She saw the raised arm and the gleam of a knife blade in the weak glow of the lantern.

"NO!" she screamed and at the same instant snatched up the Colt in both hands.

The black figure whirled to face her and she saw the lower half of a colorless face; the rest hidden by the wide brim of his sombrero. But she recognized the same dark figure that had invaded her room behind the café! Knife in hand, he spun back upon Lintell who had stirred and struggled to set up. Without further thought Hannah thrust the Colt out eye-level and thumbed back the hammer. She closed her eyes and pulled the trigger. A brilliant white flash of flame leaped out of the muzzle, and the accompanying boom nearly deafened her. She didn't know where the bullet went, but it obviously missed hitting the intruder. Emitting a loud curse, the man darted to the door, and disappeared into the night. Lintell was on his feet gun in hand and stumbled to the door.

"Jack, don't go out there," she cried, leaping to her feet, but he was already gone, out into the blackness in feverish pursuit.

A blue-white streak filled the valley below the cedars with weird light, and a boom of thunder rent the heavens. And before the booming echoes ceased rumbling, another flash of lightning streaked across the inky blackness, and the rain came in torrents. Hannah came to the door, peered out. Wind ripped through the cedar branches pelting her with rain drops. Lightning flashed and mere seconds appeared between the illuminating flashes as rolling thunder mingled continuously.

"Jack!" she yelled.

Only the rumble of thunder and the loud patter of rain driven on the wind answered her.

★

CHAPTER NINE

The shock of wind and rain pounding his person brought Lintell to a halt. A vivid flash of lightning illuminated the cedar grove in lurid detail. The boom of thunder followed quickly reverberating across the heavens. Wind whipped through the cedars driving before it the torrent. He stood a moment as though stupefied. He was barefoot and coatless. What the heck was he doing? The intruder could be anywhere out there and he was an easy target clearly visible with each flash of lightning standing in the open as he was. Lintell turned his back to the cold rain pelting him and lurched back toward the cabin. Reaching the door where Hannah stood framed by lantern light he staggered cold and wet back inside. He huddled just inside the door casting Hannah a foolish glance as raindrops ran down his face and dripped from his clothing. She slammed the door closed.

"Why in the world did you chase him out in the storm?! With a fever! Oh, you are the most exasperating person I have ever known," she sighed. "You have to get out of those wet clothes," she insisted undoing the buttons and slipping the wet shirt off his shoulder. "Hurry, take off your overalls."

He sank onto the bed, pulling down his overalls. She caught a flash of white muscular thighs before averting her gaze. Picking up his wet garments where he had dropped them, she hung them over one of the chairs and placed it near the stove as he slid under the blankets and pulled them up to his chin. His eyes were dark shadows as he stared up at her, his body quaking violently, his teeth chattering.

"Can't g-g-get w-w-warm," he stuttered.

Hannah spread both her blankets over him, tucking them snuggly about his shivering body. She fed more wood to the stove until it glowed red but still, insensible to his surroundings, his violent trembling rattled and shook the bed frame. In desperation she slid beneath the blankets wrapping her arms about him and pressing her warm body against his hard muscled frame. Eventually the chills began to subside and Hannah could sense by the relaxing of his muscles that he had fallen into an exhausted sleep. She was afraid to stir, afraid she might wake him, and so she stayed very still listening to the pounding rain on the roof of the cabin and the feel of his rock-solid body against her own softness. The wind buffed the cabin and the lashing of raindrops swelled louder. Now and then a flash of lightning turned the blanket over the window transparent, revealing the black outline of storm-lashed cedars as dull thunder reverberated across the sky. But it was warm and cozy here under the blankets pressed against his back and she felt her heavy eyelids droop.

She woke in the dark shadow before dawn; her arms still about him. Yellow flame glimmered from where the lantern sat on the table. She lay there not daring to move for a long moment aware of his deep steady breathing, the hard muscles of his long lithe form. Stealthily she raised her head and peered down at his sleeping face, thankful that he was still dead to the world, and prayed he wouldn't awake before she extricated herself. Holding her breath she slowly eased from the bunk. Retrieving one of the blankets she wrapped it about herself and curled up on one of the chairs and waited, deep in thought, for morning's light.

Sometime before daybreak Hannah was aware that the storm had abated, and later when she peeked from the partly opened door, saw that the sky was fast clearing and the air fresh and keen. For a moment she peered out at the rain-drenched landscape before walking back to her chair and setting down and drawing her feet up beneath her. What had happened to the mysterious dark figure she wondered uneasily? There was little doubt in her mind that he was still out there somewhere, waiting and watching.

Lintell's fever had left him sometime during the night leaving him with the disturbing memory of her warm body pressed close to him. Warily he raised himself on one elbow studying her where she sat curled on the chair, slowly letting his gaze travel from the crowning glory of her hair, slightly mussed from sleep, noting the coppery glints gleaming amid the gold, over her face, features now intent, serious. Her finely arched brown brows elegantly framed her eyes, large and well set, presently downcast deep in thought, the fringe of her long, lightly curling lashes casting lacy shadows across her delicately molded cheekbones. Her nose was small but uncompromisingly straight, her lips the very opposite; lush, the upper well-bowed, the lower distractingly full. Her face was an oval, her chin with its slight cleft, a sculpted curve. He wondered what held her attention so thoroughly that she hadn't sensed his prolonged appraisal.

"Good morning," he said.

Startled, Hannah glanced at him. She stared for several heartbeats seemingly transfixed by what she saw.

"Good morning," she finally said and smiled. "You need a shave."

"Yeah, I reckon," he drawled rubbing his chin. He started to throw back the blankets but remembered he wasn't wearing anything.

She noticed his hesitation and reached to feel his shirt and overalls draped over the chair close to the stove.

"They're dry," she said and turned her back. She heard the rustle of blankets as he slid from the bed. "What do you think he'll do now?" she asked keeping her face averted.

"You mean our visitor from last night?"

"Who else," she flashed.

"Yeah, well, I reckon that's a stumper," drawled Lintell with a dubious shake of his head. "It's a queer deal that's for shore. He's after something and he believes you have it. All right, I know we've been over this before, but let's put our heads together. We know it's not the missing money, so what is it?"

Hannah slowly shook her head as she pulled on her boots. "I have no idea. But why isn't it the money? You said yourself that he must think I have what he's after."

"I reckon you got a point there."

"Maybe my cousin Edward just hates me—"

Lintell shook his head. "That doesn't make sense. This man is after something. Think, girl. Figure it's not the money. Could you have taken some thing with you, maybe inadvertently—?"

"I only took a few things, a change of clothes, small items, personal things that would fit in that little valise. You searched it. You ought to know. In the last few weeks since leaving San Antonio I've taken things in and out of it a dozen times or more. I know what's in there—"

"There has to be something," he insisted as he struggled to pull on his boots.

She got to her feet, chin in the air. "I'll fix breakfast," she said by way of answer. "Would you like beans with your biscuits?"

That low reply, tinged with sarcasm, effectually checked further comment from him. That's all they had had the last three days . . . beans and biscuits.

Lintell eyed Hannah from beneath the brim of his sombrero as he saddled his horse. The morning was clear and bright, not a cloud in the sky which was a welcome sight after the days of rain. The girl was smiling and talking to her horse, looking, Lintell thought, the picture of health, cheeks vibrant with color, eyes clear and shimmering with youthful enthusiasm. He slung blanket and saddle onto the roan's back. They had eaten the last of the beans and flour biscuits that morning. Hannah had kept back a small amount of the dough, however, to use as a starter for when they reached a place to buy supplies, which had better be today, Lintell figured. Finished saddling her horse, Hannah turned and gazed a long moment at the cabin.

"In a way I kind of hate to leave this place," she said.

He halted in the process of tying his war-bag behind the cantle and folded his arms over the seat of his saddle and watched her swing onto her horse.

"What?" she demanded, seeing him staring at her.

He grinned but only shook his head and finished securing his war-bag.

"Well, it's true," she quipped.

He mounted and started down the incline toward the trail. Hannah fell in beside him. Lintell's keen eyes searched the surroundings knowing that their mysterious stranger was still out there somewhere. They had not gone far when Lintell caught a glimpse of movement and color through the cedars. He drew rein and held a hand out halting Hannah. He half-turned in the saddle, finger to his mouth silencing her. Bending low in the saddle he stared through the low cedar branches. On the far side of the narrow basin he sighted moving figures. He had only a glimpse of lean wild forms and ragged mustangs but it was enough.

"Mescalero Apaches," he whispered.

Hannah's face was as white as if it had never worn a golden tan, her eyes large, dark. Lintell deliberated. The Apaches appeared headed south, but they were proceeding slowly, cautiously, obviously bent upon mischief. They had not spotted them. That was a good thing. As best he could tell there were maybe ten savages. There could be more he realized. He waited listening, watching for some minutes. Hannah never made a sound. The Apaches were between them and the trail to Guadalupe. If the Indians doubled back it would be better to remain at the cabin. Within the sturdy stone building they could stand off a larger force of Indians than this one.

Suddenly the crack of a rifle broke the quiet. An instant later came two more shots in rapid succession. Lintell darted a glance at Hannah. She stared back, eyes wide, lips compressed. The rifle shots, Lintell determined, came from a Winchester, and from not far distant. Even as they waited there came another rifle crack, followed by the loud boom of what Lintell figured was a buffalo gun. The Apaches had sprung an ambush on some unsuspecting individual by the sound of it. Suddenly Lintell had a lightning-swift realization of his liability in this situation. His code as a Texas Ranger left him no alternative. He had to go to the aid of the poor soul ambushed by the savages. But he had an obligation to protect the girl also.

"Hannah, go back inside the cabin, and lock yourself in," he said voice low.

"Why, what are you going to do?"

"Hannah, please don't argue with me now."

"I'm not arguing. I just want to know what you are planning to do . . . you're going to get involved aren't you?"

"I have to Hannah."

She nodded. "All right, then I'll go with you," she said calmly.

"Damn it, woman, don't you ever do what I ask?" he hissed angrily.

"Of course," she said giving him a dazzling smile. "You know I'll be safer with you, than alone in the cabin."

"We'll leave our horses here," he sighed, stepping to the ground and pulling his Winchester from the saddle boot. He extracted a box of cartridges from his saddlebags. "Stay behind me," he ordered.

The Winchester cracked again, seemingly on top of them, as they slipped silently down through the cedars. Lintell dropped down to one knee, motioning Hannah down. Lintell crawled a few paces keeping low. Drawing up short he saw down the slight incline a small clearing. The first thing to catch his eye was a saddled horse lying on its side unmoving. A thin whiff of smoke rose from a smoldering campfire a few feet away. Then from behind a tree close up to a rock outcropping spouted a puff of smoke as the Winchester cracked. Apparently the ambushed rider was still alive. Lintell looked back over his shoulder at Hannah. She was kneeling; neck craned trying to see over his head. He reached back and unceremoniously grabbed her by the nape of her neck and jerked her down flat on her stomach.

"Stay down!" he hissed.

Lintell turned his attention back to the clearing. He saw several Apaches slipping among the cedars, flitting from one tree to another firing as they advanced upon the lone gunman behind the tree. At least three of the savages, Lintell realized had Winchesters and one had a buffalo gun as its loud report reverberated through the trees with predictable tempo.

At this juncture Lintell grimly entered the engagement. Three Indians scarcely a hundred feet below him were seeking to slip around the left side where they could get a clear shot at the man behind the tree. Lintell drew a quick bead on one of the Apaches and fired. Without waiting to see the Indian's fate he sighted on one of the other two and fired seeing him fall. The other quickly melted into the brush before he could fix a bead on him. Lintell swung his rifle back up the far slope where he could see another savage, the one with the buffalo gun and fired. He went down.

Suddenly Lintell saw the man behind the tree slumped down, the rifle slipping from his grip and he realized the man had been shot. Lintell sighted upon another Indian and fired. Abruptly the firing ceased, and for several moments all was eerily quiet. Then Lintell counted seven ragged figures fleeing up the slope through the cedars. He fired several rapid shots after them and knew he connected with one though the Apache continued on disappearing with the others among the trees. Lintell waited listening. Hannah edged up beside him, her little hand creeping to rest on his arm as she stared down at the tragic scene below.

Lintell wasn't too concerned that the remaining few Apaches would return, nevertheless, he cautiously approached the clearing counting as he did so four dead Apaches. They were all young, lean and ragged looking.

"Are they all—dead?" Hannah asked in a small strangled voice.

"I reckon," Lintell answered.

But then a choking rattle of blood in a man's throat belied that. Lintell reached the man slumped on his side next to the tree and eased him over on his back. The man was of middle age wearing dark shirt and pants. He was alive, conscious, but Lintell knew he was dying.

"Are they—gone?" he asked huskily.

"Yeah," Lintell answered. "But I reckon you're dying."

"I—know," the man grunted, staring up at Lintell, and then his head lolled to the side where he gazed intently at Hannah. He blinked.

"Give—me a—drink?" he asked. "Canteen on—my saddle."

Hannah hurried to the dead horse and retrieved the canteen and brought it to the man. She held it to his lips where he attempted to drink, but coughed, the water spilling down his chin.

"What's your name?" Lintell asked.

"Breen—Jeff Breen—Harlan—hired me—"

"Ed Harlan?" Lintell asked.

"Yeah." He made a strangled sound, clinched his eyes tightly closed. "Give—me another—drink?" he rasped.

Hannah put the canteen to his lips, but as before he only choked as he attempted to swallow. His eyes sought Lintell. "My boots—pull them off—please."

Lintell did as he bid which seemed to bring some comfort to the man. Breen's eyes singled out Hannah.

"Sorry," he gasped blood oozing from the corner of his mouth. "He—wanted me—'te kill you after—" His eyes rolled to take in Lintell. "But you—came along—queered the deal—"

"After what?" Lintell demanded. "What is it you're after?"

He stared, stupefied, up at Lintell, then his gaze flickered to Hannah.

"Don't yu—know?"

She shook her head, eyes wide.

"Be—damn—" he guffawed, then his body stiffened, his eyes rolled back in his head and he uttered a long shuddering breath, and lay still. Jeff Breen was dead and his passing left more questions than answers. Lintell stood and gazed around. His first thought was to leave everything as it was, but then figured he probably ought to make a report.

Lintell buried Jeff Breen. The Apaches he left lying as they had fallen. The grave was shallow for the ground was hard and Lintell's strength, having not fully recovered from his wounds, quickly gave out. Hannah helped gathering stones to place on the small mound to protect it from wild animals. As she worked, Lintell rested and watched her, a slight, slender girl with bedraggled shirt and disheveled hair, her face a rich golden-brown, her small tan hands strong and supple.

It suddenly occurred to him that saving this girl, proving her innocent, meant more to him than any task he had ever assumed. First it had been partly to mollify himself for his initial impulsive judgment of her guilt, and partly from a human feeling to aid an unfortunate girl falsely accused. But lately, however, had come a different sense, a strange one, with something personal and warm and protective in it.

Twilight had come when again they rode out into the open. The trail led out over open grassy range, with a few straggling juniper and clumps of mesquite. Selecting a camp-site, Lintell went about unsaddling the horses. After hobbling both animals, he turned them loose. Hunger made him more than usually keen-eyed with the result that he soon espied a cottontail rabbit. It ran off a few rods and then stopped and squatted. Lintell shot it through the head. It wasn't long before a second rabbit fell to his aim, and then a third. He skinned and dressed the cottontails and returning to the campsite found that Hannah had a fire going. She broiled the rabbits to a nice brown. A touch of salt made it a toothsome meal.

After supper, for a time they sat quietly around the fire, each seemingly deep in their own thoughts.

"I guess we'll never know what that Mr. Breen was looking for," Hannah sighed.

"Yeah," he nodded in agreement. "But we know your cousin Edward sent him. That tells me something."

She looked at him quizzically.

"Edward doesn't have the money, but thinks you do."

"Very queer," she murmured staring into the fire. "When I arrived I saw the door of the safe standing open."

"Did Ed have a key to the safe?"

"No . . . Uncle Bob would never have given him one under the circumstances. But I knew where he kept it, he showed me," she said softly. "I regularly worked on his account books and papers keeping them in order."

"Hmm," Lintell murmured.

Later Lintell dragged Hannah's saddle under a thick bushy cedar, and spread her bedroll there. His own roll of bedding, roped in canvas tarpaulin, he unrolled near hers. Hannah sat on her bedroll, and crossing one leg over the other struggled to pull off her boot.

"Jack, I can't pull off my boots," she moaned, looking over at him appealingly. "I'm afraid my feet are swollen."

"Well, it's been a long day in the saddle, and a wet one," he said, taking hold of the booted foot she elevated. It did not come off easily, and when it did, she gave a relieved sigh.

"There are holes in your socks," he said peering down at her tiny foot. "Do you have another pair?"

She shook her head. He stripped off her worn sock and inspected her raised foot, which brought a crimson tint to her cheeks.

"Your foot's all red but I don't see any blisters. Let me check the other one."

This boot came off with less difficulty. He held the stocking-clad foot up to the firelight.

"No holes," he drawled, grinning as the pink in her cheeks deepened. "I've got an extra pair. They're way too big for you; probably come up to your knees, but I reckon they'll have to do."

Hannah lay back on her bed wiggling her bare toes watching the glow of embers and the flickering ruddy flames. The moon rose and cast deep shadows under the cedars. Lintell rolled a cigarette and lit it with a twig from the fire. Nearby; the soft clump of hooves from the grassy bench where the horses grazed, and farther away, came the hoarse ki-yiing of a coyote. Hannah closed her eyes; a sudden feeling of well-being came over her.

Finishing his cigarette, Lintell stared into the flames for a long moment as they wavered playfully upon the deepening shadows. His gaze fell upon his weapons, lying on his saddle. His rifle was a Winchester Model 1873, shiny and smooth from long service and care. His two pistols were Colt 45's. Lintell rubbed the rifle with his hands, and then with a greasy rag which he took from the sheath. After that he held the rifle to the heat of the fire. The days of rain had wetted his weapons. A subtle and singular difference seemed to show in the way he took up the Colts. His action was slow. The Colts were not merely things of steel and powder and lead. He dried them and rubbed them with care, and then replaced them in their holsters.

The camp-fire flickered and burned out, so that no sparks blew into the blackness, and the red embers glowed and paled and crackled. Lintell at length got up and made ready for bed. He threw back tarpaulin and blankets, and laid his rifle alongside where he could cover it. His coat served for a pillow and he put one of the Colt's under that; then pulling off his boots, he slipped into bed, dressed as he was, and at once fell asleep.

Over Lintell's quiet form the shadows played, the cedar boughs waved, the juniper needles rustled, the wind moaned louder as the night advanced. By and by the horses rested from their grazing and the insects ceased to hum. Hannah lay there watching Lintell as he went about his tasks, smiled to herself. She listened to the coyote's howls, wild, sharp, sweet notes. They soothed her troubled, aching feet, lulled her toward sleep, reminded her of the gold-and-purple sunset, and the slopes of live oak and cedar of her childhood, the beauty that would never change.

★

CHAPTER TEN

The next morning they were up early and after a breakfast of leftovers and weak coffee they were once again on the trail. Mid-morning they came upon a shallow roaring river where beyond laid the village of Guadalupe. The horses drank the water, foaming white and amber around their knees, and then with splash and thump they forded it over the slippery rocks. As the horses cracked out upon the trail, a covey of grouse whirred up into the air. They presently came into the town itself which consisted of a wide main street upon which stood a number of low, wide buildings. Three horses stood hipshot at the hitching rails before a building whose weather-faded sign proclaimed it as the Last Chance Saloon. Two men lounged on the porch of a long low structure opposite the saloon. Farther down the street Lintell saw a sign which read '*Wells Fargo and Co.*' A tall man in overalls and boots stood behind the counter eying them easily as they entered.

"Howdy," he greeted.

"Like two tickets on to Las Cruses," Lintell said.

In short order the tickets were secured.

"Next stage departs pronto at nine in the mornin'," the man assured them, a rough hand tugging absently on one ear.

"I reckon we'll be aboard that one," Lintell said. "That is if there's a hotel in this burg, and a stable for our horses."

"Stables down the street," he said pointing with his chin. "As fer a hotel, we gots a lodgin' house," the man replied. "Ain't much on looks, but the grub's good an' beds clean. You passed it on the way in, next to Wright's store."

"That's the general store?"

"Yep."

They rode down to the stables to arrange for boarding the horses for the night. The stable owner was a short slim man with a clean shaven square jaw, a large handlebar mustache and lively blue eyes.

"Hod do," the man greeted.

"Howdy," Lintell replied. "Say, we're fixing to catch the stage in the morning and I'd like to board these two horses here tonight."

"Shore—"

"Sir, would you buy the little bay, saddle, bridle and all?" Hannah interrupted.

"Well, let me take a gander," the man said glancing curiously at Lintell, who peered at her but said nothing. The man circled the bay, checked his mouth, ran a hand along his neck. "Fifty dollars fer everythin'."

"Fine," agreed Hannah. "Is there a telegraph office here in town?" she asked as the man handed her the money.

"Shore, down te the end of the street, yu'll see the wires."

"I got business there myself," Lintell said after they reached the street, smiling down at her.

"I know it's not the same, but since I can't return Mr. Barker's horse I'll send him the money," she said looking determinedly up at him from beneath the floppy brim of her sombrero. "No matter what you might think, I always intended to do it."

"Whatever you say," he drawled a twinkle in his eye.

Without further words they walked to the telegraph office. Lintell waited as she transacted her business with the money and then sent his own telegraph to Captain John McKenny, Austin, Texas. The missive was short and to the point, stating that he and Hannah Lea Gibson were expected to arrive in San Antonio within a week. He would wait to see the Ranger Captain in person to make his full report. Hannah was quiet as they left the telegraph office, and he gazed down at her out of the corner of his eye.

"I reckon we ought to see about rooms for the night," he said and she nodded.

Two men reclining in tall-backed chairs puffing on cigars eyed them curiously but said nothing as they crossed the porch and entered the building, Lintel's spurs clinking on the rough boards. The lodging-house turned out to be run by a buxom woman, as jovial as she was plump, who was not above making eyes at Lintell. After engaging two rooms they strode next door to the general store.

"That outfit you're wearing, it shore has seen better days. Let's see if we can't find you some new duds here in the store."

Excited at the prospect of new clothes she gave him a dazzling smile. Lintell followed her inside the cool, dim interior. But a breathless search failed to reveal any ready-made dresses. There was an abundance of bolt cloth but it had to be sewn, so she had to resort to boys' apparel. When they returned to the lodging-house some time later, along with the other articles, there was a whole new outfit for Hannah; Mexican boots, silver spurs, a buff sombrero, overalls, shirts and other items. Lintell, arms full of packages, waited while she quickly opened the door to her room.

"Let's go get something to eat," he said depositing the articles on her bed. "I saw a little café down the street."

The street appeared to be practically deserted as they walked along, Hannah still wearing her rough garb and large floppy-brimmed hat. Passing the saloon they were greeted by loud voices, and the clack of a Rolette wheel. The strong odor of liquor and cigarette smoke drifted out the open door. Hannah wrinkled her nose and gave him a long-suffering glance as they continued on. The café located in the next block was small but appeared clean and was occupied by only a few customers. They took a table in the corner where, Hannah noticed, Lintell could watch the door. Shortly they were approached by a young dusky-eyed Mexican girl.

"What would you like, *Señors*?" she asked, looking shyly from one to the other, mistaking Hannah for a boy, which for some reason failed to enthrall her.

"How about a thick beef steak and three eggs, coffee and a slice of that apple pie," he drawled, "And lay off the *frijoles*."

Hannah giggled remembering the nights on the trail where beans had been their main course.

"I reckon I'll have the same," she drawled mimicking his slow speech.

"Hannah, tell me about your dad and Captain McKenny. I recall you saying they were once partners in some ranching scheme," he said as they waited for their food.

"I didn't tell you anything of the kind," she replied gazing at him directly.

He hesitated, returned her stare. "Beg pardon. I recall now, it was Captain McKenny that told me," he drawled.

"I have very little memory of my father, or my mother," she said leaning back and staring down at the table. "I wasn't very old when I first met Captain McKenny—I called him Uncle John. He would come on occasion to visit Uncle Bob. I took to him right off. I think because he reminded me of my father; what little memory I had of him. He's always been a Ranger in my eyes. Before I even started school he would tell me stories about catching rustlers and robbers, even murderers. Old Anita, my uncle's housekeeper who helped raise me, would get so upset with him, but my uncle would just smile, and say, 'Don't take on so, woman. Maybe when she gets big she'll join the Rangers.' I never did, of course . . . get big," she laughed, self-consciously.

"How'd your folks die?"

"Murdered . . . ," she said quietly.

"How did that happen?"

She told him what had been told her, of the robbery, how they both were killed when the buggy overturned.

"How old were you when that happened?"

"I was six."

"That's shore tough. You was just a kid," he remarked kindly.

"I went to live with my Uncle Bob. He raised me; like his own daughter."

"Was your folk's killers ever found?"

She shook her head. "No one was caught that I know of."

"Uh-huh," he murmured thoughtfully taking a sip of coffee. "I was just curious."

To do the meal justice, Hannah finished all her food, including the apple pie.

"Oh, I'm going to burst!" she moaned when they reached the street.

She sagged against him pretending that she had not the strength to stand. He caught her with one arm around her waist and suddenly she clung to him yielding, unresisting, her eyes turned up to his, singularly bright beneath the dark brim of her sombrero. And then she laughingly pulled away and as quickly as it came the mood was broken.

"Jack, I'm going to ask Mrs. Barnes to send up a bath," she ventured, glancing at him as they walked along.

"I reckon that's a good idea. I shore could go for one myself," Lintell drawled.

Reaching the lodging house Hannah took off her sombrero and went to find the lodging house owner.

"Mrs. Barnes, would you have a tub of water brought up for a bath," she asked smiling, her golden curls falling about her cheeks.

"All the time I knowed you was a girl," Mrs. Barnes grinned and Hannah blushed. "I'll have Henry—thet's my colored man—tote up the tub and fill it with hot water."

"Well, I reckon I could shore use one too," Lintell, who had followed Hannah, drawled.

"Only one tub, so I reckon yu'll have to wait 'til she's done," she replied. If she had any curiosity as to their relationship she gave no indication.

Sometime later, face shiny, hair slicked down and wearing a clean shirt, Lintell knocked on Hannah's door. A long moment passed before the door opened a crack.

"You ready to go to supper?"

"Jack, I'm still full from that big meal we had this afternoon," she groaned, "And after that luxurious hot bath, I'm so sleepy I can't stay awake. I'm going to bed. I'll see you in the morning."

"All right, get some rest," he said hiding his disappointment. He went into the dining room finding he was the only guest.

"You eatin' alone tonight, huh," Mrs. Barnes observed.

"Too tired to get up. That hot bath did her in," he acknowledged.

"Ah-huh," she nodded noncommittally.

As far as curiosity on her part was concerned, he and Hannah might have lived there all their lives. The food was indeed good and Mrs. Barnes made herself agreeable. She was loquacious and in short order Lintell was made aware of the happenings in the town past and present. By the time he went to his room the sun had disappeared behind the western mountains. That night he slept in a bed, the first time for so long he had trouble recalling the last occasion, and the softness of it. It was a while before he fell asleep though, troubled by something he didn't comprehend.

★

CHAPTER ELEVEN

Awakening early, Lintell got up and leisurely washed, shaved and dressed, paying markedly more attention to his appearance. On the front porch he found a boy to shine his high top boots, and then went down to the stable and paid his bill. He rode the roan back to the lodging house and knocked at Hannah's door. It was opened immediately by the wide awake and fully dressed girl. She stood there in her new finery a look of eager anticipation on her face. Her soft blonde curls rippled and glistened with the rich texture of spun gold. Her cheeks glowed. Her eyes were large, dark, staring. Her new plaid shirt, a little too large, was open at the throat revealing the graceful swell of her neck and the slight contour of breast. He gaped, taking a step backward.

"Excuse me, I must have the wrong room," he exclaimed.

"Jack Lintell, quit your spoofing; it's me, Hannah!"

"Well, I'll be, so it is," he remarked, eyes twinkling.

"How do I look?" she beamed eagerly.

"Well, girl, I'd hate to say 'cause it might go to your head," he drawled.

Something in his look brought the vivid color to her cheeks. She suddenly appeared nervous, shy, yet her eyes hung upon him.

"Well, all I can say is you're a girl in spite of them overalls . . . and speaking of overalls, any man, with eyes could see—"

"I won't wear them," flashed Hannah.

"Sorry, little lady, I burned your old outfit. It was beyond repair. So I reckon you got no choice," he grinned. "You ready to go to breakfast?"

They had barely started breakfast when Mrs. Barnes informed them that the stage was ready to depart.

"But it's only eight o'clock. It wasn't supposed to leave until nine," Hannah protested.

The woman chuckled. "That's what the schedule says, but it ain't ever left at nine that I can recall. Usually before, but there's times it's been past nine. It's kinda when Hank's ready an' how sprite he's feelin'."

Hurriedly they gathered up their outfits. At the door Mrs. Barnes gave Hannah a large paper sack.

"Little grub I put up fer yu folks," she said.

"Thank you," Hannah said smiling gratefully.

After paying the bill they went outside where Lintell's horse was tied. Leading the roan by a halter rope they walked over to the Wells Fargo office where the stagecoach waited. The driver sat up on the box seat, a weather-beaten man in his fifties with a large bushy mustache. Lintell could hear gruff voices coming from inside the office as he tied his horse behind the coach and tossed his saddle and bedroll in the rear boot along with Hannah's; his Winchester he carried with him. The stage had four wide seats behind the driver's seat, and a top with rolled curtains, which could be let down in inclement weather. Two well-matched teams were hitched to the stage and they appeared impatient to be off.

"Climb aboard fellers," the driver called, then, "Dag-gum—beg pardon!" he snorted taking a second look at Hannah's slim graceful form attired in shirt and overalls stuffed into tall Mexican boots. Though the new buff sombrero partially shaded her face, silky strands of golden hair showed from under its brim. The driver quickly removed his sombrero. "I reckon yu shore ain't no feller, or else my eyes are shore playin' tricks on me," he chuckled.

She looked up at the driver and smiled. Lintell handed her into the stage and she settled back against the worn cushion. The seat in front was empty as was the one next to it. As Lintell started to step into the stage he glanced up to see a man hurrying across the street toward them and he recognized the telegraph operator.

"This just came in," the man said handing Lintell a folded paper. "I was on my way to find you."

Lintell took the telegram. It was from Captain McKenny and sent from San Antonio. He quickly read the words:

> *"Trouble here. Have to talk. Staying at Menger. See me immediately when you arrive. Do not let Miss Gibson out of your sight . . . McKenny"*

Lintell stuffed the paper in his vest pocket and climbed into the stage and sat down beside Hannah who looked at him inquisitively. Lintell peered off into the distance lost in thought. McKenny's telegram troubled him. What was going on back there since he had left? '*. . . don't let Hannah out of your sight?'* A feeling of foreboding that he could not shake swept over him.

Some moments later a squat man in a faded shirt wearing a large black sombrero left the stage office and climbed up on the seat next to the driver. He carried both a short barreled shotgun and a Winchester in the crook of his left arm. But the stage did not immediately get underway. Several minutes passed before two women came hurrying along the sidewalk. Both were middle-aged and one held the hand of a child perhaps five or six years old. With much fussing and huffing they climbed aboard scooting into the front seat, the child between the two. A young man in the range garb of a cowboy following behind stored several bags on top of the stage.

“Thanks Jeffery,” one of the women called to the young cowboy. “Tell your paw I’ll write soon.”

“Yes, ma’am. Goodbye,” he replied with a wave of his hand.

The stage started. The roll of the grating wheels and the clatter of hoofs drowned out all other sound. Presently they left the town limits out upon the range country. Lintell bent his gaze on the scene around him. The sun was well above the distant mountains in the east. The beauty of the morning gave the mountains a most deceiving nearness. The green and brown ridges dotted with sage and juniper extended down from the far-off ramparts like great reaching fingers. Higher the gloomy slopes rose to the distant Sacramento Mountains, snow-capped, looming colossal in the light of morning, piercing the pale blue sky.

Hannah fell into a reverie of sorts as the four horses clicked off the miles at a good pace. Cattle began to show on the wide basin and the occasional ranch house came into sight among rolling cedar ridges and dark patches of timber. Shortly she dozed, her head falling unceremoniously on Lintell’s shoulder. He reached and gently removed her sombrero and peered down at her. Her golden hair, dark with moisture where the hat band had pressed against her forehead, clung in tiny curls about her face as she lay deep in slumber as any child, helpless in his power, trusting him as she would have trusted a brother. His fingers, settling her head tenderly upon his shoulder, tangled themselves wistfully in the sun-bright hair.

The stage rolled on. Lintell pulled his sombrero far down over his eyes deep in thought. He had joined the Texas Rangers when he was nineteen, had been involved in a number of tough and dangerous cases in the five years since; fighting Mexican bandits along the Rio Grande in the Big Bend country and chasing down rustlers in the harsh territory west of the Pecos. He had been shot twice, had spent weeks in a hospital that first time, but there had never been a case comparable to this. He could not understand the oppression upon his heart. What was McKenny hinting at? He looked down at Hannah, head upon his shoulder. Sunlight streaming through the open sides of the stage appeared to cast a halo around her face. A pang rent him. Was he doing the right thing bringing her back?

The driver's voice brought an end to his troubling thoughts and he looked to see the stage pulling up before a low one-story stone building.

"Tularosa!" the driver called, "Only an' last call fer lunch."

Hannah's eyes opened and she sat up straight.

"Where are we?" she mumbled sleepily.

"A town called Tularosa," Lintell answered glancing around.

"Young man, would you be so kind as get us some ham sandwiches and soda pop?" one of the women asked Lintell extending a gloved palm in which some silver coins lay.

"Shore," Lintell said and stepped down reaching a hand to Hannah. "Climb down and stretch your legs."

They entered the tavern where a slight-built older woman delivered the sandwiches and soda pop to him. Buying some for him and Hannah they returned to the stage where the women thanked him profusely. He and Hannah ate their sandwiches and drank their drinks standing beside the stage.

"Jack, you're awful quiet," Hannah said after a while glancing curiously at him.

He shrugged, but made no reply.

"It's because of that telegram you got this morning isn't it?"

He nodded.

"It has to do with me, huh? I have a right to know."

He looked at her. "Well, I reckon it's what Captain McKenny hinted to that bothers me. He's shore concerned something might happen to you before we get back to San Antonio."

"I'll be safe as long as I'm with you," she replied, positively.

A flash of pleasure leaped up in him at her words, but he had no answer for her. A few moments later the driver shouted to board and they once again were on the road. They came to a long level expanse of green and brown across which the road, like a long thin ribbon, stretched on into the distance. The stage rolled along keeping at a steady gait. Neither of them spoke and Lintell, glancing over at Hannah, wondered how she was managing. She met his gaze and smiled. The row of freckles across her nose appeared more prominent what with the deepening of her tan, giving the impression of marvelous health and vivacity. He was struck by the change in her since that day they had first met, when her eyes, large and unnaturally black in her white face, stared tragically back at him.

The sun was low in the western sky and twilight thickening when the stage stopped at a way station where the tired horses were swapped for a fresh team. After eating a hot meal they continued on passing through the mining town of Organ arriving at Las Cruces well after dark.

Lintell untied his horse from the rear of the stage, and removed his saddle and their packs from the boot. At the train station they discovered that the train was scheduled to depart at eight the next morning. He purchased two tickets to San Antonio, and made arrangements for the big roan to be transported in a boxcar. The street hummed with busyness—cattlemen, cowboys, women in colorful gowns, and heavily armed, hard-eyed men in rough garb—desperadoes undeniably. Lintell stabled the horse for the night and after engaging two rooms at the hotel they found a table in the far corner of the hotel dining hall and sat down to eat dinner.

Midway through their meal a cowboy wearing a tall-crowned black sombrero and shiny black Mexican boots with large silver-roweled spurs entered the dining hall. He had a clean square-cut chin and sun-bronzed face. A holstered pistol rode high on his right hip. He settled in a seat on the opposite side of the room and gave Hannah a long slow look before his hard gaze shifted to Lintell who stared back, taking cool measure of the man. Finishing their meal Lintell escorted Hannah from the hall up to their rooms.

"Lock yourself in your room. I'll be just down the hall," Lintell cautioned.

"Jack, you're worried," she whispered.

"Not at all," he denied, "Just thoughtful."

"Well, I am. I didn't like that cowboy; the way he stared. There's something familiar about him. I swear I've met him before, somewhere."

"Oh, yeah?" Lintell replied.

"Maybe I'm just imagining things. My stomach's been tied in knots for weeks now."

Hannah turned and pushed open the door to her room. She paused then, turning to peer at him.

"Jack, I'm dependent upon you," she said quietly and then disappeared into the room and closed the door.

Lintell waited until he heard the lock turn and then went, with reluctant step, to his room and to bed, but he was to lie wakeful for some time. He knew absolutely, beyond any equivocation, that he had taken Hannah at her word. She was as innocent of killing Robert Harlan as he was, and he would do all in his power to prove that. The rest would take care of itself. But for all his effort he could not generate a plan and a nagging doubt continued to assail him. The cowboy in the dining hall crossed his mind. He considered that there was a remote possibility the man knew he was a Texas Ranger, or at least had deep suspicions. But it was the way the cowboy had stared at Hannah that bothered him. He decided that he must be wary, yet seem natural. Finally he was able to drift off to sleep.

They ate an early breakfast and arrived at the station ahead of time in order to load Lintell's horse aboard the box car. It wasn't long before cowboys, cattlemen, Mexican laborers and other passengers for the early train began to gather in the station room and on the platform and the hum of conversation grew dissonantly. Hannah and Lintell finally boarded the train and settled in seats somewhat isolated from other passengers. Shortly Lintell caught sight of the cowboy of the previous night. He watched him enter the car and take a seat near the front of the coach. For several moments the cowboy claimed Lintell's attention, but he appeared to give neither him nor Hannah any notice.

"Jack, I remember where I saw that cowboy before," Hannah whispered leaning her head close.

"Oh?"

"Yes, it was at the dance the night Uncle Bob was murdered. He was talking to Ted Stoes."

"Hmm," Lintell murmured thoughtfully, but said nothing further.

"So, why do you think he's on this train?" she whispered.

"Probably on a cattle buying trip," Lintell answered disarmingly.

"I suppose you're right," she sighed.

Lintell gazed past Hannah at the speeding gray and black landscape. The juniper soon gave way to sagebrush and the yellow of grass and the occasional tuft of greasewood.

"What's going to happen when we get back? You'll lock me up won't you?" Hannah asked softly as she stared out the window.

He shook his head. "I plan to speak to the judge myself to see that you get released on your own recognizance. Do you have family, a friend that would speak up for you?"

"I've no family," she replied evenly, and was silent for a moment. "I guess Eula Mae Casey is my best friend."

"Will she help you?"

"I surely hope so," she sighed leaning her head against the window glass, the clickety-clack of the train wheels a steady rhythm in her ear.

★

CHAPTER TWELVE

The conductor's voice woke Hannah. "San Antonio, ten minutes." She sat upright, heart racing. San Antonio. They were here finally; the place she had run away from frightened and alone those weeks ago. She tried to assess her feelings as she peered out the window blanketed now and then by the smoke from the steam engine. Would Uncle John be there to meet her when they stepped off the train? For some reason she dreaded to face her old friend. She could feel Jack Lintell's eyes silently watching her and she wondered at his silence. Would his attitude toward her change now that they were back with his fellow rangers? Would he revert to that cool detached lawman she remembered when first they met? She turned and looked at him. There was no change in his expression as he stared into her eyes, but his hand closed over hers and gave it a gentle squeeze, and her heart slowed its wild beating.

The train ride from El Paso had been tiring but uneventful. They saw the hard-eyed cowboy only on one other occasion and at that instance he gave only the briefest nod to Lintell and passed on apparently occupying another coach.

The train pulled into Sunset Station with screech of brakes and a loud chug-chugging of the engine. Among the several people who crowded the platform Hannah saw three men, none of whom she recognized, standing apart from the others. They all had the hard look of lawmen and she bit her lower lip as her heart again began its hurried beating. She had actually expected to see John McKenny and was puzzled and hurt by his absence.

Lintell was first to step off the train and reached back to take Hannah's hand. As he did so one of the three lawmen detached himself from the others and sauntered forward. He was small of stature, but wiry and muscular. His garments were new but fit him poorly. He wore a wide-brimmed black sombrero, and his face was smooth except for a drooping mustache. He appeared gaunt and hollow-cheeked, with an enormous nose, and cavernous eyes set deep under shaggy brows.

"Yu Ranger Lintell?" he asked voice gruff and demanding.

Lintell nodded.

"I'm Sheriff Wade Talbert," he said pulling handcuffs from his back pocket. "I'm heah te take custody of the prisoner." He turned callous eyes upon Hannah. "Put out your wrists woman—"

"Hold on!" Lintell called sharply taking hold of Hannah's elbow.

"Wha-at?" Talbert bawled, rudely interrupted, glaring at Lintell.

"Just what I said! You'll do nothing of the kind," Lintell said deliberately stepping between the sheriff and Hannah.

"Hyar, Lintell," Talbert growled, "I'm the law heah in Bexar County. I appreciate yu bringin' the prisoner back, but the killin' took place in my jurisdiction. Yu rangers got no authority in this hyar case."

"Like hell!" Lintell said glaring at the sheriff. "Back off, Talbert and heed my words. You attempt to take my prisoner and you're a dead man, sheriff or no sheriff. If you were a Texan, you'd damn well know that!"

Talbert shot a look over his shoulder at his two companions who shifted nervously plainly quailed before Lintell's steady gaze.

"Aw-right, Lintell, have it yore way . . . fer now. We'll see what Judge Bryan has te say," Talbert grunted and turning stomped off, his companions following awkwardly behind.

"I wonder how Talbert knew to expect us on this train." Lintell muttered, glancing at Hannah to find her pale and trembling.

That was true, Hannah suddenly realized, these men had no way of knowing they would be on this train, nor would John McKenny. That was why he wasn't waiting to meet her. Yet this sheriff and his deputies were. Obviously they had known because someone had told them! She thought of the hard-eyed cowboy. But what interest would he have in her?

"As soon as I get Colonel off the train we'll go on over to the hotel and meet Captain McKenny," Lintell said breaking into her deliberations.

She nodded and they walked back along the train toward the boxcar where Lintell's big roan was tied. Lintell's keen eyes spied the cowboy they had seen on the train. He paused at the door and peered at Lintell for a brief moment before disappearing inside the station.

"It's him," Hannah hissed staring straight ahead.

"Ah-huh," he grunted reminding himself to find out more about the cowboy.

"Jack . . . I'm nervous. Couldn't we stop somewhere and find a dress for me to wear?" she replied timorously looking down at her pant-clad legs.

"I reckon you best wear what you got on," he said, his eyes seemingly to take her in with new-found perceptiveness which brought a deepening flush to her cheeks. "At least until we talk to Captain McKenny and find out what's going on," he hurriedly added.

Lintell left Colonel in a corral near the station along with his saddle. Circling the station they crossed Austin Street and down Eighth Street to Alamo Avenue. Hannah hurried along; Lintell strode easily beside her, though his keen eyes were watchful. Turning left on Alamo they followed the Avenue five blocks to where the Menger Hotel was located on Crockett Street. Several buggies and horsemen occupied the wide dusty street, and nearing Houston Street they came upon a row of mule-drawn freighter's carts. Arriving at the hotel Lintell approached the clerk and asked what room Ranger Captain McKenny was staying in. They were directed to a room on the second floor. They were ushered into the well-lighted corner room by a young, lean, brown-faced Ranger.

"Howdy, Jack," he greeted Lintell though his gaze fixed upon Hannah. "Yu must be the little Miss that's got everybody as jumpy as a cat on a hot tin roof," he grinned.

"Yep," Lintell replied. "Abe Johnson, meet Miss Hannah Gibson . . . Hannah, a Ranger pard of mine, Abe Johnson."

"I'm pleased to meet you, Mr. Johnson," Hannah said coolly.

"An' I'm delighted to meet yu, Miss Gibson," Johnson drawled making a gallant bow. But his eyes held a singularly bold expression as he continued to gaze at her.

From behind a table in one corner, a man of medium height, stern-faced with piercing gray eyes and a sandy-gray mustache that drooped well past his chin hastily stood and strode forward with a jingle of spurs to take both her hands in his rough ones.

"Hannah, child, he's fetched yu back safe," Captain McKenny said forcefully.

"Oh, Uncle John, I'm so happy to see you," she cried and rose on tip-toe to kiss his weathered cheek.

"Cap, who is this Talbert feller?" Lintell asked.

"Sheriff Talbert? You've met him?"

"Yep, had a run-in with him just now at the rail station," Lintell replied. "He was waiting for us and wanted to take custody of Miss Gibson. I thought I was going to have to draw down on him."

"The devil yu say!" McKenny snorted.

"That's shore a fact. What's going on?"

"Wal, Talbert's been on his high horse ever since the Ranger's took the lead on Harlan's murder. But I didn't reckon he'd be fool enough to brace you there that way."

"Well, it shore beats me how he knew we were on that train."

"Yu sayin' somebody tipped him off? That begs the question; who and why?"

"I've got an idea who, but I'm still wrestling with the why," Lintell replied.

"Cap, Talbert's shore up te somethin'," Abe Johnson spoke up. "Yu know he's always been Judge Bryan's boy, an' lately they been closer'n two peas in a pod."

"Yeah, I reckon yu've hit it square. Bryan's made no secret of bein' against the Rangers," McKenny said.

Lintell glanced at Hannah who had settled in a chair tensely watching and listening to the men.

"Cap, the first thing we got to do is set Miss Gibson up with a good lawyer," Lintell said reading the fear in her eyes."

"I'm way ahead of you, son," McKenny replied. "Hannah, I talked te yure friend Miss Casey—"

"Eula Mae?"

"Yep, and she's arranged fer Webb, Bodkin an' Bower's office te represent yu. So don't yu fret. I heard David Bodkin's one of the best."

"I have very little money—"

"We'll worry 'bout that when the time comes," McKenny said.

"Am I to stay with Eula Mae then?"

"That's what I was figurin' on, Hannah, but that deal with Talbert's got me wonderin'. We'll have te arraign yu before Judge Bryan, an' he just might lock yu away 'til the trial, just te spite the Rangers."

"Oh!" she gasped turning anxious eyes to Lintell.

At that moment there came a loud knock on the door which caused Hannah to jump and Lintell to whirl about hand frozen above the Colt low on his hip. After a quick glance at Lintell Johnson stepped to the door and jerked it open. A tall rangy man who Lintell recognized as one of the lawmen who had been with Talbert at the rail station stood in the doorway.

"Hyar!" he exclaimed one arm raised a surprised expression on his lean face.

"Hyar yureself, Barsh," Johnson said. "What do yu want?"

"Er—got somethin' fer McKenny," he stammered, clearly nervous, reaching a hand out clutching a wrinkled paper.

“What is it?” the Ranger captain called striding to the door.

“I reckon it’s a writ of habeas corpus,” Johnson said quickly scanning the document.

“Let me see that,” Lintell said snatching the paper from his fellow ranger and staring down at the sheet.

“What’s a writ of—of habeas corpus?” Hannah asked getting to her feet.

Lintell handed the writ to McKenny and went to where Hannah stood, laying a hand on her shoulder.

“It’s a court order to Captain McKenny to deliver you to the court. It’s signed by Judge G. H. Bryan.”

“Oh,” she whispered chewing her lower lip.

Deputy Barsh stood in the doorway, hands on his hips, glancing from one to the other a smug look on his face. Without a word Johnson slammed the door in his face.

“Abe,” Lintell said forcefully, “Hightail it over to Webb’s office and make him aware of Judge Bryan’s action.”

“Right,” Johnson replied.

“Hyar,” McKenny said, handing Johnson the writ. “Take this with yu.”

Mark Webb, Attorney at Law, peered over the rim of his eyeglasses at Hannah with the air of a doting father. He was a heavy-shouldered man in his late forties, immaculately attired in a dark suit and white starched collar. His black hair, slicked back from a broad forehead, glistened oily as he leaned forward. His tall-backed leather chair creaked noisily.

"Now, Miss Gibson, tell us about the night your uncle was murdered? Remember, every fact is important, so make every effort to recall every detail no matter how unimportant you may consider it," he said, smiling amenably.

Hannah glanced at the young man seated at the end of the long oak desk. David Bodkin, a junior partner, Webb had introduced, was a young man in his mid-thirties; clean-shaven save for a thick dark brown mustache, slim, with intent hazel eyes. Those eyes at the moment were ardently studying Hannah which brought a slight heightening of color in her cheeks and she glanced quickly back at Webb. He nodded indulgently and she took a deep breath and once again related what she remembered of that night which seemed now so long ago.

"So, Miss Gibson, from what you've told me, I sense your uncle was not himself when you left for the dance."

"No—I mean, yes, he did seem preoccupied. He—"

She was about to mention the little book, the blue leather book that lay open in front of her uncle on his desk that night. How her uncle had been staring fixedly at the contents. But it suddenly occurred to her; what if her uncle had been involved in some nefarious scheme, something dishonest—of course she didn't believe that for an instant—but . . . if it was so her innocent disclosure might injure her uncle's character cast his reputation in a bad light. She bit her lip. She would never want to do that.

"Yes . . . ?" Webb prompted.

She shook her head. "Nothing," she murmured.

"Perhaps he was worried about something. Are you certain he didn't hint perhaps as to what concerned him?"

"No," she said again shaking her head. That part was true. He had told her nothing. Would he have, she wondered, if he had lived?

"This person you said you saw, lurking in the shadows, could you identify him?" Webb asked arching a bushy eyebrow.

"I'm not sure there was even anyone there," she sighed, "I . . . thought—I had this feeling someone was there watching me."

"Ah," Webb sighed.

Was he disappointed or . . . relieved. She blinked.

"I know that sounds foolish—"

"Not at all my dear, not at all," he insisted soothingly. "Such an emotional experience, you could not have been expected to act with calm rationality."

Hannah wanted to ask him if he said that because she was a woman, just a silly emotional creature. She forced her hands to relax their tight grip on each other. No, she decided, he was only being considerate. And so she smiled and nodded. He believed her. He would clear this whole matter up. She heaved an inward sigh.

When Hannah arrived at the hotel room perhaps two hours later, escorted by the young lawyer David Bodkin, Lintell from his place on the opposite side of the room, watched the two; conscious of how the young lawyer seemed to hang on Hannah's every word. He didn't miss the way Bodkin would occasionally cover one of her small hands with his own reassuringly, or the way she smiled at him; her eyes suddenly a shining lovely light. Gone was that dark and haunting shadow which had been so apparent ever since their arrival back in San Antonio.

Lintell sustained a distinct shock, not so much at the loveliness of her eyes, but at the clear intimation that the young attorney's words and presence could cause such a transformation. Impulsively he stood and took a step toward them.

"You must be Jack," Bodkin smilingly said seeing Lintell approach.

Bodkin reached out his hand. Lintell took the proffered hand finding it, as he expected, soft and supple in his own hard grip.

"You must understand, sir, that as the arresting officer it's best you have no further contact with Miss Gibson. I will accompany her before Judge Bryan this afternoon," he said.

Lintell slowly nodded eyes upon Hannah. Her lips parted as though she would speak, but then her gaze drooped, and she looked away the healthy flush receding from her cheeks. Lintell wanted to say that he would be there for her be damn the law, but something inhibited him. He knew the lawyer was right in that regard. He was on the wrong side now. Lintell must have worn a strange expression on his face as he turned his back and faced Captain McKenny, for that worthy's bushy brows knitted and after one gray glance his gaze fell back to his paper work.

Lintell left the hotel room without looking back and descending the stair, walked back alone to the rail station deep in thought. It seemed from all appearances that Bodkin was confident about Hannah's chances in court. Or at least she seemed more than just a little encouraged by his counsel. He hoped the man was right, although he could not shake a nagging doubt. It worried him that Hannah still faced the same danger now that she did before she ran away, maybe, even more so. If her cousin was the murderer—and in his mind there was no doubt—shooting his own father, he was not going to hesitate to kill her, or have it done. Still, he considered, there was the missing money. Edward Harlan dearly wanted that seventy-five thousand to get free of his gambling debts, and more than likely he still figured Hannah had hidden it someplace. She would be safe until Edward found the money, or . . . saw her convicted.

Arriving at the rail station, Lintell saddled Colonel and rode back to the hotel with all sorts of thoughts whirling about in his head. When he reached the hotel Abe Johnson was waiting for him on the front steps.

"Hey, Jack, Ed Tarleton sent a message. He wants te see yu," Johnson said casually. He stood with one shoulder propped against one of the porch posts peering up at him, thumbs hooked in his belt. His easy-going manner was misleading. There was nothing careless in the keen look he gave Lintell.

"Tarleton?" Lintell questioned, stepping down from his horse in one easy motion.

"Yep."

"He say what it's about?"

"He wants te discuss the Harlan case with yu."

"Hells fire," Lintell cursed under his breath. Tarleton was the prosecuting attorney.

★

CHAPTER THIRTEEN

Ed Tarleton, the prosecuting attorney, was waiting in his office next to the Old Courthouse on Soledad Street for Lintell the following morning. Lintell had met the man two years ago and remembered him as a relentless prosecutor. Entering the office, Lintell surveyed the short slim man who rose from behind the large walnut desk. His dark hair was sprinkled with gray as was his thick mustache. His features were homely, especially his rather prominent nose. It was a serious face that had given way to few smiles. But his most striking characteristic was his penetrating blue eyes that at the moment were keenly scrutinizing Lintell.

"Ranger Lintell, I thought I remembered the name. Now I recognize you. It was the Rankin Case, correct? Good to see you again," said Tarleton reaching out a hand. Lintell seized it in a tight grip. For a slight man the prosecutor handshake was firm.

Lintell well remembered the Rankin Case that Tarleton mentioned. William "Little Bill" Rankin was an educated man from Ohio who drifted into Texas in 1878. After working a while as a cowboy, Rankin, along with a man by the name of Hank Dover and four others, started robbing trains, one of which was the Galveston,

San Antonio train. Jack Lintell was assigned, along with Abe Johnson and two other Rangers, to track down Rankin and his gang, which was known by then as the Dover Gang. Lintell and his Rangers caught up with the Dover Gang near Bastrop, Texas. After a running gun battle that left Dover and two of the gang dead, Rankin managed to escape.

Staying put on Rankin's trail Lintell and two other Rangers tracked him to a canyon near Doan's Crossing. When Rankin fought back firing his rifle, the Rangers returned fire and Rankin was hit in the wrist by a rifle slug. Dropping his gun and running, he was hit again, in the back and the neck, but survived. He stood trial for his part in the Galveston, San Antonio train robbery. Prosecuted by Tarleton, he was sentenced to ten years in prison.

"I've been looking over this Harlan murder file," Tarleton said. "I had put it aside, but now that you have brought back the suspect it's time to precede. It seems to me a pretty cut and dried case. We have our defendant—"

"I'm not so shore about that," Lintell replied.

Tarleton arched an eyebrow. "Oh?"

"The girl didn't kill her uncle."

"What makes you so sure of that?"

"I've been with her, heard her story. She—"

"I understand she is very attractive."

"That has nothing to do with it. She's not a murderer—"

"Tut, Ranger Lintell," Tarleton chided patiently, "I have the written testimony of two witnesses. She fled the scene. What more evidence of guilt?"

"She ran away because she feared for her life!" Lintell snarled.

Tarleton walked back behind his desk and sat down in the tall-backed chair. He leaned back, his intense blue eyes unblinking as he peered at Lintell.

"My role as prosecutor is to try the accused on facts. Sentimentality has no place in a court of law," he said, voice coldly professional. "Unless you have facts that tell a different story, Ranger Lintell, I intend to try Miss Hannah Lea Gibson for the cold-blooded murder of her uncle." He pulled a pipe from a top drawer and began to fill it from a can on his desk. "I've talked to Mark Webb—"

"Who's he?" Lintell queried.

"He has the law office with David Bodkin. He has discussed the case with Bodkin and apprised me of Miss Gibson's story. You may not be aware that Robert Harlan was a very well respected citizen; one of San Antonio's old timers. He provided for Miss Gibson gave her a home, and this is how she repaid him. She has always been a rebellious girl, and he did all in his power to curb that defiant nature, but when he caught her breaking in to his safe, she shot him and fled. Those are the facts, Ranger Lintell—"

"How the hell did you come up with those set of facts?" Lintell demanded.

"That will come out at the trial," he replied puffing out a cloud of blue smoke. "Ranger Lintell, I have a great deal of respect for you and the Rangers, or else I would not have been so candid, but you have been taken in by this girl. I intend therefore, to see justice done. Now if you will excuse me—"

"I see," Lintell said, letting go his pent up breath. "Then, will you do me one favor, sir? She's only a girl. Will you ask Judge Bryan; recommend she be released to her friend Miss Casey until the trial? I'll guarantee she will appear at whatever date set. I give you my word. Jail is not the place for her—"

"I'm afraid she is already there, Ranger Lintell. There is nothing I can do. Sorry."

Without a word Lintell turned on his heel and with jaw clinched he strode purposefully from Tarleton's office. He knew he had to get out of there before he said or did something he would later regret. When he reached the street he laid a hand on Colonel's neck trying to get a hold on his thoughts. Hannah was in jail. He visualized the two story limestone building on Camaron Street. He was familiar with the jail. He had delivered several prisoners there, the last being "Little Bill" Rankin. He had to see her, to know she was all right.

Arriving at the jail Lintell was stunned to discover that Hannah was not there, but was being held in the old County jail, called the "Bat Cave" on the northwest corner of Military Plaza. The place was old and rundown with only four cells, not much better than a dungeon.

"Jack, I shore hated te see that little gal locked up," Bill Herff the jailer said shaking his gray head when Lintell arrived at the jail. Lintell had known Herff for years and had always gotten along with him.

"Why was she sent here, and not the new jail?" Lintell demanded through clinched teeth.

"The order was signed by Judge Bryan," Herff admitted.

"Where is she?" Lintell queried.

"Wal, I put her in one of the cells on the second floor. That's the best I could do. They're dry and sunny. Them on the bottom has only dirt floors, an' they's cold an' damp."

Lintell nodded grimly. "Any other prisoners up there?"

"Nope, she's the only one."

"Is there anybody guarding her?"

“Two of Talbert’s deputies, Barsh and Hall.”

“I reckon I’ll go on up,” Lintell declared and started up the outside stairs.

“Ho, Jack,” Herff called, and Lintell halted midway up the steps and peered back over his shoulder. “That lawyer feller, Bodkin, he’s up there visitin’ her.”

Lintell continued up the stairs taking them two at a time. At the top of the steps just inside the door was a wood table. The two deputies were there. Barsh sat in a chair, his feet, crossed at the ankles, were propped up on the table his spurs digging into the scarred top, apparently dozing. The second deputy was reading a newspaper spread out across one half of the table. He was the first to glance up. Seeing the Ranger badge on Lintell’s vest, he nudged Barsh who sat up with a snort, swinging his feet to the floor.

“What you doin’ hyar?” Barsh queried.

“I reckon I got a few questions for the prisoner,” Lintell drawled. “Ranger business.”

“Yeah? Wal, ain’t nobody supposed te be allowed to see her, ‘cept her lawyer—”

“Oh?” Lintell went on lightly.

“Yep. Them’s my orders.”

“Who gave the orders?”

“Why, Talbert.”

“That’s who I figured. You tell Talbert to take it up with me,” Lintell said with deceptive softness, and turning, made his way down a narrow corridor to where the cells were located. Neither deputy uttered a word.

Hannah Gibson was seated on the edge of a rusty iron bunk upon which lay a thin soiled cotton mattress. She was hatless, still dressed in boy's attire her rather tousled golden curls framing her pale cheeks. On a stool beside the bunk sat, David Bodkin, an open note pad on one knee. Hannah glanced up at the sound of Lintell's footsteps and recognizing him leaped to her feet and hurried to the bars.

"Jack!" she cried reaching a hand through the bars.

He caught hold of her small trembling member and squeezed it. She responded with a glad pressure, and warm flush as tears welled in her eyes.

"I hoped you would come. I . . ." Abruptly she paused, as if her thoughts were somehow beyond words. Lintell felt Bodkin's eyes upon them, but the man made no comment only shuffled on the stool uneasily.

"I reckon no one could have kept me away," Lintell drawled. "Are you all right?"

"Yes, but I'm scared to death," she whispered, looking at him with eloquent, appealing eyes no man could resist.

"Don't be," he said hastily and glanced at Bodkin. "What kind of defense are you putting up?" he demanded.

Bodkin got to his feet, puffed out his chest. "Be certain I intend to mount a vigorous defense, though I'm afraid I cannot discuss—"

"Ah-huh—" Lintell grunted scornfully, on the verge of challenging Bodkin about the conversation he had with Tarleton in his office, what he angrily suspected, but caught himself. He felt deeply for the girl, he had no idea how deeply, but his intelligence prompted him to proceed more slowly. He mustn't let himself be swayed wholly by primal emotion.

"David—Mr. Bodkin, has assured me that we have a strong case; that no jury will convict me," Hannah said, yet it seemed to him her voice lacked persuasion.

"Has there been a trial date set?" Lintell asked peering at Bodkin.

"Yes. August second," Bodkin replied. "I strongly renew my earlier suggestion that you stay away from Miss Gibson until then. I don't wish to color the facts or give Mr. Tarleton any more ammunition then he already has, you being the arresting officer and such."

"Keep your chin up, Sprite, we'll get you out of this mess," Lintell said squeezing Hannah's hand meaningfully before letting go and backing away a step. He gave her a crooked smile and then turned and walked to the door where he paused to peer back at her. She stood where he had left her, pale, but somehow radiant.

Back on the street, Lintell stepped easily into the saddle and started off, without conscious thought as to where he was going. He kept thinking of Hannah, how she had appeared when she first looked up and recognized him, as though some of the hell had faded from her eyes. Something like the first burst of sunrise. Light, hope, life. He took a deep breath. Had he actually seen that, or had he imagined it all. How dry his encouraging words seemed to him now. All he could think of was that she was dependent on him, and up to this point he had failed her.

Lintell rode over to the hotel where Captain McKenny was staying. He found the captain alone at his desk a stack of papers in front of him.

"Wal, Jack, I reckon yu've heard about Miss Gibson by the dark look on yur face," McKenny said.

"Yeah, I was just over there to see her. Cap, we've got to get her out of that dungeon," Lintell said helplessly.

"I just come from Judge Bryan's office," McKenny said shaking his head disgustedly. "I reckon us Rangers right now are the lass's worse enemy. Talbert's got it in fer us, and Bryan's backin' him up. I reckon the best thing fer us fer the time bein' is te lay low. The more we balk as te how this case's bein' handled, the more Talbert throws his weight around, an' Bryan gets in the act."

"Hells fire!" Lintell exclaimed staring impotently at his boss. The situation didn't appear encouraging. The only way to free Hannah, he realized, was to find the person responsible for killing Hannah's uncle. That he vowed to do, and that brought a great and heaving lift to the unknown forces deep in Lintell's breast.

"Well, Cap, I reckon I'll do a little investigating on my own, and to hell with Talbert," Lintell drawled.

"I kinda reckoned yu would," McKenny replied.

Lintell left McKenny's room and mounting Colonel rode southwest out of town on the road that would bring him to the Circle C—Big Jim Casey's Ranch. He traveled at a slow trot surveying the land, mind working all the while. He came upon a grove of cottonwoods stretching far on each side of the river. Nestled among the trees was a long low, red-roofed, red-walled adobe ranch house. Below it where the cottonwoods spread and thinned were barns and sheds, corrals and racks. The droves of horses in the pastures, the squares of alfalfa, and herds of cattle dotting the slopes and adjacent rangeland attested to the prosperity of some cattle baron who held to the old and proven customs of his generation. The corrals were new, but their style was old.

As Lintell approached the ranch house a girl came out upon the porch apparently having seen him at some distance. She shaded her eyes with one hand watching him. Riding into the yard he reined up before the girl. She had hair as red as flame piled atop her head, a strikingly beautiful face, with greenish-blue eyes which at the moment peered up at him inquisitively. She wore a brown ankle-length dress adorned throughout with tiny red and white scallops buttoned up to her throat and edged with a row of white lace.

"Howdy," Lintell drawled, "Might you be Miss Eula Mae Casey?"

"I am," she replied frowning slightly, eyes upon the silver badge on his dark vest. "And who might you be?"

"My name's Jack Lintell, Miss Eula Mae—"

"Oh, I've heard of you. You're that Ranger who brought Hannah back," she said, her frown deepening.

"Yes, ma'am," Lintell returned. "I shore hate to disturb you, but I'd be obliged if I could get down. I'd shore like to have a talk with you about Miss Gibson."

"Help yourself," she replied unable to hide her curiosity. "Would you like to come inside?"

"Yes, ma'am," he said stepping from the saddle and wrapping the reins about a porch post. He followed after her, spurs jingling musically.

The living room was spacious and comfortable. A huge stone fireplace occupied one outside wall. Two stuffed arm chairs flanked the fireplace and there was a sofa under another window with tables and lamps on either side. There were colorful vases and lacy linens on the tables, and other charming knickknacks all about that spoke of a woman's influence.

"Sit down. Would you like something to drink?"

"No ma'am, I'm fine," he said settling in one of the arm chairs before the fireplace.

"What has happened? Hannah is all right?" she asked anxiously taking a seat in the matching chair across from him.

"The judge has remanded her to jail—"

"Oh!" Eula Mae gasped. "But Mr. Bodkin said—"

"I reckon it's a long story," Lintell replied. "Do you remember anything about that night?"

"You mean the night Mr. Harlan was murdered?"

"Ah-huh."

"Well, I only heard about it the next morning. I was totally shocked. And then to hear Hannah had run away! I still cannot make sense of it."

"You gave a dance that night. Hannah was there?"

"Of course. The dance ended somewhere around two or two-thirty in the morning, so Hannah must have gotten home close to three," she replied.

"What about this Ted Stoes?" Lintell asked.

"Ted?" she said gazing at him with that curious amused smile as those lively greenish-blue eyes seemed to assess him. "He's one of Robert Harlan's cowboys—at least he was, until Mr. Harlan was murdered and Ed Harlan took over running the ranch. Have you met Ed Harlan?"

"Yeah, we've met."

"And . . . ?"

"I reckon at the moment I'm more interested in this Ted Stoes."

She laughed outright.

"Ted is Anita, Mr. Harlan's house keeper's son. Hannah has known him since they were kids. All the cowboys were in love with

Hannah, and I think Ted believes he has the inside track," she said turquoise eyes twinkling.

"Well, Miss Eula Mae, I shore reckon you have your share of fellas," Lintell drawled. "And I shore can't figure why some lucky cowboy hasn't snatched you up already."

She laughed again. "You ought to know cowboys," she replied with a dark flash in her greenish-blue eyes.

"Yeah, I reckon most cowboys are dumb," he drawled watching the way the red spots played prettily in her cheeks.

"Ah-huh," she said with a strange soft light in her eyes.

"So, what is your opinion of Ed Harlan?" he inquired.

"I asked you first."

"But you've known him longer than I have," Lintell countered.

"A crazy boy, absolutely self-centered, crafty, and vicious, who'll stop at nothing," she said flatly.

"I'll give it to you, Miss Eula Mae, you shore don't mince words," he chuckled.

"That's what I've been told. It's my red hair," she laughed, but there was a chilliness about those dazzling green eyes. "One ought not to talk about the dead, but I always thought poor Mr. Harlan's one and only fault was his stubborn idolizing of his son."

"Well, Hannah's trial is coming up and she's still wearing boy's togs. I shore was hoping you might be able to fix her up with something more fitting."

"Yes, yes, of course," the girl said and moved as though she would rise, then hesitated. "Hmm, I'm afraid none of my dresses will fit

Hannah. She and I are not close in size. But she has plenty of dresses at home . . . if Edward hasn't thrown them all out."

"Has he taken over the ranch?"

"Yes, and dad says he running it into the ground. Some of his cowboys have quit already. I'll ask one of our cowboys to go with me and drop by there today and see if I can get some of her clothes. I haven't been there since, well, since before Hannah left—"

"Why don't I come along with you," Lintell suggested.

Her turquoise eyes dilated in what he thought was amused surprise. "Yes," she smiled. "Why don't you."

★

CHAPTER FOURTEEN

Lintell rode alongside Eula Mae's buckboard as it rattled along in a cloud of dust behind two spirited blacks. He glanced admiringly at the slim red-haired girl as the buckboard bounced along. She held the reins of the blacks with a firm hand her cheeks flushed with vibrancy. Presently she turned the team smartly off the main road onto a narrower but well-traveled lane. Lintell's admiring gaze wandered over the broad acres, where the afternoon shadows were creeping. The wide green pastures were dotted with horses, and far beyond, in a larger pasture cattle grazed. Somewhere cows were lowing and calves bawling; a burro brayed his raucous call. He could see it had the mark of a fine ranch; still, hopefully, not yet run into the ground.

"That's the ranch house over there in those cottonwoods." Eula Mae Casey shouted over the rattle of the buckboard

"You expect Ed Harlan will be there?" he asked.

"I'm sure hoping he won't," she said a frown marring her lovely features. "I'll have no difficulty dealing with Anita. She'll give me whatever I ask for, unless, as I said before, Ed hasn't thrown or given all her things away."

They rode into the ranch yard without seeing any of Harlan's riders. Lintell swung from the saddle and gave Eula Mae his hand and she stepped lithely to the ground. As they stepped up on the long low porch a large, older woman, graying, dark eyed and solid-featured, came to the door.

"Hi, Anita, it's me, Eula Mae," the girl greeted and Lintell saw the old woman's eyes relax and a smile curve her tight lips.

"Well, hello. It's been a while since you've been by, Eula Mae. Do you have news of my child?" she asked hopefully.

"Yes, Anita, although it's not happy news," Eula Mae replied kissing the woman's wrinkled cheek. "She's safe, but she's in jail. There's going to be a trial—"

"Oh, my little girl never did such a terrible thing as they say!" Anita exclaimed her eyes filled with havoc.

"I know. Anita, this is Jack Lintell. He's a Texas Ranger, and he going to help Hannah," she said giving Lintell a meaningful look.

Anita's dark eyes swept nervously over Lintell from head to foot, and she slowly nodded.

"I came to get some of Hannah's dresses and things that she's going to need," Eula Mae continued. "Is Ed here?

"No, he's out, but I never know when he'll be back. You better come in and get what you need before he does."

She led them down a wide passageway to the back of the sprawling ranch house, showing them into a neat, well-kept room.

"You should have seen the room before I put it back in order," Anita said shaking her head disgustedly. "Young Harlan tore this place apart after Hannah disappeared looking for something."

"Did he find it?" Lintell asked.

"Well, if he did it didn't make him any happier," she replied.

This meant, Lintell gathered, that he never found what he was looking for. Which, Lintell guessed, must have been the seventy-five thousand dollars? According to bank records Harlan drew a draft for that amount three days before his murder. So, what the hell happened to it?

While these thoughts had been running through his mind, Eula Mae was going through the closet and chest of drawers gathering various dresses and other items and laying them on the bed.

"I remember Hannah had a little walnut toiletry box she kept on top of the dresser. It's not there. I wonder if she took that with her?" she mused aloud.

"Yeah, she did," Lintell said.

Eula Mae shot him an inquiring glance.

"I saw it, in the little valise she carried with her," Lintell clarified.

"Ah-huh," she said with pursed lips as she wrapped the dresses in a blanket along with a few silky lacy-trimmed garments. "I'll iron the dresses when I get home," she explained to no one in particular.

They had just finished loading the blanket-clad garments in the back of the buckboard when Lintell looked up to see two riders approaching on the lane. Upon seeing the buckboard and the others standing about in front of the ranch house, the riders spurred their mounts into a gallop. Ed Harlan jerked the little mustang to a skidding halt with a cruel sawing of the reins scattering gravel and dust. His companion whom Lintell recognized as George Gans, Harlan's shifty-eyed confederate pulled up beside him. Harlan's dark gaze went from Eula Mae to Lintell and back again.

"What're yu doing here?" he demanded.

"I came to call on Anita, if it's any of your business," Eula Mae retorted coolly.

"Wal, yu're not wanted, so get off my ranch," Harlan snarled.

During the exchange Lintell studied Ed Harlan. His estimation of the man hadn't changed since his first encounter with him. He wore a black sombrero, high-heeled, fancy-topped boots, tight-fitting trousers of dark material, a heavy belt with silver buckle. An ivory-handled Colt in a black holster rode high on his right hip. He had on a white, soft shirt, with wide collar, open at the neck. His face was ruddy, and shadowed by worry or discontent. His mouth and chin were undisciplined. Here indeed, Lintell considered, was a weak but crafty and vicious individual, one who would stop at nothing to achieve his purpose.

Harlan's eyes shifted to Lintell. "I remember yu," he bit out through closing teeth, as if locking them against the temptation to say more.

"I reckon you would," Lintell coolly drawled. "Jeff Breen sends his condolences. Wanted me to let you know he won't be coming back."

The comment seemed to surprise Harlan. He stared. There seemed something boyish in his lack of comprehension. Then his face paled then flushed as his temper flamed.

"What do you mean by that?" he demanded, with a strident note in his voice. "Who's Jeff Breen?" he blustered.

"I reckon you can figure it out," Lintell drawled helping Eula Mae into the buckboard and taking up the reins she chucked the team into motion.

Lintell rode alongside Eula Mae's buckboard as they started on their way back to the Circle C ranch.

"What was that all about?" Eula Mae asked tilting her head to peer up at him.

Lintell grinned, but made no reply.

"Well, you sure set Ed's teeth on edge when you said that man's name."

"That was my intention," he drawled. "I'd give a month's pay to listen in on Harlan and Gans' conversation about right now."

She gave him a strange look but said nothing in reply. Arriving back at the Circle C, Lintell helped Eula Mae unload the items before she turned the buckboard over to a tall slim cowboy who led the team away.

"I'll put these things in my room," she said taking them from him upon entering the house.

She disappeared down a hallway. He removed his sombrero and held it in both hands as he glanced about. When Eula Mae returned after only a short interval there was a frown on her face.

"All I can think about is Hannah in that terrible jail. Isn't there anything that can be done?" she asked taking a seat in the chair she had occupied before.

"Under the circumstances it doesn't seem likely," he replied.

"Well, I'm going to go see her today," she stated emphatically.

"How long have you known Ha—Miss Gibson?" he solicited settling in the chair opposite, tossing his sombrero on the floor.

"Almost forever," she answered. "You know the tragic story of her parent's death?"

"Yes," he nodded.

"I remember the day her Uncle Bob brought her to the house—I'm two years older than Hannah," she explained. "I had overheard my father the day before telling my mother about the poor little girl who had lost her parents so horribly. My mother told me she was coming to visit and I should be nice to her because she had no mother or father. We took a liking to each other immediately and have been dearest friends ever since. I admit she went through a stage when she was fourteen or fifteen that gave her Uncle Bob a few more gray hairs—"

"How's that?"

"Not now, maybe, but she grew up with as rough and tumble an attitude as any boy. I swear she could outride most of the hands on her uncle's ranch. But then in her mid-teens she became . . . rebellious I suppose. I didn't understand it at the time, not until my own mother died a few years later," she said meeting his eye a strange light in her own. "Oh, Hannah never was bad, believe me—" she said huskily. "I was always the flirt, the cat, not Hannah. She just did wild, crazy, sometimes even dangerous things. You know, once she rode down the middle of Commerce Street in broad daylight in nothing but her nightgown," she giggled, "And on a borrowed horse! But that cowboy sure didn't mind! Yours truly never had the nerve to imitate that little antic. And she wasn't above throwing a punch either when she lost her temper, which wasn't all that often, I must say. Her uncle used to say she got her fire from her mother. I guess he would know since Hannah's mother was his sister."

The sound of horses pounding into the yard in front of the house drew Lintell's attention. Then came the sound of voices. Eula Mae got quickly to her feet.

"That sounds like dad," she said peering out the window.

Lintell stood, hat in hand as boots thumped across the porch boards and a moment later the door opened and a splendid figure of a man, tall, broad, muscular, built for strength and endurance stomped into the room. His face was unduly lined, even for his age, which was near fifty, but the eyes under the arched ruddy brows were vital as a hawk's. He wore the customary garments of a cowman, broad sombrero, flannel shirt, corduroys and boots, stitched and decorated above their high heels. He carried a long-barreled Colt in a holster high on his right side. He halted just inside the door eyes taking in Lintell.

"Dad, you're back early," Eula Mae said.

"Yep, run into that scalawag Harlan and his scrawny-faced sidekick," he replied gruffly, keen eyes still appraising Lintell. "Who's this?" he demanded.

Lintell thought he knew where Eula Mae came by her direct manner of speech.

"Dad, this is Jack Lintell. He's a Texas Ranger—"

"Ranger, huh? Wal, I reckon I'm shore glad te make yur acquaintance. Jim Casey hyar," he snorted, reaching out his hand.

Lintell clasped the huge mitt in his own firm grip.

"I reckon yu got my letter," Casey said.

"You shore got me stumped, Mr. Casey. What letter?"

"Hell, the letter I sent more'n three weeks ago te Austin complainin' about the rustlin'."

Lintell shook his head. "Can't say I did, Mr. Casey. You see I—"

"If yu never got my letter, why are yu hyar?" he demanded, tossing his sombrero upon one of the chairs.

"Dad, Mr. Lintell's here about Hannah—"

"Hannah! Aw!" he grunted, hands on his hips, a scrawl on his weathered face. "Wal, I've knowed Hannah Lea since she was a youngster. So, yu're barkin' up the wrong tree if yu think anybody in this house's goin' te speak bad of thet girl—"

"Nothing of the kind, Mr. Casey," Lintell replied. "I reckon I'd like to help her."

"Thet so?" he said darting a glance at his daughter.

"That's so," she agreed.

"I reckon we ought to head to town if you're ready," Lintell said.

"I will be," she said, "As soon as I run an iron over one or two of those dresses that I think Hannah will like." She glanced at her father. "Dad, Mr. Lintell asked me to take a change of clothes to Hannah. They got her locked in that old jail."

Casey made a disgusted face. "Sounds like somethin' Talbert would do."

Eula May disappeared down the hall and the two men walked out upon the porch.

"You mentioned a run-in with Ed Harlan," Lintell said.

"Yep," Casey growled, his keen turquoise eyes assessing Lintell. "Over at Two Mile Creek. Fer yur education, thet's twenty mile off'n Bar H range. We been loosin' small bunches of cows right an' left off thet range. Runnin' cattle's no child's play of recent. An' it's getting' te the point where it ain't safe te ride alone. Lost one of my cowboys little more'n a month ago. Shot in the back and left to die alone. We found him too late, pitifully propped again a stone, the cigarette, he had tried te light te comfort him, dead in his nerveless hand."

"Are you inferring Ed Harlan had something to do with that?"

"Hell no, I ain't inferrin' thet. I know a damn sight better than te make accusations without facts te back 'em up. I'm jest sayin' its damn queer, thet's all. I figured yu Rangers ought te look inte it."

"What's Sheriff Talbert done about it?"

"Hah!" Casey spat disgustedly.

Both men glanced up to see a rider clattering into the yard.

"Howdy, Martin," Casey spoke up as the lone horsemen reined to a halt before the bottom step. "What brings yu callin'?"

The rider nodded, his sharp-edged gaze shifting to Lintell and the ranger met his look with his own keen appraisal. The man had a handsome face despite his forty years and more which showed in the streak of white at his temples.

"Vanhall, this here is Jack Lintell, Texas Ranger. Lintell, meet Martin Vanhall, a newcomer hyar in the valley," Casey introduced.

"Ranger, huh?" Vanhall grunted. He suddenly seemed uncertain, his dull gray eyes studying Lintell as though weighing the import of Casey's words.

As Vanhall swung from the saddle and mounted the steps Eula May stepped out upon the porch several dresses draped over one arm. She paused upon seeing Vanhall, then after nodding a polite greeting, glanced at Lintell.

"Ready when you are," she said. She gave her father a quick kiss on his weathered cheek. "We'll be back before dark, dad."

"Shore," Casey replied, his quick eye regarding the two as they descended the steps to the waiting buckboard.

★

CHAPTER FIFTEEN

Hannah Lea Gibson lay on her back staring up at the rough ceiling. This was her second day in the musty old jail. She had gotten very little sleep the night before, waking at every sound, in addition to constant worry over what was to happen. She had no privacy. It was sweltering hot in the day and almost freezing at night. The one tall narrow barred window afforded her a view of what she recognized as the old Spanish Governor's Place across Laredo Street. Beyond that she could see little but a few rooftops. She was suddenly aware of voices. Her ears perked and she set up. She recognized one of those voices, although she hadn't heard it in months. Her dear friend Eula Mae! She leaped to her feet and hurried to press her face close between the bars trying to see down the narrow dimly lit corridor. She heard quick footsteps and all at once Eula Mae's tall trim figure came into sight.

"Eula Mae!" Hannah shouted beside herself with joy.

"Hannah!" her friend cried rushing to the cell both girls reaching clasping hands through the bars.

"They let you in?" Hannah exclaimed. "I was so afraid they wouldn't!"

"You darn well better believe they let me in," Eula Mae said forcefully. "Of course, your Texas Ranger was a big help—"

"Jack?!"

Even as his name left her lips, Hannah looked past Eula Mae's shoulder to see that worthy standing in the doorway. She stared at Lintell with slowly dilating, darkening eyes. His lean tanned face wore a smile, and then her blue eyes suddenly shone with lovely lights and shades and she returned his smile.

"Careful, Hannah dear," Eula Mae whispered lips close to her friend's ear, "Your heart is showing in your eyes."

"So," Hannah whispered back.

Eula Mae laughed merrily. She turned to look over her shoulder at Lintell who held a large package in his arms.

"We brought you some things," she explained.

"Oh, what—" Hannah gasped excitedly.

"Some of your dresses and . . . other stuff," she replied. "Although those disgusting guards had to inspect every item to make sure we didn't sneak a gun in to you."

"Oh, thank you, Eula Mae!" Hannah exclaimed. "I've been wearing these pants and shirt for the last week."

One of the guards sauntered in, a sullen expression on his face, to unlock the cell door to allow Eula Mae to enter after which he relocked the door and disappeared down the passageway.

"Let's get you out of those pants and into one of your pretty dresses," Eula Mae said eagerly.

"I reckon I'll go back to the guard room and make shore you ladies aren't disturbed," Lintell said and retreated the way he had come.

The two girls talked, sometimes both at once, in an effort to catch up on all that had transpired since they had last seen each other knowing they had but a short time to visit. And before long it was time to go. Hannah waited at the bars after Eula Mae departed and watched, but Jack Lintell did not return to speak with her or to tell her goodbye. After a while her lips parted, her gaze drooped, and she turned away.

She sat on the hard bunk and leaned her shoulders against the wall. She must have dozed because she was suddenly aware of a voice close at hand. She came erect eyes seeking the source. On the other side of the bars stood her cousin, Ed Harlan.

"Hello Hannah," he said softly.

She got swiftly to her feet. "What do you want?" she demanded.

He shrugged his shoulders, stared at her for a moment without speaking.

"Yu know what I want," he finally said, and glanced back over his shoulder making sure they were alone.

She said nothing, only watched him warily.

"What'd yu do with the book?"

She took a deep breath, tried to still her quickening heartbeat.

"I don't know what you're talking about, Ed!"

He peered thoughtfully at her, black eyes calculating.

"I've got a proposition for yu. Yu want out of this place? I can get yu out. Just tell me where yu hid the book."

She shook her head. "I don't—"

"Damn it, yu little fool!" he declared vociferously. "Don't yu know I can see yu hanged, and I will, I swear—"

"I don't know what book you're talking about!" she said anger now edging her words. But she did know. It suddenly flashed before her eyes. She was standing in front of her uncle's desk watching him slowly close a small blue leather-bound book.

"Liar!" he ejaculated incredulously.

He stared at her for a long tense moment when she said nothing further.

"I'm gonna watch them put a rope around that white neck of yurs," he hissed. "I'm gonna watch as yur eyeballs pop out, how yur face'll turn black—"

"Get out!" she screamed. "I hate you, Ed Harlan! I hate you!"

His lips curled in a fiendish sneer. "Think it over cousin," he said his voice deceptively calm and turning on his heel disappeared down the corridor.

She sank onto the bunk in abject terror. She couldn't breathe. Wild terrible images of long ago whirled before her eyes. For the first time in her life she thought she would faint. And she welcomed the darkness.

August the second arrived and long before the appointed hour a large and boisterous crowd had gathered in front of the courthouse, which appeared equally divided in opinion as to Hannah Gibson's guilt or innocence. Most of the day was spent in jury selection and the trial was adjourned until the following morning.

Lintell couldn't take his eyes off Hannah. She looked so fetching in a pale blue silk dress adorned throughout with gold flowers. It hugged her tiny waist above an abundance of ruched panels and ruffles, swags, and ribbons. Her golden curls were swept up on her head partly hidden by a small silk bonnet edged with dark ruffles that matched the blue of her gown. She looked small and venerable . . . and beautiful.

Things looked dark indeed for Hannah, and the newspapers reported that she looked dejected as the trial began. The penalty for murder was death by hanging. Ed Tarleton, the prosecuting attorney paced before the jury as he made his opening statement laying out for the jury's mind how he would prove that Hannah Lea Gibson shot to death her own uncle. The evidence, he would show, would prove her motive, that caught in the act of stealing seventy-five thousand dollars from Robert Harlan's office safe, she shot him with his own gun; this uncle who gave her everything, who trusted her, loved her, only to fall victim to her selfish greed.

Jack Lintell listened to Tarleton's words as the parade of witnesses came forth, watched the reaction of the jury, all men, all ranchers, who knew and respected Robert Harlan. The picture became distinctly clear as painted by those on the stand, of a wayward, rebellious girl with a fiery temper, selfish, thrill-seeking. But then came the statement of Harlan's son, followed by George Gans, eye witnesses who described hearing a gunshot and rushing inside the house to see the defendant standing over the victim holding the smoking gun, the victim's own Colt .45. At Ed Harlan's testimony Hannah's chest heaved and she gulped continually.

The autopsy report was read into evidence along with the lead slug taken from the victim's corpse, which was stored in a small glass vial. The murder weapon, Robert Harlan's Colt .45 was also marked into evidence.

Then it was the defense's turn. David Bodkin, the lead defense attorney attempted to introduce testimony as to witness, Ed Harlan's debauched and dissolute character, but the prosecutor objected that it was irrelevant, that Harlan was not on trial, which was sustained by Judge Bryan, bringing a smirk to Ed Harlan's face.

Bodkin then brought forth a number of witnesses who testified to the defendant's character in an attempt to refute the damaging testimony of the prosecutions' witnesses. The testimony ended for the day in late afternoon and since it was Saturday, was set to resume on the following Monday morning at nine o'clock. The evidence was turned back over to the coroner for safekeeping. Hannah was taken back to the jail and Lintell was only able to give her a hurried smile of encouragement before she was taken away.

Lintell couldn't sleep that night getting up several times to pace back and forth in his small hotel room. The testimony of the prosecution's witnesses worried him, but there was something else that preyed on his mind, something about the proceedings that he couldn't put his finger on. Something that was said . . . or was it something he had seen? He gave up trying to recall in the early hours of the morning and finally drug himself to bed. Exhaustion succeeded where will could not and he fell into a deep but troubled sleep. He woke with a sudden start. Light streamed in through the window. His mind suddenly clear, fixed. It had come to him somehow in his sleep—the bent slug in the small glass vial!

Throwing back the rumpled sheet he leaped from the bed and began to hurriedly dress. 'If he was right—Lord, if he was right!' kept running through his mind. He stopped suddenly. It was Sunday. The coroner's office was closed. No matter, he told himself. He'd find Fred Cooper and have him open up. Yes! He would need a witness; someone besides Cooper though; someone reliable, someone above dispute. And he knew just the person. But if he was wrong—!

Fred Cooper was a tall wide-shouldered man in his mid-fifties with a dark, pointed beard and keen eyes. His wife, a small pretty woman with dark fine eyes answered the door. Lintell found Cooper at the kitchen table a coffee mug up to his lips.

"Hod do, Jack. Coffee?" he asked not getting to his feet but gesturing to a chair opposite.

"Don't mind if I do," Lintell replied taking the proffered seat. "Thanks, Mrs. Cooper," he said smiling up at the woman as she poured black coffee into a mug she set before him.

"Yu're out awful early, Jack. What's on yur mind?"

"Fred, I'd like to ask a favor of you."

Cooper tilted his head to one side, fixing keen gray eyes upon Lintell.

In a few terse words Lintell explained his proposition.

"Wal, I'm game, but the sticker's goin' te be Tarleton."

"I reckon you're right, but I got to try. There's too much to lose otherwise."

"Yu know," Cooper said thoughtfully, "Now yu got me wonderin'. This is not gonna look too good on my account if yu're right, in fact it'll be downright embarrassin'."

"It would be an easy mistake to make, Fred, if I'm right."

Tarleton was not at home. His housekeeper informed them they would possibly find him in his office. Surprisingly Tarleton consented to listen and made no comment until Lintell had finished. Even then he studied Lintell for a long moment before speaking. Lintell returned his gaze unflinchingly.

"What you propose is rather unorthodox," Tarleton finally said.

"That may be, but what harm can come if I'm wrong, nothing will have changed, but what a terrible travesty of justice it would be if I'm right and you did nothing."

"Yes, I see your point, Ranger Lintell. All right, I'll go along with you."

Tarleton joined Cooper in his buggy and they drove to Cooper's office on Soledad Street across from the old courthouse. Lintell followed on horseback. Inside the office Cooper went to a row of file cabinets and unlocking one took out a box containing an ivory-handled Colt and the small vial holding the spent slug. He held up the vial to the light studying its contents for a long moment.

"Gol-dang, yu might just be right, Jack," he said.

"Are you certain?" Tarleton demanded.

"Almost dead certain," Cooper said. "Jack, I see yu carry a forty-five. Pull the bullet out of one of yur cartridges an' let's look at 'em side by side," he continued dumping the slug out of the vial onto the table.

Lined up side by side it was easy to see that even bent the two slugs were of different size.

"44.40, I would say. It shore ain't a .45." Copper said emphatically.

"What you're saying, Mr. Cooper is that this slug you extracted from Robert Harlan's corpse was not fired from this gun!" Tarleton exclaimed after taking a deep breath.

"Yes, Mr. Tarleton, that's about the size of it—no pun intended," Cooper replied.

"And Harlan and his side-kick testified that this Colt, belonging to the victim was the one Hannah was holding in her hand," Lintell breathed. "Mr. Tarleton, this gun never killed Robert Harlan. Hannah Gibson never murdered her uncle."

"Let me think," Tarleton said beginning to pace back and forth. "Both Ed Harlan and George Gans testified that this gun had been fired. How do you explain that?"

"They're right in that regard," Cooper replied. "There was one spent cartridge in the cylinder when I examined it."

"My gut feeling is we ought to go over the crime scene once more," Lintell said.

"You have me intrigued now, Ranger Lintell. But it's been over two months since the murder. What can you expect to find there?" Tarleton replied.

"I'm hoping the killer or killers haven't thought to cover their tracks," Lintell said.

"All right," Tarleton said. "But on condition we take David Bodkin and Sheriff Talbert with us—"

"Talbert—!" Lintell exclaimed.

"Yes, Talbert," Tarleton said. "I don't want there to be any question of bias. Talbert is Sheriff of this county and Bodkin is the defense attorney. I want everything to be aboveboard and legal."

Lintell nodded forcing himself to remain calm. The more witnesses the better.

Sheriff Talbert scratched the bridge of his enormous nose with one finger and peered from under shaggy brows at the three men who had stepped into his office.

"Wal," he retorted after Tarleton had explained their presence. "I'm not shore what yu're lookin' fer, but if yur in on this Mr. Tarleton, I reckon I'll ride out there with yu."

They found David Bodkin still in bed and had to wait while he dressed. He seemed confused and slow to realize what was expected of him. Lintell attributed his perplexity to his just waking from a sound sleep and forced himself to remain patient.

The old woman, Anita let them in the house and stood by uneasily watching the men. Lintell was relieved that Ed Harlan was not at home. He didn't want to confront the man. Yet. Entering Harlan's office, Cooper walked to the large mahogany desk on one side of the room. Talbert stood back by the door, arms folded over his chest. Bodkin waited beside Tarleton. He was wide awake now and watched with keen interest.

"The body was lying here when I arrived," Cooper said standing behind the desk. "Whoever shot him was standing there about where yu are, Mr. Tarleton."

"My guess is Mr. Harlan went for his gun either before he was shot or as he was hit and got off one shot before he died," Lintell interjected. "The gun was laying near his hand according to what Miss Gibson told me. It appears he must have dropped it as he fell. Now if that's the case his bullet would have struck the wall over . . . here somewhere," he said hurriedly as he crossed the floor, turning when he was close to the wall and peered back making sure of his alignment.

"That would place it hittin' just about where that window is," Cooper said.

"Hmm, it doesn't look like any panes have been replaced," Lintell said, surveying the window and frame.

Cooper pulled the curtain aside.

"There!" Lintell cried pointing. About head high was a small black hole in the window casing.

"Mr. Tarleton, Bodkin yu're witnesses in this," Cooper said as he drew a jackknife from his pocket.

Moments later he held a crumbled lead slug in his hand. ".45," he said matter-of-factly.

"What the hell yu mean by all this?" Talbert said advancing into the room. "Harlan's gun was only fired one time, an' that shot killed him."

"That's what everybody assumed, including you, Talbert," Lintell said. "But Harlan wasn't killed by his own gun."

"He wasn't?" Talbert blinked.

"No," Lintell replied.

"He was killed by a 44.40 Caliber slug," Cooper interjected. "Not a .45."

For an instant there flashed in Talbert's eyes a desperate, calculating gleam, then it was gone.

"I'll be damn," he ejaculated.

"Well, Ranger Lintell, it seems you were correct," Tarleton said. He turned to David Bodkin. "I'll speak to the judge this morning. I'm dismissing the case against Miss Gibson."

"Well," Bodkin said taking a deep breath, clearly surprised at the turn of events in favor of his client.

"Much obliged, Mr. Tarleton," Lintell spoke up. "I hate to think of her having to stay even one more hour in that jail"

"What about the stolen money," Talbert protested.

"Under the circumstances there's no evidence Miss Gibson stole any money," Tarleton replied.

"Ah-huh," Talbert grunted. "So yu say. Wal, I don't reckon yu need me no more. I'll see yu fellers back in town."

He stomped out of the house and catching up the reins of his horse, swung into the saddle. He rode off down the lane at a fast trot. Upon reaching the road into town, however, he spurred his horse into a gallop.

Lintell found the old woman, Anita waiting in the kitchen and informed her of the news.

"You mean they're going to let my baby out of that terrible jail," she cried, a hand impulsively gripping his arm.

"Yes, ma'am," he assured her.

"Thank the Lord!" she exclaimed and Lintell thought she might faint.

Outside Lintell mounted Colonel and waited until the three men had climbed into Cooper's buggy and whipped the team into motion sending it clattering down the lane toward town. Lintell rode along beside them his heart singing as he imagined the expression on Hannah's face when he told her the news.

Two hours later Lintell held in his hand an order signed by Judge Bryan releasing Hannah from custody. Surprisingly, after listening to Tarleton, and asking him one or two questions for clarification, the judge signed the document without further comment. David Bodkin had wanted to be the one to announce the good news to Hannah, but Lintell pointed out rather forcefully that he would take care of the matter. Face flushed with displeasure, Bodkin had grudgingly acquiesced.

Lintell was about to step into the saddle when Fred Cooper approached. He stuck out his hand. "I'm rite glad it turned out like it did. My little mistake could have been a fatal one," he said shaking his head apologetically.

"I should smile," Lintell drawled taking the man's proffered hand. "But thank God it didn't."

"Say, have Miss Gibson stop by my office anytime this week and I'll release the things I took from her uncle's body that night," Cooper said.

"I'll tell her," Lintell replied. "But why hasn't Harlan's boy picked up those items?"

"Well, I mentioned it to him but he didn't seem to care, so the stuff has just been sitting here."

★

CHAPTER SIXTEEN

The cell door closed behind Hannah with a loud clank. She walked to the hard bunk and sat down eyes upon the rough floor planks. She was aware of the guard moving away down the narrow corridor, but she didn't look up. She was frightened . . . and angry, and hurt. So many lies, and she had been forced to hold her tongue all the while. She had sat and listened with parted lips and large innocent eyes fixed on them in wonder. Unaware of how Jack Lintell clenched his hands until the nails cut deep, but held his tongue and controlled his face. Until at last when she had turned to look and saw the fire in those blazing gray eyes.

She was still sitting there when they brought her supper. But she had no appetite and after only a few small bites pushed the tray away. She stretched out on the bunk but the ruffled bustle on the back of her dress made it too uncomfortable and she got up and slipped out of the dress and kicked off her black pumps. At Eula Mae's insistence the guards had blanketed off one corner of her cell giving her a small measure of privacy. She lay back down, well-covered in her camisole and calf-length drawers, pulled the blanket up to her chin and closed her eyes. It was a long while before she finally drifted off to sleep.

Something woke her. She lay there, eyes closed, unmoving, listening. The sound came again and she recognized the slow turning of the key in her cell door lock. Her eyes sprang open, her body tensing, muscles strung tight. Bright light filled the narrow window on the wall opposite. It was well after sunup. She waited for the creak of the cell door being pulled open, but all was still. From somewhere outside the window she heard sounds of activity from the street below, then a low gruff voice from close at hand.

"Compliments of a friend."

Still she did not move.

"I know yu're awake," came the low voice. "I'm leavin' the door unlocked, but yu better hurry before we change our mind."

She heard the sound of footsteps moving away and she sat upright and swung her legs over the side of the bunk. Slowly she stood and tip-toed to the door, took hold of the bars with trembling hands. She gave the door a gentle push and it swung outward a few inches. It actually was unlocked!

Her heart was pounding now. 'Compliments of a friend,' he had said. Who?

"Jack!" she gasped. "Oh, Jack, what have you done?" she breathed. "You've forsaken your honor, your career, for—me!"

Her head fell against the hard cold bars as a flurry of thoughts whirled through her head. To go to such lengths he must know she had no chance of acquittal. He was doing this to save her life! She took several faltering steps backward. The guard had said she had better hurry. Today was Sunday. The courthouse was closed. There would be no one in the adjacent building. Where were the guards? They would make themselves scarce, giving her a free path, but she had to hurry. But where would she go?

"Jack must have it all planned," she soliloquized. He would be waiting somewhere close by.

She hurried to where she had left her folded overalls and shirt next to her boots. Leaving on her camisole and drawers she quickly put on her overalls and shirt, buttoning the shirt to the throat, then pulled on her boots. She stuffed the dress she had worn that day into her little valise along with her walnut toiletry box and a change of undergarments.

At the cell door she slowly pushed it open and slipped into the corridor, her silver Mexican spurs emitting a soft jingle as she moved. She reached the door leading to the stairs. It stood slightly open and bright sunlight spilled through the thin crack. No one was at the table. Her way was unobstructed. Her hand closed about the doorknob.

It was nearly eleven o'clock when Lintell reined up before the jail and quickly dismounted. He suddenly remembered that the courthouse was closed and he would have to go around to the gate and bang on it to gain entrance. He reached an assuring hand to pat the paper in his shirt pocket beneath his vest. The neighborhood was quiet, most people getting ready for, or returning from church, he imagined as he raised his hand ready to thump a fist on the gate. He hesitated noticing that the gate stood slightly ajar. The hair on the nape of his neck bristled. What the heck was going on? Slowly he pushed open the gate and stepped inside the yard. Quickly he made his way up the steps taking them two at a time. At the door he hesitated. He could see it too stood slightly ajar. There was no sound from inside. He pulled the door open and stepped into the little room. No guards. He swallowed hard as coldness gripped him. With hard quick steps he advanced down the corridor not knowing what he would find. At the end of the corridor his eyes darted to the cell where Hannah was confined. He stopped, breath rushing from his chest. The cell door stood open.

Hannah Lea Gibson sat quietly on the bunk, hands folded in her lap. She had heard his approach and her eyes, dark in her pale face, were fixed on him. He reached the cell in two swift strides. She was on her feet and with an anguished cry threw herself into his arms.

"I couldn't do it, Jack!" she sobbed. "I couldn't let you sacrifice your honor—not for me! Oh, Jack can't we face this thing together, face whatever is to come? And beat it!"

"You crazy kid! What are you talking about?" he cried.

"Whatever you did—bribed the guards—I know you thought it best, but it's wrong—"

He held her tightly in his arms, felt her throbbing heart as realization dawned on him. Someone had arranged for her to escape, and she thought it had been him! That explained the missing guards. It had been a set up, but she had not taken the bait—thank God! He shuddered to think what would have happened had she gone out that door! He sat upon the bunk and drew her upon his knee.

"Sit down here, Sprite," he drawled, pulling the release document from his pocket. "I got something to show you."

"I don't understand," she said in genuine bewilderment after he had finished explaining what had transpired, even as she held the paper granting her freedom in her hand.

He laughed. "Well, it's simple, Sprite. The charges against you have been dropped."

"I—Oh, Jack!" she gasped her head sinking upon his breast.

"So there was no reason that you had to escape."

"I thought you had arranged it," she said tilting her head back to gaze up at him.

"No. But someone did. Someone who knew you were going to be released and wanted you on the run again, with people trying to kill you."

"Who?" she asked, eyes great gulfs.

"I have a good idea—Sheriff Talbert."

"But why?"

"That's what I intend to find out. Come on, get your things. We're not waiting for the guards to return," he said taking the release paper from her and placing it back in his pocket.

Lintell led the way down the steps carrying Hannah's valise in his left hand. No one challenged them. At the front of the courthouse, Lintell hooked the valise over the pommel and stepped into the saddle. He kicked his left foot clear of the stirrup and reached a hand to Hannah. She placed her foot in the vacated stirrup and swung with easy grace up behind him. She slipped her arms around his waist pressing her cheek against his back.

For a moment he sat there unmoving with the slender, trembling girl's arms about him conscious of an exaltation he had never known before that seemed to transcend all the dark, terrible, uncertain moods of the last few days.

Stopping at Noyles Livery Stables on Main Street Lintell rented a horse for Hannah. They rode southwest out of town arriving at the Circle C Ranch an hour later. Lintell spent nearly two hours explaining what all had occurred. Jim Casey and both girls listened, Hannah no less than the other two. Though she had heard him tell it earlier, she had been so excited that she hardly comprehended it all. Eula Mae was beside herself.

"Oh, you shall stay here with me as long as you want. Can't she dad?" she said hugging her friend.

"I reckon yu're shore welcome, Hannah," Jim Casey said.

"Whoever killed my uncle used a 44.40," Hannah said leaning forward anxiously. "All we have to do is look for someone Uncle Bob knew who carries a 44.40—"

"That's not as easy as it sounds," Lintell said. "Lots of cowboys carry 44.40's. The bullets are interchangeable with rifles of the same caliber. That way they don't have to carry two different types of cartridges on their belts."

"Oh," Hannah sighed frowning.

"Yep, the ranger's right, Hannah. Fact is I carry a 44.40 myself. Eula Mae there learned to shoot with this ole pistol," Casey said, patting the butt of his holstered gun. "And if I recall yu shot a few jackrabbits with it yourself," he chuckled.

"Shot *at* them you mean. I recall missing more than I hit," Hannah drawled, archly.

"Yeah, wal. There weren't many misses—that I recollect," Casey grinned.

Hannah flashed Lintell a look and he was happy to see that the shadow of havoc was gone from her eyes.

"I reckon two or three of my riders carry 44.40's," Casey mused. "I know Ted Stoes does, fer one."

"Is Ted riding for you now?" Hannah asked.

"Yep. He quit the Bar H shortly after—Wal, about two months ago," Casey replied. "Been with me ever since."

"Well," Lintell drawled getting to his feet, "I've some business to take care of, so I better mosey."

"Are you going back to town?" Hannah asked, rising also.

"Yep," he replied.

"It'll be dark 'fore yu get there," Casey said, "Yu're welcome te stay the night. Got plenty of room in the bunkhouse."

"Thanks, Mr. Casey, but I'll ride on in."

"Suit yerself," he replied.

Hannah walked with him to the door where he peered down at her for a long moment before nodding to the others. He stepped out on the porch. Hannah followed him.

"What's wrong?" she asked her gaze troubled as she peered up at him.

"What makes you think something's wrong?"

"You don't fool me one bit, Jack Lintell."

"Oh, is that so?" he drawled.

"Yep, that's so."

"Well, I reckon we still don't know who murdered your Uncle Bob or what happened to all that money, so I reckon you better not go any place without me and stay close to the house."

"All right," she said eagerly giving him a dazzling smile.

Lintell swung into the saddle with slow easy grace and touching fingers to the brim of his sombrero spurred his horse into a lope. When he reached the end of the lane he peered back over his shoulder. She was still standing where he had left her, a small pale figure in the gathering twilight.

Once out of sight of the house, instead of turning toward town, Lintell rode southwest. It was well after dark when he paused on a slight rise overlooking the Bar H. Only two lights shown in the otherwise darken ranch house windows; one near the front of the long, tall-gabled frame structure, and the other at the far end. Lintell's eyes scanned the remaining buildings. Lights winked brightly in one some distance from the house partly obscured by tall cottonwoods, which he judged to be the bunkhouse.

He stepped from the saddle and tied his horse well back in the cedars. Taking off his spurs he hung them over the saddle horn and after one last long look at the buildings below started down the slope keeping to the cover of the cedars. He made his way slowly, cautiously and watchfully. Some of Harlan's riders might still be out and Lintell did not intend to be seen. When he reached the cottonwood grove that surrounded the house he proceeded even more slowly. The barking of a dog somewhere near the bunkhouse halted him. The crunching of boot steps not far distant made him freeze behind the trunk of a cottonwood.

At length he reached the shrubbery that grew thickly on the south and east side of the house. Once in this dense shelter he felt safe. He recalled the house from his earlier visits and noted that the nearby lighted window was Harlan's office. The shadows were impenetrable as he moved with slow cautious steps feeling his way at one point. It was a warm night with only a slight breeze to stir the cottonwood leaves and he saw that the window sash was open several inches. He heard the low murmur of voices and once the scraping noise of a chair being pushed back. The office was occupied, and he suspected one of the occupants was most likely young Harlan. And if his luck hadn't failed him, the other person was George Gans.

Lintell wasn't certain what he expected to hear, but he was convinced the answer to Harlan's murder rested with these two men. The missing money was another thing. At length he removed his sombrero and drew himself up until he could see into the window. The first thing he caught sight of was Ed Harlan sitting at the desk directly in line with the window. Lamplight showed on his swarthy face as he leaned back in his chair with booted feet resting on the desk top. Lintell raised himself to take a keener and longer look. There didn't appear to be anyone else in the room. Harlan must have been mumbling to himself as he puffed slowly on a cigar. A thin cloud of blue smoke drifted above his head.

The sound of horse's hooves on the lane caused Lintell to duck back into the dark shadows below the window. The rider reined up in front of the house and shortly Lintell heard the thump of booted feet and jangle of spurs crossing the porch. Moments later Lintell heard the door to Harlan's office open and shortly George Gans came into his view.

"Where the hell yu been?" Harlan demanded dropping his feet to the floor. "We been waitin' fer yu!"

We? Someone else *was* in the room Lintell realized.

"Where'd yu think? I was meetin' with Buster," Gans said easily tossing his sombrero on a nearby chair. "Let me have one of them cigars."

"In the box yonder," Harlan replied with a jab of his chin.

"How well do you trust that cowboy," an unseen voice said.

Lintell craned his head without exposing himself, tried to see farther into the room. But whoever the third person was he was seated in the shadows to Lintell's left near the door out of Lintell's line of sight.

"Buster? He's been square with us so far," Gans replied striking a match to the cigar and puffing out a cloud of smoke.

"Yes, so he has. Until recently we've had a pretty good setup here."

Lintell thought he detected a note of sarcasm in the man's cultured voice.

"I reckon we still have a good thing goin'" Harlan grunted aggravated. "Usin' paw's reputation to cover this rustlin' operation has worked like a charm. An' with Buster on Casey's payroll it's been like shootin' fish. Casey an't got a clue."

"How many head have you made off with so far?" the unseen voice asked.

"I reckon 'bout ten thousand, all told," Gans said settling in a chair across from Harlan.

"Yes, that's well and good, but have you discovered the whereabouts of the book?"

"Not yet. I know the girl's hidden it somewhere. I've searched every inch of this house. It's not here—"

"Your carelessness is beginning to concern me, Harlan," again that unseen voice. "It puzzles me that you had that book in the first place. Why did you? You wouldn't be planning on double-crossing me by any chance?"

"Hell no! I an't got no reason te double cross yu. It was just gettin' too confusin' tryin' te keep track of things. I didn't know paw would go through my things—" Harlan cursed. "An' why did yu have te kill him?"

"That was unfortunate I'll admit. But Hank insists he had no choice. Foolishly your father attempted to draw on him. Besides, now the ranch belongs to you—"

"I could have got the book back from paw without yu plugging him," Harlan growled.

"I reckon it's ov'r an' done with now," came a fourth voice from Lintell's left near the door where the other mysterious voice sat, out of his line of sight. This man's voice was rough, less cultured than the other.

"The girl must have the book. Apparently she hasn't told anyone about it . . . yet. But we can't count on her keeping quiet forever. If you can't get her to tell where she hid it . . . well then, we'll just have Hank silence her. Whatever she knows will go to the grave with her."

Lintell slumped hard against the wall beneath the window his breathe expelling in a rush. He tried to clear his mind, absorb what he had just overheard. Hannah's life was in terrible danger!

A chair scraped inside the room and there came the thud of boots striking the floor.

"What was that?!"

"It came from outside the window."

"By Gawd, somebody's out there, listenin'!"

Lintell abandoned his position, and glided back into the shrubbery where he froze for several heartbeats listening. There came the thump of hurried footsteps on the porch. Stealthily Lintell moved making no sound. He parted the leaves of the shrubbery and moved noiselessly through them, away from the house. He had to feel for the trunks of the cottonwoods. One by one he passed through them, gradually gaining control over his stunned faculties as he crept toward the slope and the thick grove of cedars. At the edge of the cottonwoods he stopped to make sure of his further course. He crossed the wide dark space to the right of the cottonwoods and gained the lane. Crossing it he entered the stand of cedars.

Working his way upwards he found his horse where he had tied him, and mounting was soon out on the road headed for Casey's place. He had to talk to Hannah; had to find out about this mysterious book . . . and why she hadn't told him about it before. There was no pursuit.

Lights were still on in the house when Lintell reined up before the porch. The door opened and big Jim Casey's solid frame blocked the light. Lintell swung to the ground and threw the reins.

"Sorry to disturb you, Mr. Casey, but I've got to talk to Miss Gibson. Is she still awake?"

As though in answer Hannah's face peered from around Casey's bulk.

"Jack! What is it?" she asked and stepping past Mr. Casey walked to the edge of the porch.

"I need to talk to you."

She stepped down from the porch and came up beside him.

"Yes?" she whispered.

He glanced up at Mr. Casey, nodded, then took her arm and steered her away from the house into the shadows. She went easily with him. He stopped when they were out of hearing from the house and turned to face her. She could make out his features clearly in the light from the house. He stared intently at her.

"Why didn't you tell me about the book?" he demanded.

Her eyes widened. She blinked. "Book?" she breathed.

"Yes, the book! Where did you hide it?"

"I didn't hide it anywhere! I don't have it!"

"Then you know what I'm talking about!"

"Yes, I—I think I do. The night Uncle Bob was murdered I saw a small blue leather-bound book on his desk. He had been looking through it when I came into the room. I didn't think anything about it until Edward asked me—"

"Your cousin talked to you about it?" he questioned.

"Yes. He came to the jail. He insisted I give it to him. But Jack, I—I don't have it. I never did!"

His eyes searched hers for a long moment.

"Ah," he whispered. "It all makes sense. That's what Jeff Breen was after! Why he was following us, tried to kill me to get to you and retrieve the book!"

"I don't understand. What is so important about that little blue book?"

"I don't know. But I suspect it has a lot to do with this rustling scheme Harlan is up to his neck in."

★

CHAPTER SEVENTEEN

It was well after midnight when Lintell reached town. He left his horse at Noyles' Livery Stables and walked over to the hotel. There was no light in Captain McKenny's room so he decided to wait until morning to tell the Captain what he had learned. The thought that Hannah's life was in danger; that she would be killed because of a book she didn't even have still unsettled him and left him feeling cold. On the long ride to town he could think of nothing else. Up to that time he had been convinced one or both of the men were involved in Harlan's murder. But it seemed Harlan was at least innocent of his father's murder. What was it the mysterious voice had said . . . *'That was unfortunate, I'll admit. But Hank insists he had no choice. Foolishly your father attempted to draw on him.'* Hank, the man had called him. That's all he had to go on; a name and the sound of his voice, the voice of a coldblooded killer. And, he knew as little about the other man, the one with the cultivated sounding voice. He had detected a slight accent; Spanish, French, he wasn't certain. He was no coarse-talking cattleman or cowboy, like the other, the one he called Hank. He was apparently the brains behind the rustling, and was keen to remain shadowy, letting others' do the dirty work; obviously a shrewd individual. And this Buster character Gans mentioned was apparently an inside man on Jim Casey's payroll unbeknownst to the rancher. Well, he had something to go on, a place to start. The answer to both men's identities rested with that little book. The book Hannah's uncle must have appropriated somehow from his son's belongings, and obviously hid . . . but where?

In his room Lintell pulled off his boots and unbuckling his gun belt and hanging it over the bed post, stretched out on the mattress. Well, he thought, he had struck a hot trail. It would lead him to the murderer of Hannah's uncle and it would lead to the end of Harlan's rustling scheme. He should have felt some satisfaction, but he didn't. And he knew why. Hannah's life was in danger. The thought of something happening to her brought an icy chill to the pit of his stomach. He had to break open this case, and soon, before they targeted her. After a while he got up and undressed and got back in bed where he slept plagued by disturbing dreams the rest of the night.

Lintell was up with the sun and after washing and dressing was soon knocking on Captain McKenny's hotel room door. It was opened immediately by the old ranger captain.

"Come in, Jack. I was kinda expectin' yu," McKenny said by way of greeting.

"You had breakfast yet?" Lintell asked.

"Nope, let's go down to the dinin' room an' grab some. Then yu can tell me what yu been up te. I've heard some rumors thet have shore struck my fancy."

"What have you heard?" Lintell asked as they sat down at a table in the far corner of the crowded dining room.

"First off, thet yu got Hannah's murder charge dropped."

Lintell nodded, and went on to tell how he had been puzzled by something about the spent slug the coroner had removed from Robert Harlan's corpse.

"I kept staring at it and there just seemed something wasn't right," Lintell explained, describing how, after comparing the slug with a .45, confirmed that it was a 44.40 and could not have come from Harlan's gun.

"I reckon thet was some fine police work, son. Yu can bet thet'll go in my report te headquarters," McKenny said.

"Cap, did you receive a letter from a rancher by the name of Jim Casey complaining about rustlers?" Lintell asked after the two men had given their orders to the waiter.

"Yep, as a matter of fact I was goin' te talk te yu about thet, but seein' yu was all tied up in the Harlan case I assigned the matter te Johnson."

"Hmm, I reckon it's turned into something a hell of a lot deeper than just common rustling," Lintell replied.

"Ah-huh," McKenny murmured keen gray eyes on Lintell.

Lintell proceeded to tell McKenny how he had paid a night visit to Harlan's ranch and what he had overheard as he listened at the open window.

"Wal, I'll be gol-dang!" McKenny exclaimed plainly taken aback by the news. "What are yu gonna do?"

"Well, I reckon we could go in and arrest Harlan, break up this scheme, but that wouldn't get us the ring leader, and his hired killer." Lintell said shaking his head, "And Hannah would be in greater danger than before. They'd for shore try to shut her up. Cap, I don't have to tell you I'm worried."

"Ah-huh, I shore see yur point. What're yu thinkin'?" McKenny said.

"Harlan has an inside man on Casey's payroll. The only name I've got is, Buster. But I reckon it won't be hard to identify him."

At that moment the waiter brought their food and talk was abandoned for the next several minutes as each man attacked his breakfast with gusto. Midway through their meal they were joined by Abe Johnson who settled his lanky frame down in one of the chairs and ordered coffee. As Johnson sipped the hot black drink Lintell told him about what he had learned.

"Wal, wal," Johnson said, shaking his head, eyes darkly keen.

"We have to move on this bunch," Lintell replied. "And in the process we can't let anything happen to Hannah."

"Shore, yu're right about that," Johnson agreed taking another sip of coffee.

"I reckon yu'll have te devise a trap an' catch Harlan red handed. Thet'll lead us te the rustler boss." McKenny interjected. "I want him as bad as Harlan. Besides, that's the only way to protect Hannah."

"Ah-huh," Lintell acknowledged. "Abe, are you up to the old trick we used over Pecos?"

"I heard that this Casey has a redhead daughter whose shore a heart-stopper," Johnson drawled. "Any truth te that?"

"Yep, I reckon you heard correct," Lintell replied eying his fellow ranger shrewdly.

Johnson smiled broadly. "I reckon I'm shore game," he declared. "Yu keep an eye on that sweet little Hannah an' I'll have a go at that red head—"

"Is that all you think about, Abe—girls?" Lintell said more gruffly then he intended. His friend had struck too close to the truth.

"Pard, sometimes I just wonder if yure mother knows yu're out," Johnson drawled.

"Hah!" Lintell growled. Clearly his worry over Hannah was wearing on his nerves.

"Aw right, I'm with yu," Johnson said coolly though there was still a twinkle in his eye.

"I'll ride on out to Casey's place this morning and clue Casey in. You ride in later and hit him up for a job—"

"Shore, I know the game," Johnson returned. "I'll get a line on this Buster; get on his good side an' invite myself in on the action."

"Abe, watch yourself. Harlan's not the brains behind this rustling scheme. We don't know who this fellow is we're dealing with. A careless slip could be deadly."

"Don't worry, pard. I've got eyes in the back of my head."

It was mid-morning when Lintell reached the Circle C. Nestled among the cottonwoods stretching far on each side of the river was the long low, red-roofed, red-walled adobe ranch house. He stood in his stirrups shading his eyes as he took in the droves of horses in the pastures, the squares of alfalfa, and herds of cattle dotting the slopes and adjacent rangeland.

"Whew," he soliloquized admiringly. "I reckon Casey shore has a fine looking spread."

He settled back in his saddle eyes upon three riders emerging from the trees and starting toward him. When they were within a hundred yards or so, Lintell recognized the big man in the center of the trio, Jim Casey.

"Howdy, Mr. Casey," Lintell greeted, as the three reined to a stop before him.

“Lintell,” Casey said, “Been expectin’ yu.”

Lintell glanced at the two riders bracketing Casey. He didn’t want to say too much in front of these men, not until he found out who he was talking to.

“This hyar is my foreman, Charlie Reed,” Casey said indicating a tall stooped-shouldered, bronze-faced rider somewhere in his early forty’s. “And this sorry lookin’ cuss with the sad eyes is Bud Jackson. Charlie, Bud, meet, Jack Lintell, Texas Ranger.”

Reed and Jackson nodded but said nothing, their keen eyes taking in Lintell.

Jim Casey fell in beside Lintell and they sat their horses as Reed and Jackson continued on to the corral.

“Mr. Casey, do you have a rider on your payroll that goes by the handle of Buster?” Lintell asked after the two riders had passed out of earshot.

“Shore do,” Casey replied. “Fact is we was just talkin’ ‘bout him the other day when yu was here. He used te ride fer Harlan, had been with him since he was just a youngster. He got the nickname Buster since he came te work fer me. That boy’s one hell of a rider! There ain’t a bronc livin’ that he can’t bust. His real handle is Ted, Ted Stoes. I reckon yu met his ma, Harlan’s old housekeeper, Anita?”

“Ah,” Lintell breathed. “How come he stopped riding for Harlan?”

“Wal, I reckon he didn’t take te the way young Harlan was runnin’ the ranch since his paw was killed,” Casey replied, then after a moment’s hesitation, “I got a hunch yur ‘bout te tell me somethin’ I don’t hanker te hear.”

“I’m afraid so, Mr. Casey,” Lintell said. “Your Buster’s taking a salary from you, and at the same time he’s rustling your cows.”

"The hell yu say!" Casey cursed. "Yu talkin' true?"

"Your Buster is double-crossing you, Mr. Casey. He's been helping steal your cows. His job is to stick with you and be a spy for whoever bribed him to ditch you. He'll keep these rustler pards of his posted on where and when your outfit rides and the movement of your stock. Damn clever! We've identified a dishonest rancher that's in on the deal, but there's a shadowy figure who happens to be the key player, the brains behind this deal, whose identity we haven't pinpointed yet. We're keen to get him."

"Be damn!" Casey ejaculated. "How do yu know all this?"

"Well, Mr. Casey, you wrote asking for the rangers to look into the matter of your stock being rustled—"

"Be damn! Yu rangers don't waste no time!"

"That's our business, Mr. Casey. But we've got to catch Buster red handed so he can lead us to the man behind the rustling." *Something we wouldn't have to fool with if we had that damn book*! But he didn't voice his thoughts. "Therefore, I'm asking you to keep what I just told you under your hat until we catch our man."

Lintell went on to explain that one of his rangers by the name of Abe Johnson would show up asking for a job. "He'll be working undercover, so play along with whatever he does or says," Lintell elucidated.

Casey nodded his head slowly, thoughtfully. "I can't get over that friendly, easy-going boy betrayin' me. Why would he do thet?" he asked.

"I guess the big persuasion is money," Lintell replied. "I've known cowboys without a bit of yellow doing it for that reason. A big roll of greenbacks shore talks loud. Our rancher knows this and he's found a cash-strapped cowboy to be a mole for him rustling Circle C cattle."

“I reckon it’ll be hard te keep my trap shut whenever I happen on Buster, but I’ll manage I reckon,” the rancher said.

“I reckon it’s a good idea that my man doesn’t meet up with Hannah though,” Lintell said.

“Oh?”

“She’s met him once and knows he’s a ranger.”

“I get yu,” Casey replied.

★

CHAPTER EIGHTEEN

Late evening three days later found Lintell camped in the foothills east of Uvalde. Earlier that afternoon he had ridden down into this valley where a lonely cabin nestled, having followed an old, blazed trail that wound up the course of a brook. The water was of a color that made rock and sand and moss seem like gold. He saw no signs or tracks of game. A gray jay now and then screeched his approach to unseen denizens of the woods. The stream babbled past him over mossy ledges, under the dark shade of clumps of spruces, and it had grown smaller as he had progressed upward toward its source. At length it was lost in a swale of high, rank grass, and the blazed trail led on through heavy pine woods. Here he had halted and was now leaning back against the rough logs of the old cabin before a small fire.

The hour was sunset, with the golden rays and shadows streaking down the rolling sage hills, all rosy and gray with rich, strange softness. Lintell gave the appearance of lazy ease as he sat there, but all the while his senses were tuned to the sounds around him and shortly there came to his ears the soft thump of horse's hoofs. Moments later a rider emerged from the trees and entered the clearing. Lintell stood waiting for Abe Johnson to ride up before the fire.

"I was beginning to wonder if you'd make it before nightfall," Lintell said as his friend stepped easily from the saddle.

"Me too," Johnson replied. "I shore didn't hanker havin' to find this old cabin in the dark."

"Nobody followed you?"

"Nope. I made shore of that."

"I brought some grub; sandwiches I had made up at the hotel, and there's coffee in the kettle. I reckon you're hungry."

"Yu bet I am," Johnson said squatting before the fire in the easy manner of range riders.

"Well, what's the news?" Lintell asked as the two ate.

"I reckon I'm in good and solid. It wasn't hard. They shore are lousy about hiddin' their goings-on. Damn shore of themselves. So, I let on right off that I was aware of somethin' shady goin' on, an' wanted in on it. Wal, it turns out there's a big drive in the works in the next day or two. I reckon Buster's tired of them small drives an' is pushin' fer one big'en that will shore as hell ruin, Mr. Casey."

"Hmm, how many involved in this scheme?"

"I ain't met them all, but I reckon five or six. Let's see, Smoky Hill, another one of Casey's riders, an' Pete Small; he's the old man of the bunch, but young in years, I was told, an' I reckon the one te watch. I peg him as a coldblooded killer. One of them who just enjoys killin'. There's Jim Tasker. He goes by the handle, Durango. He's another deep hombre that shore bears watchin'. The rest I ain't crossed paths with yet as they was out on a drive. But this Buster's a deep hombre. I reckon there's more on his plate than rustlin'," Johnson finished.

"How you mean?" Lintell queried.

"He needs money, and that's drivin' him. I reckon he's the one pushin' fer this big drive, and from what I gather he's buckin' the head honcho. And I figure one of them girls is at the bottom of it—"

"Which one?" Lintell demanded quickly.

"Why, your little Hannah. It shore wasn't hard te figure that one out once she wasn't hangin' out with that redhead, Eula Mae. Hannah's been stickin' close te the house, which is good, an' me, I been makin' myself scarce around her so as she won't see me an' let the cat out of the bag about me being' a ranger. But that ain't kept me from studyin' our boy, Buster. Whenever your little lady comes outside, pacin' in the yard or loungin' on the porch, or whatever, our Buster goes all stiff, like a watchin' jack rabbit that thinks he ain't seen. When he's around the others he acts happy-go-lucky, but out in the dark he walks up and down under the trees like a hounded man. I don't like it, Jack. He's plannin' somethin' regardin' that girl or my name ain't Abraham Archibald Johnson!"

"Abe, that's shore what I been afraid of," Lintell said worriedly. "There's a good chance he's been given the order to silence Hannah and he's getting up his nerve."

"Shore, that make's sense."

"When you get back don't let Buster out of your sight. I'll ride in to the ranch first thing in the morning. I've got to get Hannah away from there, out of danger, Lintell said dumping the remains of his coffee tin on the ground.

"Yu got it," Johnson replied.

Night had settled down over the quiet foothills by the time Lintell reached town. He found Captain McKenny in the hotel dining room eating dinner where he proceeded to tell him of his meeting with Abe Johnson.

"I don't like the look of it. I'll never forgive myself if somethin' happens te Hannah," McKenny huffed.

"I intend to ride out there in the morning and bring her to town. I'll put her up here in the hotel where she'll be safe until this is all over," Lintell said.

"Hmm," McKenny murmured thoughtfully, "I reckon Johnson was took-to awful quick. Thet might be good an' it might not. I reckon I've heerd of thet Pete Small 'fore."

"Oh?"

"Yep, and I reckon his name suits him. He's a little feller, but shore one of them bad-tempered, cross-grained types. Not one yu'd want te meet in a narrow, dangerous place. He keeps a gun in each inside vest pocket, an' I reckon he don't hesitate te use 'em."

"I reckon that's Abe's estimation. He told me as much," Lintell replied.

It was late when the two finished eating and both retired to their rooms. Lintell undressed and laid down where he reviewed the events of the day and evening. That occupation afforded him little pleasure. What further plot was Stoes hatching? Was it simply that he intended to double-cross Harlan, and the rustler boss? Abe calculated that Stoes was greedy for money—cash that would set him up with his own outfit somewhere else where he wasn't known? That would be the easiest to deal with. He strongly suspected though that it concerned Hannah, and that troubled him. Had he been ordered to kill her? Or did it have nothing to do with Harlan and the mysterious book; but some hot-blooded scheme on his own to kidnap Hannah!

His thoughts turned to her. He closed his eyes, trying to visualize vivid lips, the glory and gleam of her golden curls, of dancing, laughing blue eyes, warm, beautiful, fearless, of her pulsing vitality. He sighed into the darkness. He couldn't let anything happen to her.

Lintell woke with the first sifting of sunlight through the lace curtains on the window across from his bed. He dressed and went down for breakfast. Captain McKenny was already there, seated at a table in one corner of the crowded room. Lintell joined him and ordered breakfast.

"Wal, son I've got a company of rangers standin' by when yu give the word te move in on them rustlers," McKenny said.

"I'll meet Abe this evening. Hopefully he'll have the information we need to move in," Lintell replied.

"How many we're facin'?"

"Abe said there's six or seven in the gang, maybe more. He's not run into the whole bunch yet."

Their talk was interrupted at that moment with the approach of Fred Cooper.

"Morning gentlemen," Cooper said, "Mind if I join yu?"

"Not at all," McKenny replied.

"Wal, I won't take long," Cooper said, "I'm on my way te the courthouse, but I saw Lintell here an' just wanted te remind him about old man Harlan's property I'm still holdin'—"

"Dog-gone," Lintell exclaimed, "I plumb forgot to tell Miss Gibson you said she could pick it up."

"I wouldn't be naggin' yu, but I'm running out of room te store evidence," Cooper said.

"I'll ride out there today," Lintell replied. Cooper's request would give him an excellent excuse to see Hannah; not that he needed an excuse, he smiled to himself. "You'll be in your office this afternoon?" he asked.

"Yep, shore will," the coroner answered.

It was early dawn at the Circle C. The sun was not yet up behind the eastern ramparts. The cottonwoods whispered in the dawn breeze, the spring beneath the milk house talked and murmured. Out in the big corrals the cattle were beginning to stir and bawl. In the kitchen Eula Mae and Hannah had breakfast waiting for Jim Casey.

"Mornin' gurls," the big man said entering the kitchen and dropping heavily into the chair at the end of the table.

"You look tired, dad," Eula Mae returned. "Didn't you sleep well last night?"

"Not so as yu could say," the big rancher replied.

"What's worrying you, dad?"

"Nothin' te upset yu. Just ranchin' business."

"We're losing more cows aren't we?" Eula Mae exclaimed.

"What's fer breakfast?" he queried putting an end to further questioning.

Finishing eating, Casey stomped out of the house making his way down towards the barn. Hannah walked to the window and peered out. Two cowboys were at the corrals. She recognized Ted Stoes. The first rays of the sun that was rising over the eastern hills shown on his boyish face. His gaily studded belt and riding cuffs, his spurs and the vanity of silver on his wide hat caught the glow and sparkled brightly.

Ted had changed, she thought, since she had last seen him the night of the dance. She couldn't remember him in the past being so flamboyant in dress or manner. She took a second and less hasty look at him. He wore high-heeled, fancy-topped boots, tight-fitting trousers of dark material, a heavy belt with silver buckle holding an ivory-handled Colt in a fancy holster, and a colorful shirt, with wide collar, open at the neck. Yes, he had changed from the reckless boy she had once known.

She didn't care at all for his new guise. Nor the way he stared at her whenever she went outside. Oh, she had been aware of his piecing gaze, remembering the night they were on the way back to the dance after changing her gown, how he pulled the buckboard up under the tall cottonwoods and tried to kiss her. At first she had been so shocked she had not immediately objected. But his rough, unbridled manner forcing her down on the hard seat, his fingers groping, had roused her fiery spirit and she managed to free one hand and struck him a hard blow to his jaw which brought an end to his amorous advances, but not his angry indignation. He had been in a temper, moping about, the remainder of the night, and she had willingly avoided him.

He had not approached her since her return, but only stared at her from a distance, which distressed her even more leaving her feeling uncertain and vulnerable. Her attention turned to the other man with Stoes. He was older and had the dress of a cattleman. She didn't know him. The two appeared to be deep in some heated discussion. She turned from the window, caught Eula Mae's eye.

"Who's that man talking to Ted?" she asked.

Eula Mae peered out the window, gave a grim knowing smile. "That's Martin Vanhall," she replied tersely. "He came to the valley about two months ago, just about the time your uncle was murdered."

"Oh?" Hannah said, looking askance at her friend, then back at the cattleman. "I get the feeling you don't like him."

"I don't dislike him," Eula Mae denied. "It's just that he makes me uncomfortable; the way he looks at me. I think he's trying to get up the nerve to court me," she shrugged, "But he's just not my type."

"Hmm," Hannah mused thoughtfully. "Come on, I'll help you wash dishes."

As Lintell drew near the house the front door opened and Hannah and Eula Mae, both wearing fashionable summer gowns, walked out on the porch watching him approach. Lintell was struck by the contrast between the two women; Eula Mae, tall and statuesque; Hannah, small, petite, with all the appearance of a fragile golden flower. Lintell caught sight of Jim Casey approaching from the direction of the corrals. He waited until the rancher came up to him.

"Anything I should know?" Casey asked peering with keen eyes up at Lintell.

"Things are moving smoothly," Lintell replied.

"Fer yu maybe, but I'm losin' cows right an' left."

"I know, but don't get discouraged. A few more days and it'll be over."

"I hope yu're right," Casey retorted and the two continued on to the house.

Hannah walked to the edge of the porch, graceful, big-eyed, strangely disturbing, at least to Jack Lintell.

"Morning, Jack," she said gaily.

"I come to see if you wanted to ride into town," Lintell replied. "The coroner, Mr. Cooper has some property of your uncle. He asked me if I would see you in to his office so he can release it to you. He's running out of room to store evidence. Do you feel up to it?"

"Of course," she said with a dazzling smile.

"Well, are you going to ride a horse in that garb?"

"I most certainly will not!" she retorted wide-eyed. "I've sworn off boy's togs—at least for a year," she laughed.

"Then I reckon yu'll have to take the buckboard," Casey said stepping up on the porch beside the girls.

"Thanks, Mr. Casey," Lintell replied.

A cowboy brought up the buckboard hitched to the same spirited blacks of a few days ago. Lintell helped Hannah to climb aboard then climbed in and took up the reins. The lane went for a mile or more before striking the road into town, the same road that continued on southwest to the Bar H.

"What were you and Mr. Casey talking about on the way up to the house," Hannah suddenly asked her blue eyes wide. "His face was pale. It's not like him."

"You're shore a sharp-eyed little sprite," Lintell returned. "Mr. Casey has lost some cows to rustlers. He's asked the rangers to look into the matter."

"Jack Lintell, I grew up on a ranch you might remember! I'm a western girl, so I know about rustlers. Ranchers lose cows all the time to rustling. It's part of the business . . . So what were you really talking about?"

"I bet when you get married you're gonna be one of them carping wives," he replied with pretended irritation.

"Oh, dear," she cried, blushing. "Do you really think so?"

He gave a loud chuckle.

"Don't laugh, Jack. It's not funny," she pouted.

They rode on in silence for several moments before she spoke again, seemingly willing to change the subject as she asked him many questions about himself, wanting to know about his family, his mother and sisters. Before he realized it they were pulling up in front of the coroner's office on Soledad Street.

Jack Lintell helped her down from the buckboard and walked beside her into the coroner's office where Fred Cooper met them, a broad smile on his lips.

"Miss Gibson, I'm happy things turned out as they did," he said taking her hand.

She smiled. "Me too," she replied.

Hannah was glad she was not alone, that Jack was with her to retrieve the property found upon her uncle's body the night of the murder. For it was as she knew it would be, a very emotional moment. The items were in a large paper sack which she took with trembling hands after signing the release form.

Inside the sack were the clothes her uncle had been wearing that night, a few coins and a small brass key attached to a thin chain. She avoided looking at the clothes, still smelling of the musty odor of blood. Instead her gaze fell upon the small brass key.

"Oh, Jack, would you look here! It's the key to the small drawer in my walnut toiletry box," she exclaimed. "I wondered where it had disappeared to. I can't imagine why Uncle Bob would have had it in his pocket! All I kept in the drawer were a few sheets of stationary and one or two envelopes."

★

CHAPTER NINETEEN

Hannah slipped the chain holding the tiny brass key over her head and tucked the key inside her blouse. Her mood had changed. She had become strangely quiet. Lintell gathered up the sack with the remaining items and after thanking Cooper they walked outside. Nothing more was said about the brass key, but Lintell's mind was actively pursuing a disturbing thought; why did Harlan have the key to his niece's toiletry box in his pocket the night he was murdered?

"It's past noon, let's stop somewhere and get some lunch," Lintell suggested.

"I'd like that," she replied looking him in the eye. "And I know just the place."

She held one hand out to Lintell and with the other lifted the hem of her ruffled skirt in order to place a dainty slippered foot upon the wheel hub. She stepped gracefully up, tucking her skirt out of the way of the wheel and settled confidently upon the seat of the buckboard. Lintell released her hand and climbed up beside her.

"Where we headed?" he asked.

"Mexican Joe's, it's over on Laredo Street. Uncle Bob used to take me there whenever we came to town. He has the best *Chili Verde* ever."

"Mexican Joe's it is," Lintell drawled, and with a slap of the reins the team started off.

Mexican Joe was a little wizen-faced bright-eyed Mexican not much taller than Hannah. His restaurant was small but clean and filled with mouth-watering smells. Upon seeing Hannah he hurried forward to greet her, a huge smile on his face.

"*Señorita*, how you been? Joe worry about you when me hear what happen to *Señor* Roberto. Your uncle, he was a very good man," he said.

This eloquent tribute elicited a grave smile from Hannah.

"Thank you. Joe, this is Jack Lintell. He's a Texas Ranger," Hannah said peering up at Lintell.

"Me very happy to meet you, *Señor* Jack," Mexican Joe replied. "Come, you and the *Señor*, please, set down. Angelica will serve you," Mexican Joe went on waving the two to a table against the wall. It was where she and her uncle always sat when they ate at the little restaurant.

They were no sooner seated when they were approached by a plump, sweet-faced Mexican girl of sixteen who took their order. After the girl had departed, Lintell leaned back in his chair giving Hannah a long keen look.

"I know what you're thinking. Me too," she said fingering the key through the cloth of her bodice. "Why did my uncle have this key in his pocket?"

He nodded. “I think the answer is in that toiletry box.”

“Yes. That tiny drawer is just big enough to hold a small leather book.”

Hannah was quiet as they rode back to the Circle C and Lintell made no effort to break into her thoughts. When they arrived at the ranch Eula Mae met them at the door. After a quick greeting Hannah went straight to her room. Lintell followed after turning the buckboard over to a cowboy. Inside her room she closed the door behind them and took her toiletry box from its place on the dresser. Holding it in her hands she sat upon the bed and pulled the brass key from inside her bodice. She looked up at him hesitantly as though not certain she wanted to go on. He nodded encouragingly. With a sigh she slipped the key into the lock and turning it slowly drew the drawer open. Slowly, with trembling hand, she picked up the small blue leather-bound book. She looked up at him, eyes large.

“May I see that?” he asked dropping down beside her.

Lintell slowly leafed through the pages, pausing now and then on a particular page to study more closely the series of figures jotted down in a rough hand.

“That looks like Edward’s writing,” Hannah interjected peering over his shoulder.

“Are you shore?” he asked flipping to another page where he halted again studying the column of figures.

“Yes,” she gulped.

“Whew-ee,” Lintell whistled. “He’s kept first-rate notes on all the drives he’s made; the dates and number of head, even the initials of the ranchers he’s rustled the cows from. He’s been involved in rustling long before your uncle was murdered. I shore understand why he wanted this book back! And here, these initials—M V,” he deliberated, keen eyes scanning page after page. "Dog-gone! I'll bet my saddle these are the initials of our mystery man!"

"Do you think?" Hannah gasped.

"Yep. See here. He's jotted down meeting places and dates. Looks like he shore didn't trust this M.V."

He got quickly to his feet. Hannah rose also.

"I've got to get this book to Captain McKenny. There's enough information here to break this case wide open!"

He started for the door, then froze, turned and stared hard at Hannah. "Sprite, don't leave this house! Not for anything! Not until I get back! Understand?"

Hannah nodded peering wide-eyed up at him. She slowly slumped back upon the bed as the sound of his boot steps echoed down the hall.

"Gracious," she sighed. "I've been carrying that book around with me all this time."

She reached to push the toiletry box drawer closed, but hesitated as her gaze fell upon a single sheet of paper. Picking it up she gazed at the words written in her uncle's rough hand.

"Hannah, child,

I reckon I ain't done a good job with Ed. I know it and yu know it, so I ain't gonna beat around the bush. As much as I love my son, and as much as it breaks my heart—I reckon this is something I got to do. Yu'll find out soon enough when everything comes to light. But before thet I want yu to get away—leave Santone. It won't be safe hereabouts. I left some cash for yu thet ought to hold yu over. I couldn't take the chance of leaving it in the safe. Yu

> remember thet game we use to play . . . our secret hiding place? I'm jest sorry for what it'll mean to yu, child, but I reckon yu'll hold up yur head proud like. I'll most likely be gone when yu get home, as this business will take me to—"

Hannah blinked, stared at the note. It was not signed. Something or someone had interrupted him at that point.

"He must have had only a moment to hide the book and the note in my toiletry box," she whispered. "Whoever murdered Uncle Bob must have broken into his safe and . . . and was still in the room when I found him!"

She leaped to her feet rushed out into the hall and out upon the porch. She halted, staring down the lane, but Jack Lintell was nowhere in sight.

"Hannah, what is it," Eula Mae asked following her out upon the porch.

"I—I forgot to tell Jack something," she replied.

"He's probably half way to town by now," Eula Mae laughed, "the way he was riding. What did you say to him?"

Hannah shook her head, turned not meeting her friend's eye and slowly walked back inside the house. Once in her room she flopped on the bed, stared unseeing out the window. She picked up her uncle's note.

"'*I left some cash for yu thet ought to hold yu over'*—the seventy-five thousand! That had to be it!" she gasped. '*Yu remember thet game we use to play . . . our secret hiding place*?'

Of course she remembered. It had been years since she had thought about that little cubbyhole, and even longer than that since she had opened it. She had been eight when she discovered it, and purely by accident. The memories came rushing back. How lonely she had been, lonely and frightened, when they had first brought her to her uncle's ranch, an orphan. She had hid; hid in the far corner of the store room, huddled there protected by the dark. She had heard them calling her and had scrambled back farther in the corner. She had bumped something and the shelf she was leaning against fell in making a perfect hiding place just big enough for her small body. She had crawled inside and pulled the board back in place; and had stayed there, falling asleep. Hunger had finally brought her forth. Her uncle had been worried, she remembered with a sad smile. She never told anyone about her secret place, slipping away to it often. She realized much later that her uncle knew where she went and it became their little secret, until the time came when she no longer needed the protection it gave her. Yes, she knew the secret place although the thought of it had been buried deep in her memory for all these years.

Her uncle had not expected to die that night, she thought blinking at the tears that sprang to her eyes. He had intended to leave the note where she could find it. But things had gone terribly wrong. Was the money still there, in the little cubbyhole, or had Ed found it? She doubted very much that he had. As far as she knew only she and her uncle were aware of the secret place.

She got quickly to her feet and set about changing out of her gown into riding clothes. Moments later she slipped out the back door. She didn't want to have to explain her business to Eula Mae. She hurried to the corral and a short time later was riding up through the cottonwoods out upon the open range in the direction of the Bar H. On the way she said a prayer that Ed wouldn't be there.

She rode into the yard and leaping from her little mustang, threw the reins and mounted the steps to the porch, so familiar, though it seemed now a life time since she had trod them. She didn't bother knocking crossing the room to the hall and the kitchen. The old housekeeper Anita must have heard her for she was on her way to the front of the house when Hannah met her.

"Oh, my child!" the woman gasped, hands clasping her cheeks in wonderment. "Is it really you?"

"Yes, Anita, it's me," Hannah said automatically reaching to take the woman's now outstretched hands.

"I talked to that ranger; he told me you were released from that terrible jail."

"Yes," Hannah replied taking a step back. "Anita, is Ed here?"

The old woman shook her head.

"Anita, I came after something I left here when—when I left before."

"Yes, yes," the woman nodded.

Hannah stared at her suspiciously. "You—?"

"No," she replied as though reading Hannah's mind. "Though I knew there was something. Young Harlan tore this house apart looking for it. But he never found it."

Hannah squeezed the woman's hand and started for the kitchen. The woman caught her hand.

"I'll keep watch," she said.

"Thank you," Hannah whispered and continued down the hall to the kitchen. The last time she had been here was when George Gans had locked her in the storeroom. Opening the door to the storeroom she stepped inside. Moving quickly she knelt before the shelf in the far corner. With trembling fingers she pulled the board back a few inches, enough to reach her hand inside—and encounter the rough surface of what she recognized as a canvas bag! She let out her pent-up breath. It was still there! She started to pull the board all the way back when the sound of horses' hooves reached her ears. Ed! There was more than one rider. George Gans must be with him. She pushed the board back into place and stood. She would never get past him with the money bag. It had been safe there these many months, a few more hours or days would make little difference. She stepped out of the storeroom, softly closed the door and hurriedly crossed the floor to the door and—right into the arms of Ted Stoes.

"Wal, it's shore nice of yu te come te me," he sneered.

A pack of roving coyotes visited Lintell, and sat in a half-circle in the shadows beyond the campfire a short distance from the old cabin. They howled and barked, but he paid them little heed, his thoughts were deeply engrossed in what tomorrow would bring. Abe Johnson had departed moments ago to meet with the rustler gang at their camp deep in the hill country. It was rough but beautiful country. Grassy hills, with groves of live oak and juniper, and a scattering of mesquite, where a rider could easily get turned around, even lost unless he knew the country. But now, thanks to Abe Johnson, he knew the location of the rustler camp. Tomorrow at first light they would strike the camp. With any luck they would catch young Harlan at the camp, but if not they knew where to find him, and he would lead them to the mysterious "M V"; and put an end to the rustler organization, and finally close Robert Harlan's murder case.

It was still dark when they set out; ten grim-faced riders, each armed with pistol and rifle, garbed in black silent and keen-eyed. They had been on these rides before and knew what awaited them. There would be bloodshed this day.

★

CHAPTER TWENTY

Hannah Lea Gibson's hands were tied in front of her. The string of horses of which she was second in line trudged along the narrow trail winding along the edge of a cedar belt. In front of her was Ted Stoes. Behind rode a little man with cold eyes. He had been with Stoes at the house. Stoes had called him Pete. And to the rear of them, nudging close, was another rider leading a string of three packhorses. Hannah had heard Ted refer to him only as Smoky. He had deep-set, serious, thoughtful eyes, which had avoided Hannah's.

It was twilight when they came upon the camp. All day they had traveled, up steep live oak-covered hills where wild broken fastness lay before them; down into mesquite cloaked valleys halting sparingly. One of the darkly garbed figures about the campfire rose and took a quick step toward them. She gave a strangled gasp as she recognized Abe Johnson; Jack Lintell's Texas Ranger partner! She opened her mouth to call out to him, but there was something in his eyes, something that she thankfully identified, and she bit her tongue, dropping her gaze, hiding her thoughts. There was a reason Johnson, a Texas Ranger, was here with these hard-eyed men. Five men had been at the small camp including Abe Johnson which now brought the gang to eight in number. All were shifty-eyed, dusty-booted men who radiated little civility.

"What the hell yu doin' bringin' a woman hyar?!" Johnson demanded.

"Don't get yur hackles up, Montana," Stoes grinned. "This hyar's my sweetheart. We aim te get hitched after we make this last big drive."

"I'm not his sweetheart," Hannah protested contemptuously staring wide-eyed at Johnson. "This blackguard has stolen me! I—"

"Shut up!" Stoes snarled face flushed, no longer his easy-going self.

"Wal, I reckon Buster has double-crossed us," Johnson sneered.

"Buster," Smiley cursed, "Yu can't saddle us with this gurl! We got a big herd te drive. Wait 'til the boss finds out—"

"The boss ain't got nothin' te say about this deal," Stoes said menacingly.

"He will when he finds out!" Smiley argued.

"By then them cows will be on a cattle train headed te Kansas City," Stoes replied smugly positioning himself by the little man with the cold eyes. "So, I say the gurl stays."

There were a few mumbled curses, but no one else of the little gang protested.

"Reckon yu been plannin' this caper fer some while," Johnson remarked.

"Yep, yu could say that," Stoes grinned.

He said this last as he advanced upon Hannah. He reached up and pulled her from the saddle.

“Let go of me!” she hissed.

“Ha! Yu may as well get used te thet,” Stoes muttered.

Holding her arm he shoved her toward a little hut of mesquite branches. He jerked her hands upward and with a flick of his knife cut the rope binding her wrists.

“Get inside,” he ordered. “I’ll fetch yur bedroll. Yu hungry?”

“Water,” she replied rubbing her wrists as she dropped her forehead upon her drawn up knees not wanting to look at him.

As Stoes shuffled off Hannah’s eyes flitted over the dark figures milling about the campfire searching for the wiry form of Abe Johnson. Though she was exhausted by the physical and mental stress of the last several hours and frighteningly aware of what Ted Stoes intended to do to her, the presence of the Texas Ranger gave her hope. She was not entirely alone. She glanced back into the dark hut and shivered.

Stoes returned carrying a bedroll over one shoulder and a tin of water in his other hand. He tossed the bedroll beside Hannah and handed her the cup.

“I reckon yu best eat somethin’. Smoky’s hatched up some grub fer yu. I don’t want yu wastin’ away on me,” he chuckled seemingly in fine humor.

She made no reply but took the cup and drank from it. She was very thirsty. And as much as she hated to admit it she had to eat; keep up her strength. She was not about to let Ted Stoes get the best of her.

“Spread the bedroll inside the hut. And don’t fret, I cleaned it out; no snakes or spiders,” he snickered.

“Buster,” one of the men called, “How’d the little lady stand the ride?”

"I reckon she's all in."

"Say, Buster, yu aim te sleep in thet hut with her?" queried Durango who had not spoken before. His tone was peculiar.

"No, if it's any of yur mix," Stoes replied, after a considerable pause.

"Ah-huh. I was jest curious."

Hannah let out a pent-up breath. She crawled inside the little hut and unrolled the bed. A shadow crossed the entrance and she looked quickly up to see the rustler Smoky Anderson. He squatted and handed her a cup of coffee and a tin with a slice of cold meat and a biscuit.

"Sorry, miss; it ain't much, but I reckon yu gots te eat."

"Thank you," she whispered taking the proffered food and drink. She was hungry, and drained; more so than she wanted to admit.

It did not take her long to consume the cold meat and biscuit. She sat for a while peering out the opening of the hut watching the men within the camp fire circle of light, sipping the hot coffee. She sat the empty cup down next to the tin plate finally and leaned back on the blankets. Tired as she was she refused to stretch out on the blankets no matter how inviting they looked; she might fall asleep, and she was determined to fight Ted Stoes with every fiber of her being. She didn't believe for one minute he wouldn't try to join her in the hut. Perhaps when everyone had fallen asleep . . .

A rustling sound just outside the entrance of the hut captured her attention. She sat up straight listening.

"Miss Gibson," came a tense whisper, "can yu hear me?"

She recognized Abe Johnson's voice.

"Yes."

"Keep up yur courage. Fight him if—"

"I intend to. I'm not afraid of him."

"Good gurl. Listen, if yu can hold on till morning things will be fine."

"What do you mean?"

"Wal, 'bout first light a company of rangers will come down on this place."

"Oh!"

"Thing is, I don't reckon Jack knows yu're here, and fer shore they'll be a lot of shootin'—"

"What about you?"

"We arranged a signal so the boys'll recognize me; a red bandana tied to my sombrero." She heard a faint noise, the sound of ripping cloth. "Here, tie this round yur sombrero."

She felt and caught the piece of bandana as he thrust it into the opening.

"I reckon this might come in handy too," he whispered and cold metal brushed her hand. "Yu know how te use thet Colt I reckon."

"Yes," she breathed clasping the heavy pistol.

"When the lead starts te fly, stay down out of sight 'til it's all over."

"I will," she breathed as a sudden surge of gladness swept over her. Jack was coming to rescue her!

"Get some rest. I'll keep watch," he whispered and in the next instant she heard the soft crunch of his boots as he moved away.

At length sleep came to Hannah, though fitful and teeming with strange dreams. She woke suddenly to the sound of the camp coming alive. Dawn was just breaking. She peeked out the opening. Heard the gruff sound of a man's voice, a voice she recognized. Sheriff Wade Talbert.

"They're 'bout a mile back; headed straight fer hyar! Get a move on!"

"How the hell'd they know te find us?" Stoes cursed.

"Cause yu got a double-crossin' stoolie in yur outfit!"

"What?!"

"Yeah, yu dumbhead! That tall drink of water thar is a Texas Ranger!"

All eyes turned upon Abe Johnson who slowly got to his feet. Hannah sat paralyzed, breath caught in her throat. Stoes stared, mouth agape as though he could not believe his ears.

"Yu—Montana!" he choked.

"Be damn!" the little man, Pete cursed. With blurring speed his hand flashed inside his vest and a gun appeared in his fist. A shot rang out and Johnson was sent stumbling backward to collapse outstretched in the dirt; a splotch of red materialized suddenly on his chest. Hannah clinched her jaw tightly closed stifling a cry as she stared in horror. Stoes suddenly came to life.

"No time te waste," he yelled. "Saddle up! Get them pack hawses loaded!" He turned to Hannah, jerked her to her feet. "Roll up yur bedroll!"

"No!" she said.

His hand shot out smashing into the side of her cheek sending her crashing into the side of the hut which crumbled inward in a haze of dust.

"Oh," she gasped tasting blood.

"I ain't gonna tell yu again!"

She glared up at him. There was a deathly white line about her lips, but her eyes blazed with the fire that had characterized them from birth, the flickering, unfathomable flame that came and went. Stoes scowled at her for several heartbeats, then his pale eyes waivered and he glanced away.

"Smoky, get her gear together," he ordered.

"What yu gonna do with the gurl?" Talbert demanded.

"Why, I reckon she comin' with me."

"She knows too much. The boss wants her silenced."

"Wal, I reckon thet ain't gonna happen," Stoes sneered.

Talbert's shaggy brows went up and his eyes took on a curious gleam. Then he shrugged. "Suit yurself," he muttered.

Some moments later, found Hannah's hands again tied in front of her and mounted on her little mustang being led out of the clearing.

"Drive the packhorses behind me an' keep 'em movin'," yelled Stoes and started off leading her horse paying not the slightest attention to her.

Hannah peered back over her shoulder, eyes clouding as she stared at the prone lifeless figure outstretched beside the smoldering campfire. She didn't see Sheriff Talbert among the riders strung out in a line behind her and calculated he must have slipped away, probably heading back to town. He must have ridden all night to warn Stoes.

The wash that Stoes led them into was shallow and dusty. The dry streambed afforded easy progress. Hannah could not see any sign of a trail or even an old hoof track. But she had no doubt Stoes knew his way. He rode as one familiar with this mesquite and live oak-infested terrain. The streambed began to drop becoming rough and the horses kicked up dust in a ruddy cloud. Hannah began to cough as the dust clogged her nostrils. The sky had darkened, and a rumble of thunder came on the sultry air.

An hour or so later they broke out upon a river lined on each bank by narrow strips of sand. They struck out alongside the river, which at this season was low, less than a foot deep. Before long Stoes led the small cavalcade into the river where they splashed along downstream and Hannah was aware they left no trace of their tracks now. For the remainder of the morning they stuck to the river not stopping even to eat. Only late in the day did Stoes leave the water. It was at a spot, Hannah noticed, where the ground was rocky and hard. Thunder was now rolling over the brakes, and gray veils of rain drifted from purple clouds off to the east.

"I don't reckon my luck's run out jest yet," Stoes sneered peering up at the darkening sky. "The storm's travelin' this way an' it'll wash out what little tracks we leave."

Between the intervals of mumbling rumble of thunder there was a penetrating quietness, a sultry suspension of air where even the stomp of horses' hooves lost their harshness. Night had nearly fallen when the group came upon a dark outcropping of rock that seemed to suddenly leap out of the deep twilight shadows. Stoes drew to a halt.

"Smiley, light up them torches," he hissed.

The rider swung from his horse and with a clink of spurs disappeared into what looked to be a black hole in the face of the outcropping. Hannah stared. It was as though the mouth of a great beast had swallowed him. Moments later a flicker of flame flashed which grew brighter illuminating the rock wall of what she now saw was the entrance to a cave. The rustler emerged from the cave a torch in each hand.

“Hawk, grab one of them torches and lead the way.”

The man rode forward and took one of the flaming torches. For an instant his dark bird-like gaze touched Hannah’s before he pushed on past. As the cavalcade moved forward jagged rock walls closed in surrounding them. Heat and dust vanished and a coolness swept over Hannah as the column moved deeper into the cave descending at a noticeable pace. The winding path fell away sharply forcing the horses into a single file as it sank deeper and deeper into the earth. The clink of the horses’ shod hooves on the rocky path echoed jarringly in the narrow confines. At one point they had to slow nearly to a halt as they edged around the rocky path that made a tight turn back upon itself. Down, down, they traversed and with each passing moment the air grew chill and musty. Finally the path opened upon a large cavernous room. In the winking torchlight Hannah saw the black remains of several campfires. Glancing upward she was startled to see, far above, the glimmer of stars through a circler opening. A flash of lightning illuminated the sky. Rain would reach the center of the cavern where a giant rock sat, but the rest of the huge room would be dry, she realized, evinced by the powdery slit under the horses’ feet.

“Hyar we are,” Stoes called out. His voice echoed hollowly. “Smoky, rustle up a fire and put a pot on so we can have some coffee. There’s heaps of cold pure water. Then hatch up some grub fer us. I reckon we’re all a tolerable hungry.”

“There’s firewood down hyar?” one of the men asked skeptically.

“Plenty of firewood,” Stoes said. “Had enough te last a good week packed down hyar along with horse feed. We’re safe hyar fer the time being. Hawk, in the morning yu go on up and keep a lookout. Sounds carry a long ways down hyar. Sing out if yu spot anythin'. But fer now we can relax."

Stoes came up to Hannah and jerked her out of the saddle. Holding her arm he shoved her along, thrusting her into a shadowy hollow in the rocky wall. He cut her wrists free and she sank to the stone floor. She looked up as Midnight Hays dropped her bedroll beside her.

"Hyar yu air, miss. I'll lay out yur bed fer yu," he said voice low, and he unrolled the blankets arranging them in the small rocky recess.

She sat on the blankets her head hanging wearily upon her chest, the sight of Abe Johnson's bloody lifeless form etched in her mind.

Before long a blazing fire lightened the dark corners of the cavern. Over the sounds of the men tossing saddles and dropping packs Hannah heard the tinkle of water close at hand and the musical flow farther away and down which signaled the presence of an underground river.

A chill swept over her which had nothing to do with the cold dank air of the cave. Whatever tracks they had left, the coming storm would wash away. She was on her own. Her hand crept to the gun hidden in the waist band of her pants under her shirt.

★

CHAPTER TWENTY-ONE

The first thing that drew Jack Lintell attention as he cautiously entered the small clearing ahead of a half-dozen other rangers was the still figure of a man lying out stretched on the ground. His heart thudded in his chest as he recognized the lifeless form of his friend, Abe Johnson. With a sick feeling in his stomach he knelt beside Johnson, stared down at him. Blood covered his chest, but it still rose and fell with his labored breathing. He was still alive! He bent over him; laid a hand on his shoulder.

"Abe?"

Johnson's eyes flickered open. "Jack?" he moaned.

"How bad are you shot?"

"Bad, I reckon," he breathed. "Chest burns like fire."

As Johnson talked Lintell was busy unbuttoning his shirt, laying it open.

"Be damn," Lintell cried. "Abe, by God, you ain't gonna die, at least not from this wound. I reckon your badge saved your life. The slug glanced off the star and bounced off your ribcage. You lost some blood, but I reckon you'll live."

"Won't wonders ever cease," Abe grimaced. "I reckon I owe it te thet Pete feller fer bein' a crack shot. Thet badge was pinned inside my shirt right over my heart."

Lintell was busy untying his bandana, folding it in a square that he pressed over the wound. "Somebody give me your bandana so I can tie the pad on tight."

Someone thrust a scarf in his now bloody hands. Abe suddenly clasped Lintell's wrist.

"Jack, Stoes kidnapped Hannah. He's got her with him—"

"She's—with his outfit?"

"Yep, spent the night in that little hut yonder—alone—before yu go all cold in yur gut."

"Damn," Lintell cursed, his expression grim.

"She's a fighter, Jack. Stoes ain't about te get the best of her. And I gave her one of my Colts. I reckon she'll use it—if she's got to."

Lintell's lips blanched and a tremor ran over his frame, a release of swift passion. But he controlled himself.

"What happened; how'd you get shot?"

"Talbert—he bust in on us 'bout daylight. Let the cat out of the bag. Told Stoes yu was comin'. Then thet little weasel, Pete Small threw down on me 'fore I could move. He's fast."

"Sheriff Talbert!" Lintell hissed. "Somebody must have let it slip we were riding out."

"I should smile."

Lintell glanced up at the darkening sky to the east. "Abe, I'll have two of the men see you back to town. The rest of us are going after that rustler outfit."

"Not a chance," he grunted. "I reckon I'm goin' with yu."

"Look, you stubborn cuss—"

"Stow it, Jack. Jest get me on my feet and set me on a horse."

"Shore enough," Lintell grinned.

"Jack—Stoes mentioned a hideout, a cave—"

"Cave?"

"Yep. I got the feelin' it wasn't far off."

"Jim," Lintell called to one of the men. "You grew up hereabouts. Know of any caves?"

"Shore do. Thar's caves all 'round these parts. I reckon thar's a fair size one 'bout twenty miles southeast of hyar."

"What about provisions. I don't reckon we figured on bein' out hyar more'n a day," one of the men spoke up.

Lintell nodded. "Thompson, you and Smith head down to Casey's place. Pick up enough supplies to last a week. You should be back by midafternoon if you push it."

"Right," Thompson said nodding to Jeff Smith. They both swung into the saddle without another word and struck off down the narrow trail. Lintell watched them until they disappeared from sight.

"Abe, I don't reckon I can cool my heels here until they get back," Lintell said.

"I didn't figure yu would."

"I'll take Jim with me and see if we can pick up Stoes' outfit's trail. I don't like the idea of a storm coming. It could wash away any trace of their trail, and they just might not be headed for this cave."

"Alright, I'll come with yu—"

"No. I want you to rest and build your strength back. You come after us when Thompson and Smith get back with the supplies. We'll mark the trail so you can track us."

The tracks of the seven riders and three packhorses in the dry streambed were easy to follow. Reaching the river Lintell saw that the tracks of the rustlers disappeared in the water.

"Which way?" Lintell asked.

"Left," Williams replied with a jab of his chin in that direction.

They rode into the knee-deep water following the current. Lintell glanced back over his shoulder. The storm was trailing them, and moving rapidly; working toward the northwest, trailing gray curtains across the low hills. The tail of the storm, when it reached the upper end, would flood the river turning it from this narrow, shallow watercourse into a torrent of rushing water, making it impassable. After five miles or so they left the river and continued on skirting the scrub cedar and brush growing along the bank.

Huge, scattered raindrops were pattering down on the sandy ground, great spattering drops that kicked up a smell of dust as they entered a heavy growth of cedar and live oak. They had traveled nearly ten miles by Lintell's estimation since leaving the river and the sky had darkened forbiddingly.

"I reckon we're mighty close," Williams said, voice low, bending to peer through the trees.

Both men had donned slickers as the rain was falling heavily now.

"We best leave the horses here," Lintell replied in an equally low voice.

They could not hold to a straight course through the thick growth of brush and trees. After some time Williams, who was leading the way, suddenly halted a hand held low palm out.

"Ah," he hissed.

Lintell peered over his shoulder. Rising above the mass of juniper and live oak covering the hillside was a rocky outcropping, gray, grim and weather-worn.

"If they're in there they'll shore have a lookout posted," William whispered.

Raindrops spilled from Lintell's hat brim as he squatted on his haunches his intent gaze searching the dark opening. Williams crouched beside him.

"What yu figurin' on doin'?" Williams asked.

Lintell shook his head. "She's down there with those coyotes, all alone," he muttered as though talking to himself.

"I'm acquainted with most of these caves," Williams said, "Explored them as a kid. There's two other openings to this one that

I know of. An' I'd wager this Buster's aware of at least one of them other ways in. I don't reckon he's dumb enough te hide out someplace with only one way in an' out."

Lintell stared at him. "Can you find them, the other ways in?"

"Shore. But yu're not figurin' on goin' in there are yu?"

"Yep. But you'll need to get on back and lead the gang in," Lintell said as though there was no other way about it.

"Alright, yu're the boss," William replied and eased off through the trees.

Not far to the north thunder rolled, and to the south faint mutterings arose as they made a long circuitous hike through the thick brush and scrub oak, leading their horses, bypassing the rocky outcropping. Every so often Williams would halt and peer about as though looking for a familiar landmark. The rain continued to fall and Lintell surmised the gray wet day was affecting Williams' sense of direction. Twilight was upon them now, darkening the distant hollows, and appeared creeping up out of them. A little farther and Williams seemed to have gathered his bearings.

"Right up yonder," he whispered pointing up the slope.

William moved with growing confidence up through the trees. He suddenly halted.

"Hyar!" he hissed.

Lintell found himself standing at the edge of a brush-covered depression. Leaning forward he saw a dark opening in the ground about ten feet across.

"Watch yurself," Williams said, voice low. "It slopes down, but it's steep."

“Ah-huh,” Lintell breathed.

Hannah slumped back against the cave wall watching Smoky’s stooped-shouldered figure, a dark silhouette against the flickering firelight as he approached.

“Howdy, Missy, I brung yu somethin’ te eat,” he said.

She took the tin plate containing beans, a slice of cold meat, and a biscuit.

“Thanks, Smoky,” she said softly.

He nodded. “I’ll be back in a bit te get yur empty plate,” he said and retreated.

She was starved and so she ate every last bite, licking clean her plate. Setting the plate aside she stared morosely into the dark shadows beyond the wavering flames of the fire. Her gaze was drawn to the figures about the fire happening upon the little outlaw Ted called Pete Small and she shivered. She still found it hard to believe. Abe Johnson that boyish-faced Texas Ranger, Jack Lintell’s friend, was dead, shot in cold blood by that evil little man. The violence of the sudden and ruthless killing had shaken her more than she cared to admit.

She peered back at the dark forms within the campfire circle of light, searching out Ted Stoes. What did he intend to do with her? She was afraid she knew the answer. But he wouldn’t find her a shrinking violet quaking in fear. Her hand closed about the grip of the pistol Abe Johnson had given her hidden in her waistband. She knew how to use it and she wouldn’t hesitate to do so. She may be his prisoner but she wasn’t helpless.

She suddenly thought of Jack Lintell. He didn’t know she had been kidnapped. Nobody knew. But if he didn’t know why was he riding for the rustlers’ camp? The incriminating book, of course! There was enough evidence in that book to round up the rustlers, bring them to jail. Which brought her back to her first thought;

nobody knew she had been kidnapped. She'd have to get herself out of this jam.

Getting to her feet she moved a short distance along the cave wall trying to see past the large rock in the center of the cavern where the horses were corralled, measuring the distance to the bottom of the path leading upward. What were the chances she could slip past everyone and escape up to the entrance and freedom? She shook her head. It was foolish to even consider escape in that direction. She was trapped, cornered.

She started to turn back when a chill waft of air touched her face. She halted, tilted her head in the direction of the strong draft of cool air. For a moment its significance didn't register. She stared into the dark shadows coming suddenly alert. She took a deep breath. Of course, she gasped, that draft of air came from outside the cave! Yes! Ted wasn't stupid . . . There was another way out! He would never think of hiding down here if there was even a remote possibility he could be trapped. A shadow blocked the firelight and she recognized Smoky's dark form coming to get her empty plate. She ducked and quickly scurried back to her bedroll.

"Yu ate it all. Good gurl," Smoky smiled cheerfully.

Hannah smiled in return. The man's happy-go-lucky manner was catching. He squatted before her.

"Missy," he said in a low voice, "I ain't keen on what Buster done bringin' yu along like he did; this ain't a fittin' place fer a woman an' all. But he shore claims yu're in love with him, an' air jest bein' a female—"

"Hah!" she snorted. "Love him! I despise him, Smoky. The skunk kidnapped me; I sure didn't come with him of my own free will!"

"Wal, I reckoned thet seein' yu was tied up like yu was."

"Hyar, what yu jabberin' about old man?"

Smoky straightened as Ted Stoes' shadow fell across them.

"I was jest complimentin' the little Missy on finishin' her dinner," Smoky said easily.

"Yeah? Wal, why don't yu get on back an' clean up them dirty dishes," Stoes declared.

Without a word Smoky got to his feet and shuffled off whistling a tune as though he hadn't a care in the world. Stoes leaned his shoulder against the rocky wall and peered down at her. A flash of lightning illuminated the cavern in lurid detail followed immediately by the crash of thunder. Hannah shivered. Stoes peered up at the dark opening above.

"I reckon we'll hold up hyar fer a while 'til the weather clears," he remarked easily.

She said nothing keeping a wary eye upon him. He straightened, glanced around, then his intent gaze fell upon her.

"The boss ordered me to kill yu," he said.

She caught her breath stared wide-eyed at him. He reached and removed her sombrero, tossed it aside.

"Where did yu hide the book?" he demanded.

For once she knew what book he was talking about. She stared at him silently debating whether she should admit it; threaten him with her knowledge, but an inner voice of caution held her tongue. He seemed to read her thoughts.

He squatted next to her; laid a hand on her raised knee.

"Get your hand off me!" she hissed jerking her leg away.

"Yu always was pigheaded," he sneered. "I'm tryin' te save yur life."

"Hah!" she snapped.

"It's thet book the boss wants. Turn it over te him an' everything'll be fine."

"You'd let me go?"

"Wal, yu know I couldn't do thet, Hannah," he said grinning engagingly.

"Humph," she snorted.

"I'll take care of yu. After this deal I'll be set fer life."

"Ted, I don't have the book." That was the truth. "Do you think I'm loco? My life's not worth some silly book."

His eyes searched hers for a long moment. "Yeah, I reckon yu ain't lyin'," he said softly.

He reached out his hand and cupped her chin, tilting her head up peering down into her face. She tried to jerk away but he held her chin in a tight grip.

"No use te fight me, Hannah. Yu know I'll take good care of yu. Once I close this deal, yu an' me, we'll go away, just the two of us."

"I don't want any part of your lowdown scheme, Ted Stoes, and I sure don't want anything to do with you," she declared forcefully and she flung her whole young strength against his grip wrenching herself free of his fingers. The quick, tremendous effort left her breathing heavily. Stoes' eyes narrowed evilly. Then they became calculating.

"Yur comin' with me no matter yu like it or not," he avowed. "The boss wants yu dead . . . and I'm the only one thet can save yu from bein' buzzard meat, yu dim-witted gurl!"

"You want me to believe you'll double-cross your boss," she sneered, "For me?"

Fire flashed in her blue eyes as she spoke. For an instant Stoes' eyes narrowed drunkenly. He suddenly caught her shoulders with both hands and drew her against him his mouth seeking her lips. Hannah gasped like a swimmer sinking. She twisted her face away and at the same time kicked out hard with her booted foot and was rewarded by a loud painful grunt. Half-doubled over one hand to his groin he stared red-faced at her. Fury distorted his handsome features.

"Yu little bitch!" he hissed.

Her lips were pale as ashes with sudden rage.

"If you ever—touch me again, I'll—kill you!"

He got clumsily to his feet eyes glinting maliciously. He stared at her a moment longer, then turned and in a half-crouch stumbled away still holding himself. She sat unmoving, heart pounding, suddenly cold. She stared into the dark shadows trying to slow her racing heart. She had to escape, and she had to do it now before he returned. She would never survive the night. She rose on her knees bracing herself to slip off into the blackness where she prayed she would find a corridor large enough that she could make her way through and up to the outside. Once in this passageway though she would not be able to see; it would be pitch black. How long would it be before they discovered her missing and come searching for her—with a torch! Peering at the dark forms within the campfire circle of light, she realized that if Ted or one of the others happened to glance in her direction they could easily see she wasn't there and would be after her in a flash. She looked at the jumble of rocks nearby. Quickly scooting over to the rocks she rolled one as large as her torso over on top of the bedroll. She got three smaller ones which she placed in a row keeping a watchful eye on the group around the fire as she did so. Taking one of the blankets she spread it over the rocks.

"There," she breathed. Without close inspection it would look like she was resting beneath the blanket.

Hopefully Ted wouldn't return too soon. Taking a deep breath and with one last glance at the men around the campfire, she crept toward the dark shadows. Again that chill waft of air touched her. She was certain she was right; this opening must lead to the outside! Hope surging, she slipped into the darkness. For an instant panic nearly overtook her. She could see nothing, not even her hand in front of her face, only inky blackness. Running her fingers along the rocky surface she slowly inched her way, stumbling occasionally over rocks, some as big as her head. The blackness was disorienting. Even though it felt as though she was going upward—she wasn't positive—she had the sense she was going in circles, but she kept telling herself that couldn't be true. She knew though that she was going much too slow; it would take her hours to reach the top! Every little sound she made, even her breathing seemed to carry and she paused every now and then, holding her breath, to listen, fearful that she would hear the thud of booted feet that would signal pursuit.

The darkness began to weigh on her, closing in upon her and the unnerving feeling of panic returned. The darkness imprisoned her in impenetrable blackness and her only link to reality became the rough surface of rock beneath her fingertips and the crunch of dirt under her boots. She began to talk softly to herself gaining courage from the sound of her own voice. She lost track of time; her only thought to keep moving.

Suddenly, warned by some sixth sense of another's presence, she froze, breath caught in her throat. An instant later, before she had time to react, a rough hand closed over her mouth and an arm slid around her waist. She felt faint. She didn't understand. How could Ted have caught her so quickly? She hadn't even heard the sound of his approach.

★

CHAPTER TWENTY-TWO

Handing Jim Williams his Winchester, Lintell unfastened his spurs and eased himself over the lip of the small opening slimy with mud from the steady rainfall. The slope was steep and he slid downward digging his heels into the soft dirt. Rainwater ran in rivulets down his slicker. Shortly he struck a hard surface which leveled off slightly before angling downward again, though less precipitously. He stood for a moment trying to see as far as he could down into the tunnel before it was immersed in darkness. He peered back up at the round hole above him at Williams' silhouette.

"I'm going ahead down," he called in a low voice. "But you better toss the end of my lariat rope down and tie off your end. I reckon it's too steep to climb back out.

"Comin' up," Williams said and disappeared.

In a moment he was back and a lariat rope came snaking down striking Lintell's shoulder. He clasped the rope.

"I'm set, Jim. Head back and meet up with Johnson and the others and lead them here," Lintell called softly.

Williams waved his hand and was gone. Taking a deep breath, Lintell moved ahead cautiously making his way down into the yawning blackness. Bracing his hands on the cave wall he took one careful step after another his ears alert to sounds ahead in the dark. A strong current of cool air streamed up through the tunnel bringing with it the hazy odor of wood smoke, and the nearly indistinct scent of . . . perfume—Hannah's perfume. At the same moment that registered his ears picked up the faint sound of a woman's voice. He halted holding his breath as he listened. Who was she talking to? he wondered. She was moving toward him, drawing closer; he could now hear her shuffling steps and he realized abruptly that she was talking to herself.

He smiled as he waited hardly daring to breathe. He couldn't see her but he sensed she was nearly upon him. Suddenly she stopped and he heard her quick intake of breath. She felt his presence, knew someone was there, and was going to scream, he just knew it. Judging where her mouth would be by her gasp, his hand shot out and clamped over her lips.

"Hannah, it's me," he whispered mouth close to her ear.

He felt her shudder, her whole body going lax, and he slowly removed his hand from her lips.

"Oh God!" she sobbed, throwing her arms about his waist and pressing her face against his rain-drenched slicker. "Jack! Jack!"

She clung to him as though her life depended on it, and he slowly wrapped his arms about her, holding her trembling form in a secure embrace.

"Jack, how did you find me?" she cried, her voice muffled against his chest.

"It's a long story, and we'd better get out of this place."

"Yes. Yes," she whispered, taking a step back but not releasing him.

He caught her hand in his. “Come on.”

Holding her hand in a tight grip he led the way back up the sharply ascending path, his other hand sliding along the rocky wall. The sound of falling rain grew louder and the damp scent came strongly to Hannah’s nostrils. Soon she could make out the opening to the surface, a gray oval outline midst the black of the cave. Lintell halted drawing Hannah close.

“We’re almost there,” he said voice low close to her ear. “How did you manage to escape?” he asked as though in wonderment.

“Well, I knew Ted wouldn’t hide in a cave if there wasn’t another way out. He’d not get himself trapped. So when I felt a draft on my face, I knew there was another opening, so I just followed the path.”

“Smart girl,” he murmured, and she knew he was grinning although she couldn’t make out his features. “But there must be a third way out cause you could never get a horse out this way and they’d shore want their horses.”

“Oh. You’re right,” she whispered.

“Here, it’s a steep climb,” he said.

She looked at the pale oval above her. “Gosh, I don’t think I could have climbed out by myself.”

“Me either. That’s why I had Williams toss a rope down.”

“Williams?”

“Another ranger.”

“Oh.”

“Hold on to this rope. I’ll have to boost you up. Put your foot in my hands,” he ordered.

She put her hands on his shoulders, hesitated.

"Jack, how *did* you find me?" she asked incredulously.

"Abe, he told me you—"

"Abe, Abe Johnson? But I saw that evil little man shoot him—"

"I reckon you could call it a miracle. The bullet hit his badge pinned inside his shirt and bounced off. He only suffered a flesh wound."

"Thank God," she whispered.

"Now, put your foot in my hands," he hurriedly said.

Balancing herself, hands on his shoulders, she felt with her booted foot and quickly located his cupped hands. She took hold of the rope.

"Ready?" he hissed.

"Ready."

He hoisted her upward and clutching the rope she hauled herself up hand over hand. Grasping the rim of the opening, she caught a handful of wet grass and pulled herself up on her elbows. Swinging one leg up over the top she scrambled out. She turned and leaned her head over the opening.

"Are you coming?" she called softly.

"On my way," he replied in the same low voice, and bracing his feet on the muddy side he worked his way up and was soon on top. Rain fell with a steady patter. He slipped off his slicker.

"Here, get into this," he said.

She thrust her arms in the sleeves. It enveloped her, dragged on the ground.

"I'm lost in it," she twittered.

"You need to stay dry. This rain doesn't look like it's going to stop anytime soon," he answered as he untied the rope and coiling it tied it to his saddle.

"What about you? You're going to get drenched."

"I'll be fine. Climb aboard," he ordered pointing to his horse.

"Humph!" she exclaimed.

Turning to the big roan, she mounted, but nearly fell owing to the cumbersome coat. He reached one hand and braced her and she swung into the saddle. He started off leading the horse down the slope. Although only mid-August, the rain was cold as it steeped through his shirt and vest, and he shivered. Lightning ripped across the sky and thunder crashed. For an instant the cedar and live oak-covered slope turned as light as day.

"Are you all right?" Lintell asked peering back over his shoulder. Her sombrero was pulled low on her head bent against the driving rain.

"Yes! Oh, just to be free," she called squinting at him through rain-bedewed eyes.

"I'm not shore of this country," he said, water dripped from his sodden hat brim. "I could get lost easy in the dark and this rain doesn't help. We need to find someplace where we can get out of the weather until it gets light enough to see."

"You know best," she replied.

He continued down the slope trying to get his bearings. He swung to the right weaving his way in amongst the dense growth of trees and brush. The sound of rushing water reached his ears, and shortly the river lay before them. But it was no longer the shallow placid stream of earlier. It now rumbled and rushed in a muddy torrent. Uprooted trees twisted and thumped in the current. In the dark Lintell couldn't tell how wide it was but guessed fifty yards or more. It would be reckless folly to attempt to cross the roiling flood. He turned and looked up at her huddled form.

"We can't get across," he said simply.

She nodded sending a stream of rain water pouring from her sombrero brim. He followed the course of the rushing river keeping it to his right. He remembered passing a stretch of rock outcroppings on the way earlier with Jim Williams. The rocky ledges had been quite a distance back from the river. But when he suddenly came upon them, like gray spectral ghosts, he realized that the overflowing river had risen considerably reaching within yards of the rocky ledges. He led the way up the steep slope and under a low caverned crest which gave immediate shelter from the cold drenching rain.

"We'll be dry here," Lintell said stepping next to Colonel's shoulder and reaching a hand up to her.

Essaying to dismount wrapped in the too large slicker Hannah fell into his arms.

"Oh," she gasped.

He caught her, his arms wrapping about her.

"Can you stand?" he inquired.

"Of course I can stand. It's this damn slicker. I'm lost in it."

Her hands clutched his shoulders as she leaned her head back to peer up at him.

"You're soaking wet," she said.

"Yeah," he replied.

"You're going to catch a dreadful cold," she accused.

"I'll survive," he remarked.

She made no move to step away continuing to gaze up at him.

"Jack," she breathed. "Thank you, for saving me . . . again."

"We're not out of the woods yet," he scoffed gently stepping back from her.

He wrapped Colonel's reins around a large rock. He didn't figure the horse would wander off, but he wasn't going to take the chance. Untying his bedroll from behind the cantle, he unrolled it against the back of the cavern for them to sit on. Hannah unbuttoned the slicker and slipped it off shaking off the large drops clinging to it. She sat down with shoulders and head resting against the slant of the rear wall. Lintell settled beside her and she spread the slicker over them both as a gush of wind sent a mizzle of rain under the overhang. The shelter would do alright unless the wind picked up and drove the rain in on them. Lightning slashed across the sky in undulating brilliance displaying the rain-engulfed scene before them in lurid detail. The crash of thunder resounded overhead then slowly rumbled away into the distance.

It was going to be a miserable night. Lintell was cold and wet . . . and troubled. Every now and then a fine misty rain blew in on his face. They hadn't gotten very far from the rustlers' cave but it was too dangerous to continue on in the face of the storm. Stoes must by now have discovered her gone. He would realize too that she had help getting out of the cave. But he wouldn't risk chasing them in the dark with the storm raging and the chance of getting lost. Not with knowing that rangers were on his trail and probably had identified his hiding place. No, in all likelihood he would run the other way; but not before morning when hopefully the storm abated. What worried

Lintell at the moment was the rising water. It blocked their escape and prevented Johnson and the others from pursuing the rustlers.

"I'm so tired," Hannah said in a faint voice barely heard over the pounding rain. She had slept only fitfully the night before; fearful that Ted would force his way into her little hut. "But I'm too excited to sleep."

"Try to get some rest anyway," he encouraged. "You'll need all your strength come tomorrow."

"I know," she sighed laying her head on his shoulder.

Lintell stared out into the night. No stars showed. Flares of lightning ran across the sky revealing the black churning river and shadowy skeleton of trees bent in the wind. He glanced down at Hannah. She had removed her sombrero and as the lightning flashed and flashed it appeared to cast a halo around her pale face, but he knew that was the gold sheen of her hair. Much of his life since he was sixteen had been spent in the open. But there was never a night comparable to this. No, it wasn't the storm, not the cold wet night. No, without a doubt, it was the golden-haired girl huddled against him. He took a deep shuddering breath. He would protect her with his life. He would never let anything happen to her. He bent his head close to hers listening to the sound of soft breathing. She had fallen asleep.

Under the cliff the deep shadows grew gray as dawn approached. A thin rain fell quietly almost soundless. The storm of the night before had passed on to the north. Lintell glanced down at the small figure slumped weightily against his side a tiny hand wrapped about his arm. She sat exactly as she had fallen asleep six hours before. Colonel lifted his head shook himself whickering softly. Slowly Lintell uncrossed his cramped legs. Hannah's eyes opened and she stretched arching her back languidly. Then she sat up straight glancing around before casting him a questioning look.

"The storm's past," he said. "But the river's still too high to cross."

"Oh," she groaned as she lurched to her feet and stomped her feet bringing circulation back to her sluggish limbs.

His hand grabbed her arm pulled her against him while at the same time his other hand covered her mouth.

"Shh!" he hissed.

She froze, eyes darted to where he was looking. Riders broke from the trees less than a hundred yards distant. She recognized them immediately; Ted Stoes and behind him at the head of a string of horsemen, the little killer, Pete Small.

★

CHAPTER TWENTY-THREE

Lintell edged Hannah back against the rear of the rocky ledge, cautioning her to silence. She sank to her knees. Crouching, Lintell reached Colonel and laid a hand on the horse's muzzle. He didn't want the horse neighing and calling attention to their location. From where he stood Lintell could plainly see the riders, but realized now that it would be nearly impossible for them to see into the cavern. He watched as they made their way up the brushy slope moving away; intent on escaping. Hannah stood, stretched in an effort to better see the riders.

"Stay down!" Lintell hissed.

"Damn," she cursed softly. "They're taking my little mustang!"

He came up behind her peering over her shoulder as the riders disappeared over the long slope of cedar and live oak.

"Looks like they're clearing out," he muttered.

"They're going to get away!"

"I don't reckon there's any way to stop them," he grunted. "Abe and the others can't get across the high water—"

"We could follow them; leave signs along the way for your rangers—"

"Where'd you come up with this 'we' stuff anyhow? I'm shore not going after them with you with me—"

"But we can't let them get away!"

"Ump-umm," he objected forcefully.

"Jack, haven't we been through some bad stuff together?" she asked sweetly. "Driving off that band of Indians and—and facing down horse thieves—you getting shot—"

"Hold on there! Just who was it that got me shot in the first place?"

"Humph! I knew you'd get around to bringing that up sooner or later; blaming me for your recklessness. But it won't work, Jack Lintell. Blast it! I want to stop those rustlers and catch Uncle Bob's murderer just as much as you—even more! So there!"

"Sprite, it's too dangerous."

She tilted her chin, just stared at him.

"We only have one horse," he argued.

She raised one eyebrow. That was a weak argument he knew. Colonel was a big strong horse, and she weighed hardly anything at all.

"We don't have any provisions," he said certain that would put an end to the discussion.

"I saw some food in your saddlebags," she said smugly.

"Two cans of peaches," he snorted. "And some biscuits."

"I like peaches," she said with a dazzling smile.

"Aw," he capitulated and turning walked to his horse. "I reckon I best feed Colonel."

"Go ahead. I'll get out the peaches and biscuits," she said following him.

After slipping the bridle from the tall gelding, Lintell scooped up two heaping hands-full of oats from a canvas sack stuffed in one side of his saddlebags and dumped the grain on the rocky floor of the cavern for the horse to eat.

"Hell's bells," Hannah moaned.

Lintell looked up to see her staring dismally at the remnants of water-logged biscuits oozing like porridge from between her fingers.

"Your saddlebag leaked," she said disgustedly.

"Toss me a can of peaches," he chuckled pulling his jackknife from his overall pocket.

It didn't take them long to consume the peaches. He watched her lick her fingers. She glanced up and saw him watching and grinned.

"What?"

"You're still hungry."

She shook her head. "I managed to eat something last night before I slipped away. But you . . . ?"

"I'll live," he shrugged getting to his feet. "We best get going if we're going to keep Stoes and his bunch in sight."

Lintell mounted Colonel and reached a hand down to Hannah and swung her up behind him. She wrapped both arms around his waist and they started off. The rain had stopped altogether, and as Lintell headed down the slope Hannah suddenly spoke.

"Jack, I just thought of something."

"Yeah?"

"Ted said they were going to make one last big drive. He meant they were going to rustle a big herd; even hinted he was going to double-cross his outfit and with the money make his getaway. He intended to take me with him."

"Ah-huh . . ." Lintell murmured, and Hannah felt his muscles tighten beneath her arms.

"Well . . . and this is what's got me thinking. They'd have to move fast wouldn't you think; to move all them cows?"

"I reckon you're on to something, Sprite. Figuring they got some of their bunch working on the inside, they could easily have a large herd already set up waiting to be moved—"

"Right!"

"I reckon you know this country. Any guess where they'd bunch these cows?"

"Let me think . . . Blue Valley, that's a possibility or, Cripple Creek . . . My guess though is Blue Valley." She well remembered the park. It was several miles across and half as many miles long, covered with tall, waving grass, and it had straggling arms that led off into the surrounding belt of live oak and cedar. "It's out of the way . . . and it's an easy drive from there to the railroad depot at Hondo."

"Can you get us there from here?"

"Of course," she replied confidently.

"Then we'll leave a trail for Abe to follow. Maybe we can catch that rustler bunch with the herd. That would shore settle their hash."

"Jack," she said after a moment's hesitation, "I think I know the identity of the initials 'MV', you know, in that little leather book."

"Oh yeah?" Lintell queried peering back over his shoulder.

"Martin Vanhall."

"Vanhall . . . say, I remember that name; handsome hombre, in his forties, white streaks in his hair."

"That's him. Where'd you know him from?"

"He dropped by Casey's ranch a few days ago while I happened to be there. What makes you so shore he's our man?"

"Well . . . Eula Mae doesn't like him for one thing . . . and I trust her estimation. And second, I saw him and Ted together one day. They were in a heated discussion that I could tell they didn't want anyone else to overhear. Doesn't that seem odd? And third, Eula Mae said he showed up in the valley around the time Uncle Bob was murdered."

"That's shore something to think about, but we'll need more than that to go after him."

"Yeah, I suppose so," she acknowledged laying her cheek against his back and tightening her arms about his waist. "But I still think he's the mysterious rustler chief."

Mid-morning found them topping a rise of scattered live oak and mesquite miles beyond the little cavern where they had spent the night. The sky was blue, the sun bright and warm after the rain storm. There had been a trail here once proved by a depression on the dusty earth. Below them opened a wide winding valley. Tall grass green as emerald waved in the breeze. Only in the distance it stood out blue under the hot sun.

"Blue Valley," Hannah cried. She scrambled up on Colonel's back, hands on Lintell's shoulders, cheek next to his. "I think we beat them here!"

Lintell rode toward this, keeping somewhat to the right. Soon he rode out beyond one of the projecting line of trees to find the park spreading wider in that direction. Far down this part of the valley he espied the brown mass of milling cattle and imagined he could hear their bawling.

"Sprite, hand me my glasses out of my saddlebags."

Lintell took the binoculars and focused on the herd of cattle.

"I'd guess about three thousand head," he announced.

"Three thousand! Good grief! That will just about wipe poor Mr. Casey out!" Hannah exclaimed.

"Yeah," he muttered still scrutinizing the herd.

"Oh," she sighed dejectedly. "What are we going to do?"

Slowly he moved the glasses up into the trees where he had spotted a thin column of smoke. "Looks like there's an outfit camped up in them trees yonder. Hmm . . . I'll wager Stoes has left two or three punchers to keep an eye on them cows to make shore they don't drift until they're ready to make the drive. Either that or Stoes got here quicker than I'd have estimated."

"You think we beat his bunch here?"

"Yep, that's my guess. But not by much, so we best get a move on. I figure Stoes will try to throw off pursuit by heading north then after a spell double back and make tracks for here. That'll give me some time."

"What are you planning to do?"

"Well, I'm thinking if I could stampede that herd, scatter them up into the brush that would just about fix Stocs' hash. He'd have a devil of a time rounding them up, and shore by then Abe and the others will be here."

"That's your plan! How could the two of us, on one horse, stampede that big bunch of cows?"

"I reckoned you'd not be along."

"Oh? Well, what about that outfit up in the trees? You think they're just going to let you ride down there and scatter that herd like nothing at all?"

"Yeah, I reckon that's the only kink in my plan."

"You're loco, Jack Lintell."

"Thanks for the vote of confidence, Sprite," he grinned. "But you just gave me an idea."

"What?" she queried eyes searching his.

"I reckon I can throw down on them hombres—I don't reckon there's more than three—and persuade them to help me stampede the herd."

"Now I know you're loco!" she burst out. "You'll get yourself killed!"

"That's shore not part of the plan, Sprite," he drawled.

The flame in her blue eyes leaped and flickered, and the tawny brows gathered into a puckered glower.

"You're not leaving me behind," she said through clinched teeth.

He opened his mouth to protest but immediately closed it. He knew by now there was no use arguing with her; not when she had that look in her eye.

★

CHAPTER TWENTY-FOUR

Lintell guided Colonel along a tortuous course through thickets of oak and patches of cedar, winding in and out. They slowly worked their way in a wide circle coming finally to a break which commanded a view of that end of the basin. Beyond a low incline ran up to a ridge top where a few rods down on the other side the belt of timber ended. Lintell drew Colonel to a halt back from the edge of the trees. The sound of cattle was plain.

"I see their camp," Hannah whispered.

"Yeah. We best leave Colonel here and go on from here on foot."

Lintell swung his leg over the pommel and dropped to the ground. He reached and caught Hannah as she slid off the horse's back.

"Here, take this," he said and drew his rifle from the saddle boot and handed it to her.

Fastening Colonel securely to an oak sapling he reached in his saddlebags and pulled out a box of shells and stuffed it in his pocket. Bending he took off his spurs and hung them over the saddle horn. Hannah clutched the Winchester tightly in both hands as she watched him.

"Luck's with us," he said sniffing the air. "The wind is blowing toward us. Follow me and don't make any noise."

"You're going to hold them up?" she whispered.

"I'll say I will."

"And if there's a fight?"

Suddenly he faced her and there was a commingling of fear and pang, it seemed, all in one throb as they stared wordlessly at each other for a long moment.

"If they go for their guns you dive for cover and stay down. Promise me?" he whispered hoarsely.

"I promise," she quickly replied nodding her head vigorously.

Taking the rifle from her, Lintell slipped off under the cedars. Hannah followed at his heels. He picked his way, walking stealthily, and after proceeding a hundred steps or more he halted to listen. After a moment he seemed satisfied and started on. Hannah put one foot forward after the other as if she was fearful of stepping on broken glass. Patch after patch of dark cedar were passed, and thickets of live oak that rustled in the cool soft breeze. Every few feet now Lintell halted listening for several moments before starting on. After a moment he froze. He glanced back over his shoulder, touched his nose and Hannah could smell the pungent odor of wood smoke and . . . the soft murmur of voices! Her breath quickened and she laid a trembling hand upon Lintell's arm. He peered into her eyes.

"Wait here," he whispered his lips next to her ear.

She shook her head fiercely and he glared at her a long tense moment before again starting off now more guardedly than ever.

He halted suddenly and Hannah peered past his shoulder and saw a beautiful glade before her. A small camp fire burned in the center of the glade and Hannah could see the dark forms of three men. Beyond them some hundred rods or so several horses peacefully grazed. She heard voices plainly now and a coarse laugh that sent a chill along her spine. Her breathing came fast. She looked at Lintell's broad-shouldered back. She prayed there would be no fight even as she eased the Colt Johnson had given her from her waistband. She didn't want to kill a man, but she knew she might be forced to if one of them attempted to pull a gun on Lintell.

Lintell halted behind the trunk of a sturdy live oak and motioned Hannah to stay down. The open glade before them offered no further means of concealment. The camp fire lay no more than a hundred feet distant; so close that Lintell could smell coffee and the juicy aroma of ham.

"What do yu care if old man Casey looses a few head?" rang out a loud voice.

"I told yu I weren't stuck on this job," replied another man.

"Hell, Gans, three thousand ain't a few," came another voice.

"What yu beefin' about? Yu'll get yur cut, an' I reckon yu'll be settin' pretty," imposed the first voice, which Lintell identified as George Gans Edward Harlan's sidekick and the leader of the trio. He was of average build with sharp features shaded under a black sombrero.

"I don't know . . ."

"Wal, Laigs, yu ain't thinkin' of turnin' sideways air yu?"

"I reckon not. I cum this far ain't I?" the man answered.

"Hyar, listen te my hawse," called the third man, in a different tone of voice.

"Aw, he just smells the ham," chided Gans.

"Like hell he does," the man retorted. He sat with his back to Lintell and was looking at the horses.

Lintell realized the horses had scented him. Leaning his rifle against the tree he drew both Colts and stepped from behind the tree.

"Hands up!" he yelled, "Texas Rangers!"

Two of the rustlers shot their hands into the air and sat paralyzed. Gans, however, made a lightning-swift grab for his gun. Lintell shot a second before Gans' gun blazed. Lintell heard the sickening rend of a bullet striking flesh behind him. Lintell never waited to see Gans fall but whirled to see Hannah sprawled upon her back.

"Good God!" he cried holstering his Colts.

He sank to his knees beside Hannah reaching to lift her head. Bright red blood bubbled up soaking through her shirt. Behind him he heard the scuffing approach of the two rustlers. But he didn't care.

"Hannah!" he cried all else forgotten except the girl lying in his arms. Her face was white, sweat beaded her upper lip. Blood bathed her shirt wetting his fingers as he fumbled to unbutton the garment. He pulled the cloth back baring her shoulder and the swell of one small milk-white breast. He grimaced at sight of the wound. Someone took hold of his arm.

"Hyar, Mister, take this," one the rustlers said and Lintell looked to see him holding out a brightly colored bandana folded in a square. "It's clean," he insisted. "I jest got it out of my pack."

Without a word Lintell took the cloth and pressed it on the wound.

"Here's another one," the second rustler said kneeling beside Lintell. "Tie the pad tight."

Hannah's eyelids fluttered open. They were glazed with pain.

"Oh—Jack . . . Jack—I—I'm sorry," she whispered her voice hoarse.

"Hush," he scolded gently. "Don't try to talk. I'll get you to a doctor."

"Jack . . . am . . . I bad . . . shot?" she asked weakly. A tear leaked from the corner of one eye and trickled slowly down her cheek.

"No. No, Sprite," he gulped biting back a cry of anguish. "You'll be just fine."

She seemed to take comfort in that. Her gaze fastened on the rustler kneeling at her side.

"Laigs Keene," she whispered. "Is that you?"

"Yeah, Missy. It's me," he answered voice husky. He wiped at his eyes with a rough callused hand.

Slowly she shifted her gaze to the other rustler crouched on one knee next to Lintell.

"Brazos . . . Smith," she sighed and she frowned. "Rustlers?"

"Missy, I'm—plum ashamed," Brazos said voice catching.

"You . . . ought to . . . be," Hannah retorted weakly. "Hasn't . . . Big Jim always . . . treated you . . . decent?"

"Yes, Missy," and a sob broke from his lips. "He's been more'n white te me."

"Why . . . then?" she asked.

"It were drink," he said in a strangled voice. "Laigs and me, we jest got in over our heads, and Gans there, he got te us in a weak moment."

"Sprite, don't talk anymore," Lintell pleaded. "Fellers, I've got to get her to a doctor."

"Brazos . . . Laigs," Hannah implored, her eyes misty. "Stampede . . . don't let . . . them rustle—"

"We'll to it!" Laigs asserted forcefully. "If it's the last honest thing I ever do. So help me Gawd!"

"Don't yu fret, Missy. We know what te do. We'll pull it off," Brazos said eagerly.

"Where'd yu leave yur hawses?" Laigs questioned.

"Only one. A big roan. Back yonder, about a half mile or so."

"I'll fetch him," Brazos declared.

Lintell stared down at Hannah. Her eyes were closed, her face a ghastly white. All he could do was hold her as he waited for Brazos to return. It seemed an eternity, but in a matter of minutes Brazos rode up leading Colonel. Lintell slid one arm under Hannah's knees, the other around her back and rose to his feet. She screamed. Her head fell against his shoulder.

"Reckon she's passed out," Brazos said. He held Colonel's bridle as Lintell, clasping Hannah against his chest, stepped into the saddle. Cradling her in the crook of one arm, Lintell looked from one to the other of the two reformed rustlers.

"There's a company of rangers tracking Buster and his bunch—"

"Get goin'," Laigs ordered gruffly giving Lintell a piercing look. "We'll take care of things hyar. Yu make shore thet little lady don't die."

With a curt nod to the two, Lintell started off. Hannah was still unconscious. He carried her in front of him, cushioning her as best he could from the jolt of Colonel's hoofs. Lost to him was the beauty of his surroundings. His thoughts were only on Hannah and they swept over him with astounding significance and spurred him to urgency. If he lost her—No! He would not deign to think of that. Hannah was all that mattered. He should have taken the bullet. She'd been shot because of his foolish stubborn pride. He'd known the risk, and still he went ahead with that stupid, stupid plan when his first concern should have been Hannah's safety. He stared down at her colorless face. Blood was still seeping through the pad over the bullet wound. Every now and then at a jarring bump a soft whimper would escape her lips. And he would release an echoing groan of helplessness.

The afternoon waned. Colonel plodded on. Hannah was a dead weight in his arms. Down out of the timber he rode. The foothills waved away to the west and the low open range appeared. Sunflowers burned a riot of gold against the green and star-eyed daisies sprang in luxuriant profusion out of the earth. And with every step Colonel's hoofs sank deep, to come forth with a huge cake of mud.

Every glance at the corpselike girl in his arms caused Lintell's heart to sink deeper into despair. It seemed her face grew paler, her breath shallower with each plodding step of his horse. How far yet to town? Was he anywhere near? Colonel labored out of the mud to higher ground. He knew the horse was wearying and he urged him on with quiet words. Despair had nearly seized him when he topped a rise and saw below him the road and he suddenly knew his surroundings. The town was just beyond the wide bend.

Lintell's mind was frantically trying to recall where he had recently seen a doctor's office as he rode into town and started up Flores Street. As though in answer to an unspoken prayer, a shingle in front of a flat-roofed adobe structure, which read: *Renn McEachern, General Practitioner*, caught his eye. A woman holding a child by the hand was exiting through the gate when he reined up before the small office building.

"Is the doctor in?" he called.

The woman looked up, eyes widening with alarm as she saw the bright red blood staining Hannah's shirt, and gave a gasp. She nodded mouth hanging open. Then whirling and dragging the boy in tow hurried back into the house. Holding the unconscious girl close to his chest, Lintell swung to the ground letting the reins drag. By the time he reached the gate a short thin man with thick graying hair came hastening to meet him. He wore a dark suit that hung loosely on his bony shoulders. Concern showed in his eyes.

"You the doc?" Lintell demanded.

"Yes. What is wrong with the woman?"

"Bullet wound," Lintell answered tersely.

"Bring her inside," he ordered and turning quickly led the way.

Once inside, the doctor directed Lintell into a side room. Lintell was aware of two or three people seated in chairs staring wide-eyed as he carried Hannah into the next room where he saw a narrow bed about waist high. White painted cabinets lined one wall. Next to the bed was a small table containing shinny steel instruments.

"Lay her on the cot," the doctor said assertively.

As he began examining Hannah a woman briskly entered the room and stood by the cot upon which Hannah lay. She was slender with a smooth pale complexion and wore a starched white apron over a dark dress. She appeared much younger than the doctor. She smiled reassuringly at Lintell. Bending over Hannah the doctor raised one eyelid and in doing so Hannah's other eye, glazed with pain, opened.

"Ah, she's awake. That's good," he murmured.

Gently pulling the shirt off her shoulder he lifted the bloody pad and grunted. The wound began to bleed. With quick movements he picked up a stethoscope from a small side table and leaning his head close he placed the end of the listening device to her chest. Raising his head he glanced at Lintell.

"I was concerned the bullet might have nicked her lungs since it's so close, but thankfully her lungs sound clear. I am Doctor McEachern, and this is Nurse Madison," he said indicating the young woman.

Lintell nodded. "Jack Lintell."

"Is this your wife?" the doctor asked as he poured water into a basin and began to wash his hands.

"I—no," Lintell answered huskily.

The doctor looked sharply at him.

"The bullet will have to come out," he said. "Are you able to give permission to operate?"

Lintell found himself staring at the row of bright sharp instruments laid out on the white-cloth-covered tray on the small table. There was no real choice for Lintell to make. Hannah was dying.

"She has no family—but me. Operate," he said in a hoarse voice.

"What is the young woman's name?"

"Hannah Gibson."

"Miss Gibson, can you hear me?" the doctor asked bending close.

Her eyes remained closed but her lips moved. "Yes," she whispered.

"I'm going to remove the bullet. But first I'm going to anesthetize you so you won't feel a thing."

He nodded his head to the nurse and she picked up a clear glass bottle with two outlet taps, ending in a calico covered hood mask and a figure of eight shaped rubber hand pump bellows. She arranged the hood over Hannah's nose and mouth.

"Just breathe naturally, dear," she instructed.

"You had best wait in the other room," the doctor said turning his attention to Lintell.

"I'm not leaving," Lintell said emphatically. "I'm staying with her."

The doctor gave him a keen look but said nothing further and turning back to Hannah he took the forceps the nurse handed him and leaned over Hannah.

As the doctor went to work Lintell couldn't take his eyes off Hannah's motionless form, as quiet as death, stretched out on the small table, at her tiny pale hand limp at her side. He swallowed the lump in his throat and reached and softly closed his hand over hers. She couldn't die. It wasn't right! He should have taken the bullet!

"This is the reason the flesh about the wound was so mangled," Doctor McEachern said holding up a flattened chunk of lead on the end of bloody forceps.

"It's over?" Lintell breathed.

"Yes. I'll clean the wound. It will require a few stitches," he replied.

"She's not moving," Lintell said worriedly.

She lay so still, so vulnerable, face colorless.

"She'll regain consciousness soon," he assured him. "She will perhaps experience some nausea when she wakes. That is the result of the chloroform. Give her only small sips of water. The queasiness should clear up within an hour or so. It appears to me that the bullet struck a hard object and ricocheted losing some of its force before entering her chest. Otherwise that size of cartridge would have propelled the bullet all the way through her."

"You seem to know a lot about gunshot wounds," Lintell replied recalling vaguely Gans' gun tilted downward as he fired, a jerk-reaction to Lintell's slug striking him. How ironic that chance slug glancing off a hard surface and hitting Hannah!

"Well, lad, before I came to your country, I've dug bullets for years out of every man, woman and child in Ireland. And there seems no loss of opportunity here, mind you," he finished a cynical smile on his lips. "You were fortunate you came to me."

Lintell was thankful too. He wasn't going to tell the doctor he just happened to see his shingle as he rode along the street.

Cleaning the blood from his hands Doctor McEachern proceeded to wash the area of the wound with alcohol. After closing the wound with several stitches, he covered it with cotton pads and bandaged it tightly with strips of gauze before arranging her shirt over the bandages.

"She has lost a lot of blood. What she needs now is rest. I see no reason why she shouldn't make a full recovery." He paused, peered at Lintell. "I do not know the situation of her injury, but I feel it necessary to inform the authorities."

"I'll take care of that," Lintell informed him producing his badge. "It's police business. I'm a Texas Ranger."

"Ah, I see," the doctor sighed.

★

CHAPTER TWENTY-FIVE

Eula Mae burst into the hotel room like a small tornado skirts whipping about her legs her eyes round with dread. They searched Lintell's face as he quickly got to his feet. Big Jim Casey stood in the doorway behind her. He had driven the spirited blacks hitched to the buckboard hard arriving at the hotel in record time after Eula Mae had received Lintell's note briefly explaining that Hannah had been wounded. Eula Mae's gaze darted beyond Lintell alighting on the slight figure stretched out in the bed a blanket tucked about her chin. She flew past Lintell and dropped to her knees beside the bed.

"Hannah!" she cried squeezing the hand which had slid from under the blanket.

Hannah smiled weakly, a tear gliding from the corner of one eye in obvious joy at seeing her dear friend.

"Eula Mae," she whispered.

Casey took off his sombrero twisted it nervously in his hands as he slowly approached the bed to stand beside his daughter and stare down at Hannah. Lintell came to the foot of the bed.

"It was my fault," he said huskily.

"What do you mean?" Eula Mae asked eyes narrowing.

"No," Hannah insisted. "It was my fault."

"I shouldn't have braced them rustlers, not with Hannah along," Lintell continued ignoring Hannah, and in a terse voice he related how they raided the rustlers' camp early in the morning four days ago.

"The gang was warned that we were coming by that low down rotten sheriff, Wade Talbert—"

"Talbert! I might have known!" Casey interjected forcefully.

"He tipped off Stoes that Abe Johnson was one of our rangers working undercover—"

Eula Mae looked quickly up at Lintell.

"Dad, that new cowboy you hired last week; the one they call Montana; he's a Texas Ranger?" she said looking from Lintell to her father.

Her father nodded after a quick glance at Lintell.

"Go on. What happened?" Eula Mae said.

"Well one of the gang got the drop on Abe and plugged him—"

"Oh!" Eula Mae exclaimed. "That poor boy."

"Thankfully it was just a flesh wound. He was mighty lucky. He told me that Hannah had been kidnapped by Ted Stoes."

"Oh, so that's what happened," Eula Mae exclaimed peering sternly down at Hannah. "I looked for you after Jack left but you weren't in the house. Sunset Smith said he saw you ride off. I was surprised you didn't tell me you were going riding. When you didn't return by dark I started worrying, and the next morning I was frantic."

"I'm sorry," Hannah said weakly squeezing her friend's hand. "Jack told me to stay in the house until he got back. But there was something I had to do. I'll tell you about it—but not now." She looked from Eula Mae to Lintell. He watched her quietly making no reply.

Eula Mae nodded as though she understood. She glanced up at Lintell. "You were saying . . . ?"

"Well, me and Williams tracked the gang to a cave. I sent Williams back to lead the other rangers in," Lintell said and went on to tell of how he entered a second entrance to the cave and how he and Hannah had met in the dark passageway and made their way out of the cave, their finding shelter from the storm, which had flooded the river preventing them from reaching the ranger camp. He explained how the next morning, after seeing the rustlers ride off, Hannah had made a lucky guess that it was Blue Valley where Stoes was probably holding the herd as they gathered more cows, and how they had arrived there before Stoes' gang, and finally the vain attempt to foil the rustlers by stampeding the herd wherein Hannah had been struck by a stray bullet meant for him.

"Oh, Hannah," Eula Mae exclaimed, "What an experience! You were always such an adventurer! But how are you feeling?"

"I'll be fine," Hannah insisted. "The doctor said he would check on me regularly and that I should rest and gain my strength back, though it would take a while."

"When I read Jack's note, I nearly fainted," Eula Mae shuddered. "I couldn't get here fast enough."

"I'm so glad you came," Hannah said, and in a low voice only her friend could hear, "And I hope you brought a change of clothes. I'm naked under this blanket . . . except for the bandages."

"Hannah!" Eula Mae cried, shocked, hand to her mouth. "Did Jack . . . ?"

"Of course not, silly!" she gasped, blushing. "Mrs. Finch helped me to bed. I can't move my right arm at all. Oh, Eula Mae, I'm terribly weak all over, and it hurts like hell—but don't tell Jack," she continued in a whisper. "He's worried enough as it is. He's so set on blaming himself."

"Yu say they was bunchin' three thousand head to drive off! By God thet'll ruin me fer shore!" Casey cursed interrupting Hannah and Eula Mae's low-voiced conversation.

"I don't reckon they had any luck doing that," Lintell said, and told how the two rustlers had a change of heart and how Hannah had convinced them to stampede the herd. "I don't reckon they was too keen on this rustling deal to begin with. Hannah knew them both and shore they knew her, and they shore was ashamed of what they had become. So, I'm figuring that Stoes and his gang won't have time to round up them cows before my rangers brace them."

"Wal, I'll be doggone," Casey exclaimed staring at Hannah. "Hannah, girl, I got a feelin' I know them two cowboys."

"Don't ask me, Big Jim," she said with a wary smile.

He grinned. "Shore," he replied. "Whatever yu say."

Now that Eula Mae had agreed to stay with Hannah Lintell was free to get back to his job chasing rustlers and solving the Harlan murder. He strode down the hall to Captain McKenny's room and knocked on the door. It was opened immediately by the ranger captain.

"Howdy, Jack. Come on in. How's Hannah?"

"She's still abed, weak as a new born kitten, though she insists she's not. I reckon it'll be a while before she's back on her feet. But she's shore a game kid. Miss Eula Mae's there with her now," he replied. "Say, any news from Johnson?"

"Nothin'," McKenny said shaking his head in disgust. "I was kinda hopin' yur knock was one of the boys with a report."

"Hmm," Lintell grunted. "Cap, I don't reckon we ought to move on Sheriff Talbert until Johnson gets back."

"I reckon yu're right," McKenny agreed. "Goin' after another lawman, we'll need a strong case."

"That's what I figured," Lintell said. "In the meantime, though, I reckon I ought to ride out to Harlan's place. From what Abe told me Harlan wasn't with the gang, and he wasn't with Gans when I braced those three. I don't want him to skip out on us."

"Alright. I'd ride out there with yu, but I best stay hyar in case there's news from Johnson."

Lintell drew up in the cedars overlooking the Harlan ranch and surveyed the scene below him. The house stood quiet. Lintell swung his gaze to the bunkhouse, but as with the house he saw no activity. Several horses grazed in the far pasture. He wasn't sure what to make of the idleness. Had Harlan driven off all or most of his honest riders?

Lintell slowly descended the slope and entered the yard. For some reason he suddenly felt he wasn't going to find Harlan here. Dismounting he tied Colonel's reins to one of the porch posts and ascended the steps. Crossing the porch he knocked on the door and waited listening hard for any sound from within. All was still. He knocked again louder. Usually the old woman Harlan's housekeeper was quick to answer the door. He waited a moment longer, then reached and tried the door handle. It moved easily and he slowly shoved open the door. He stepped inside and paused.

"Howdy, anybody home?"

No reply. A strange heaviness hung in the air. It was the smell of death. Lintell knew it well. He moved down the hallway drawn inexplicably to Harlan's office. The door stood open and he peered cautiously into the room. Edward Harlan sat upright in his chair; head slumped on his chest. A black hole encircled by a splotch of red was plainly visible on his white shirt over his heart. He hadn't bled. He died instantly. The odor of gunpowder still hung in the air. Lintell stared at the dead man. Harlan was unarmed; his gun was in its holster hanging on a clothes tree in the corner behind him. The expression on Harlan's face, frozen at the time of death, displayed surprised disbelief.

A floorboard creaked at the far end of the hall and Lintell's gun leaped into his hand. Someone else was in the house. The killer? The housekeeper? He waited. Suddenly a door slammed somewhere in the rear of the house, then the hard slap of booted feet running away. Lintell hurried down the hall and into the kitchen. The clatter of hoof beats reached his ears as he thrust open the backdoor in time to see a dark rider astride a big bay horse disappearing into the cedars on the far side of the lane.

"Damn!" Lintell cursed.

The killer had still been in the house when Lintell entered. Lintell sprinted back down the hall, out upon the porch, leaping the final steps where he snatched up the reins of Colonel and sprang into the saddle. As he cleared the back of the house he saw the flash of movement high in the cedars. He spurred Colonel and the big roan broke into a run up through the trees. The dark rider had too much of a head start and Lintell quickly lost sight of him. At the top of the ridge he scanned the ground for signs. Mixed with those of deer and cattle he saw the imprint of fresh horse hoofs.

Lintell started off following the tracks. This dark rider had shot Ed Harlan—only moments before Lintell's arrival. But why kill Harlan? There was no sign of a fight. He had shot him in cold blood. He suddenly had a pretty good idea why. The heat was on the rustler gang and it would soon be busted wide open! How many of the gang actually knew the identity of the rustler chief? Talbert, he supposed; Gans and Harlan for certain. But Gans was dead and now Harlan; killed to silence him.

Lintell rode six miles along the divide at his estimation. The killer was sticking to the cedars where the thick needles made distinguishing the tracks difficult. On two occasions he had to back track in order to pick up the trail again. He was almost at the point of giving up when he saw that the tracks left the cedars striking a course down into a valley. Lintell moved slower now, eyes keenly watchful. At length he caught sight of a cabin. He came upon it abruptly and quickly jerked Colonel back out of sight from where he surveyed the small log structure and surroundings. The cabin was well hidden in a thick grove of live oak and mesquite. A spring trickled from under a low cliff. But for the horse tracks he had been following Lintell would not have found it easily. A lazy column of blue smoke from a stone chimney curled up toward the sky, to be lost there. A corral sat a little ways from the cabin and Lintell counted three horses. One was a big bay and it looked as though it had been ridden recently—hard. It appeared to be an old hunter's or prospector's cabin, probably with a dirt floor, and a fireplace and chimney. He could see it had a door and two small openings serving as windows. They looked as if they had been intended for port-holes as well.

Lintell expected the rustlers to have someone of their number doing duty as an outlook. So he kept uphill, above the cabin, and made his careful way through the thicket of mesquite, which at that place were dense with matted clumps of live oak. No one was in sight. There might be a dog. But at length he decided that if there had been a dog he would have been tied outside to give an alarm.

Lintell had now reached a point some eighty paces from the cabin, in line with an open aisle down which he could see into the cleared space before the door. On his left were thick live oak with low-spreading branches, and they extended all the way to the cabin on that side, and in fact screened two walls of it. Lintell knew exactly what he was going to do. No longer did he hesitate. Laying down his rifle, he looked to his Colts. Stooping low, he entered the thicket of live oak. Swiftly and silently he approached the cabin till the brown-barked logs loomed before him, shutting off the clearer light.

He smelled a mingling of wood and tobacco smoke; he heard low, deep voices of men. Resting on one knee a moment he deliberated. The door of the cabin was just around the corner, and he could glide noiselessly to it or gain it in a few leaps. Either method would serve. But which he must try depended upon the position of the men inside and that of their weapons.

Rising silently, Lintell stepped up to the wall and peeped through a chink between the logs. Sunshine streamed through the slit of one window. The door stood open. A man sat on a chair tipped back against the wall, full in its light. He was in his shirt-sleeves. He was hatless, and Lintell recognized him—the cowboy on the train. He had been in the room that night when Lintell had listened below Harlan's window to the conversation between Harlan and Gans, and the mysterious rustler chief. This Hank was the hombre who murdered Hannah's uncle, and moments ago, shot Harlan in cold blood.

Two other men were seated at a table. Lintell's keen eyes took this in at a single glance. The man in the chair by the wall was armed, and the other two wore gun belts. Lintell gave a long scrutiny to the faces of these men as though to assess what he had to expect from them.

Lintell drew both Colts, then stooping low; he softly swept around the side of the cabin and in two noiseless bounds was inside the door!

"Don't move!" he called.

The surprise of his appearance, or his voice, or both, stunned the three men.

“We ain’t movin’,” burst out one of the men at the table.

“Who’re yu, an’ what d’yu want?” challenged the other.

The cowboy from the train slowly lowered the legs of his chair to the floor.

“I reckon yu’re lookin’ at a Texas Ranger,” he drawled. “He’s the one I was tellin’ yu about.”

“Ranger! Damn yu Hank Barlett! Yu led him hyar!” one of the men at the table, red-bearded and large of frame and wicked and wild-looking, ejaculated hoarsely, “Say, Barlett, or whatever the hell’s yore right handle—is this hyar a game we’re playin’?”

“Shore, Smith,” put in Barlett, not improbably he had encountered such situations before. “His name’s Jack Lintell an’ I reckon he set on bustin’ up this rustlin’ game.”

“Aw, is thet a fact,” replied Smith, contemptuously.

“Yep,” returned Barlett.

The other rustler at the table had not spoken since his first query. He was small, swarthy-faced, with sloe-black eyes and matted hair, evidently a white man with Mexican blood. Keen, strung, furtive, he kept motionless, awaiting events.

“I’m here to arrest this man for the murder of Robert Harlan,” Lintell said gaze shifting to Barlett. “You’re coming to San Antonio with me to stand trial.”

That was the gauntlet thrown down by Lintell. Barlett seemed to expect it. Lintell wanted to take him alive. He wanted to know the name of the rustler chief, how they operated.

Smith’s eyeballs, however, became living fire with the desperate gleam of the reckless chances of life.

"Ranger, I've been a gambler all my life, an' a damn smart one, if I do say it myself," declared Smith, "An' I bet yu ain't up te takin' on all three of us."

Barlett stared in cool suspense at Lintell. Knowing Lintell was on his trail Barlett had led him here for this very confrontation. There ensued a silence fraught with suspense, growing more charged every long instant. The balance here seemed about to be struck.

Barlett; cold blooded killer he might have been, but he was brave. Quick as a cat he grabbed for his gun. A tense, surcharged instant—then all four men flashed into action. Guns boomed in unison. Spurts of red, clouds of smoke, ringing reports, and hoarse cries filled the cabin. Lintell had fired as he leaped. There was a thudding patter of lead upon the walls. Lintell flung himself prostrate behind the bough framework that had served as a bedstead. It was made of spruce boughs, thick and substantial. He peeped from behind the covert. Smoke was lifting, and drifting out of door and windows. The atmosphere cleared. The dark-skinned little man lay writhing. All at once a tremor stilled his convulsions. His body relaxed limply. As if by magic his hand loosened on the smoking gun. Smith was on his knees, reeling and swaying, waving his gun, peering like a drunken man for some lost object. His temple appeared half shot away, a bloody and horrible sight.

"Pards, I got him!" he said, in strange, half-strangled whisper. "I got him!"

His reeling motion sent drops of blood flying from his gory temple. He pulled the trigger. The hammer clicked upon an empty chamber. With a low and gurgling cry of baffled rage Smith dropped the gun and sank face forward, slowly stretching out. Barlett had leaped behind the stone chimney that all but hid his body. The position made it difficult for him to shoot because his gun-hand was on the inside, and he had to press his body tight to squeeze it behind the corner of ragged stone. Lintell had the advantage. He was lying prone with his right hand round the corner of the framework. An overhang of the bough-ends above protected his head when he peeped out. While he watched for a chance to shoot he loaded his empty gun. Barlett strained and suddenly darting out his head and arm, he shot. His bullet tore the overhang of boughs above Lintell's face. And Lintell's answering shot, just a second too late, chipped the stone corner where Barlett's face had flashed out. The bullet, glancing, hummed out of the window. It was a close shave. Barlett let out a hissing, inarticulate cry. He was trapped.

"Give up, Barlett!" Lintell called.

"Haw! Haw! Haw! An' hang! Nix! I'll take my chances here an' now!" he sneered.

In his effort to press in closer Barlett projected his left elbow beyond the corner of the chimney. Lintell's quick shot shattered his arm. Still Barlett did not cry out. Then with a desperate courage worthy of a better cause, and with a spirit great in its defeat, Barlett plunged out from his hiding-place, gun extended, his handsome face now fierce and baleful. Lintell's gun blazed and Barlett pitched headlong over the framework, falling heavily against the wall beyond. Then there was silence for a long moment. Lintell stirred, looked around. The smoke again began to lift, to float out of the door and windows. In another moment the big room seemed less hazy. Lintell rose gun in each hand, and slowly he approached Barlett's inert body. Barlett's eyelids fluttered open. He was still alive. Lintell knelt by his side.

"Barlett, you're dying."

"I . . . reckon I . . . know," he choked, blood oozing from the corner of his mouth. "Yu did . . . me in, ranger. Gut shot . . . slug went . . . clear through . . . I reckon . . . my luck's . . . run out. I bet . . . on a . . . bad hand. Shore didn't think yu could . . . take all three of us."

"Barlett, you haven't got long," Lintell said, not unkindly.

"I . . . reckon not. What do . . . yu want . . . te know?"

"Who is MV?"

"It . . . *was* yu . . . listenin' at the . . . window . . ."

"Yeah, it was me."

"I reckoned . . . right."

"MV?—Who is he?" Lintell persisted.

Barlett mouthed a name as though he was reluctant to say it aloud.

"That doesn't figure, Barlett. The initials—"

"Real . . . name. Ed Harlan met . . . him on a cattle buyin' trip te . . . Kansas City . . . four years ago . . . They hatched up . . . this rustlin' scheme. When . . . he came here . . . changed name. But . . . Harlan knew . . . real name."

"That's why you killed Ed Harlan—to silence him."

"Yeah . . . and . . . old man Harlan . . . He had the . . . book . . . Fool drew on me."

"Who else knows his real name?"

"I reckon now . . . only me . . . yu—"

"What about Talbert?"

"Daid."

"You . . . ?"

"Yeah. Saved yu . . . the trouble . . . of . . . arrestin' him. Talbert would . . . have squealed . . . his head . . . off."

"You're telling me no one else, besides me, knows who MV is?"

"One . . . more . . . I reckon—"

"Who?"

Barlett inhaled a deep gasping breath then coughed a froth of blood. Lintell pulled out his bandana and wiped the blood from his lips.

"Yu . . . know—" Barlett choked. His eyes rolled back in his head. Lintell stared. Barlett was no longer breathing.

Lintell slowly got to his feet struggling to make sense of Barlett's words. His thoughts were interrupted by the roll of horses' hoofs coming up to the cabin. He drew his pistol and stepped to the door, peered cautiously out from around the edge of the frame. A voice reached him.

"Yu there in the cabin! Yu're surrounded! Come out with yur hands in the air!"

Lintell recognized the speaker. He holstered his Colt and stepped into the sunlight.

"Wal, I'll be dog-gone! Jack! What're yu doin' here?" bawled Abe Johnson.

"Settling the score with one Hank Barlett," Lintell replied coolly.

"Huh?" ejaculated Johnson.

Lintell grinned as he surveyed the four rangers mounted on lathered horses, guns drawn, on either side of his friend; faces only now relaxing their grim countenance as they recognized Lintell. Off to one side sat Laigs Keene. Next to him, Brazos Smith. They both were beaming like school boys on a lark. Dust covered all the riders and bits of brush and cedar stuck in their chaps. The odor of the range clung around them.

"Hank Barlett; he killed Robert Harlan and shot Ed Harlan in cold blood this morning," replied Lintell. "I trailed him here and braced him and two of his cronies. They're dead," he said grimly nodding with his chin back toward the cabin.

"Hell," Johnson protested, "Yu could have waited fer us."

"I shore would have if I'd of known you were on your way," Lintell drawled. "How'd you know to find this place?"

"Them two hombres," Johnson said pointing to Laigs and Brazos.

"Howdy fellers," Lintell said.

"Mornin'," drawled Laigs innocently.

"Where's the rest of the bunch?" Lintell asked surveying the four rangers surrounding Johnson.

"Thompson, Smith, Williams and McCoy are escortin' Buster an' two other rustlers inte Santone. Buster's shot up some but I reckon he'll live to stand trial," Johnson replied. "Walters was bored, but not bad."

"Belmet and Evans?" Lintell queried.

Johnson lifted his face to the sunlit sky for an instant. "I reckon they didn't make it," he said with a grim shake of his head.

"Ah-huh," Lintell managed. Belmet was only twenty. He had married his sweetheart a little more than a month ago. "The rest of the rustler gang?"

"Daid," Johnson replied. His eyes narrowed to blue dagger points. "I reckon thet short dumpy little gunman weren't as fast as he thought."

★

CHAPTER TWENTY-SIX

Hannah Gibson gingerly swung her legs off the mattress placing them on the floor all under the watchful eye of her friend Eula Mae. She put out her hand and Eula Mae clasped it and she slowly stood. This was the second day in a row Hannah had gotten out of bed. The first time she had walked the few feet to the overstuffed chair and sat down with a breathless sigh. It had been good though, despite the pain, to get out of bed. She was so tired of just laying there.

"Are you sure you're not overdoing it?" Eula Mae demanded intently surveying her friend's wan countenance.

"Do you think Jack will come by today?" Hannah asked ignoring Eula Mae's anxious inquiry.

Eula Mae shrugged her shapely shoulders. "I don't know," she replied.

"You did ask Captain McKenny?"

"Yes. But he was kind of vague."

"Oh, I know Jack must be very busy," Hannah sighed. There was no hiding the disappointment in her voice. It had been four days since Eula Mae had arrived; the last time Hannah had seen Lintell.

Hannah circled the room and seemed to gain strength as she went leaning less on Eula Mae's arm.

"It's nearly noon. Are you hungry?" Eula Mae asked.

"Starving," Hannah replied.

"Well, that's a good sign," her friend said. "Here, sit down and rest and I'll go down to the kitchen and bring something up."

Hannah settled gently in the stuffed chair and smiled up at Eula Mae.

"I won't be gone long so don't try to move around on your own."

"I'll behave," Hannah promised.

As the door closed behind Eula Mae, Hannah's thoughts returned once more to the incident in which she had been wounded.

"If only I hadn't been shot,' she whispered aloud. "Then we could be searching for Uncle Bob's murderer together."

She laid her head against the chair back and closed her eyes. She really enjoyed watching him struggle to control his anger when she talked back to him. She smiled to herself. He was such a proud man, never wanting to admit he could be wrong. But he wasn't wrong very often. An impish smile curved her lips. Of course, she'd never tell him that. No, she'd tell him . . . well, she'd tell him she was sorry she'd disobeyed him. That she wished . . .

The door opened and Eula Mae slipped hurriedly into the room. She carried a linen-covered tray which she quickly placed on the table and shoving the door closed hastily locked it. She turned to Hannah, her cheeks slightly flushed.

"What is it?" Hannah asked.

"Nothing . . . I suppose," Eula Mae said and went about uncovering the tray.

"Eula Mae?" Hannah persisted.

She glanced at Hannah smiled sheepishly. "Well, I met Martin Vanhall in the corridor. He . . . well, I think he has been spying on our room."

"Spying?" Hannah gasped straightening, and then grimaced as the stitches in her chest pulled painfully.

"Yes. He didn't see me at first, and seemed startled when I challenged him."

"Oh," Hannah gulped glancing furtively at the door. "Is he still out there?"

"Why, Hannah, you look absolutely terrified!" Eula Mae ejaculated.

"Oh, Eula Mae, you must find Captain McKenny—"

"What is it?"

"Eula Mae, I've reason to believe Martin Vanhall is the boss of the rustlers! And he . . . believes I have . . . something that can prove it."

"Mr. Vanhall?! Oh, Hannah, how in the world—"

"Eula Mae! It's true! Uncle Bob found a small book in Edward's room. He was reading it the night he was murdered. It was a journal that Edward kept of . . . all his rustling activity. He named names, and identified the mastermind behind the stealing—"

"Edward named Mr. Vanhall!"

"Well, no, not by name, but his initials . . . M.V."

"Oh—*MV* . . . Martin Vanhall!" Eula Mae shuddered. "I thought he was trying to get the nerve to court me. But in reality he was hanging around the ranch to meet—talk to Ted Stoes—?"

"Yes! I don't have the book anymore, but he most likely doesn't know that. Eula Mae, he wants that book back and if he can't force me to give it to him, he'll . . ."

"Oh, dear!" Eula Mae replied sinking onto the bed.

"So, you must send word to Captain McKenny. His room is at the end of the hall. Have him tell Jack."

"Yes, I'll do it," Eula Mae said springing up from the bed. She went to the door and unlocking it, opened it a crack and peered out. In a moment she closed it. She turned to Hannah. "I don't see him. Maybe he left."

"He won't stop you. He's after me."

"Yes, alright, I'll go, but I wish I was as brave as you."

She took a deep breath and slipped out the door. Hannah eased off the chair and stood. She walked slowly to the door and slid the lock. She remained there waiting for Eula Mae's return, her head resting against the door, heart pounding. If only Jack were here! Time passed. Only the tension of the moment kept Hannah from collapsing. Then the door handle rattled.

"Hannah started. "Who is it?" she demanded.

"It's me," Eula Mae called.

Hannah threw the bolt and opened the door stepping back as Eula Mae slipped inside.

"Well," Hannah asked breathlessly.

"I knocked but there was no answer at Captain McKenny's room. I went down to the clerk and he said Captain McKenny had gone out early this morning and had not returned," Eula Mae informed her.

"Did you see Vanhall?"

Eula Mae shook her head sliding her arm around Hannah's waist. "He was nowhere in sight. You had better sit down. You're as white as a sheet."

"Alright," Hannah agreed letting Eula Mae escort her to the chair where she slowly sat.

"Maybe you're wrong about Mr. Vanhall—"

"No chance!" Hannah insisted adamantly.

"You think you could eat?" Eula Mae asked eyeing the tray of food.

"Yes," Hannah sighed.

Eula Mae scooted the table over in front of the chair where Hannah sat. But neither girl seemed as hungry as they professed, although they did manage to eat everything. Eula Mae was clearing the dirty dishes when there was a knock on the door. Eula Mae glanced sharply at Hannah who took a deep breath and nodded. Eula Mae went to the door.

"Who is it?" she called.

"McKenny," came the muffled answer.

With a sigh of relief she slipped the bolt and opened the door.

"Howdy, Miss Casey," the ranger captain said. "The clerk said yu was askin' fer me."

"Uncle John," Hannah called, "Come inside, hurry!"

McKenny stepped into the room removing his sombrero as he did so.

"Hurry, close the door—lock it!" Hannah ordered.

McKenny looked from one girl to the other. "I reckon yu must have heard about young Harlan," he grunted.

"Ed?"

"I don't reckon yu heard then."

"What about Ed?" Hannah asked.

"Daid."

"Oh," Hannah gasped. "How did it happen?"

"Wal, his housekeep found him late last evenin'. Shot clean through the heart. She sent one of his boys in te town with the word. Seems nobody could find Sheriff Talbert, so they notified the rangers. Thet's where I've been all mornin'."

"Do you know who shot him? Was there a fight?"

"No te both yur questions. Harlan was shot settin' in his chair. He weren't armed. It was a clean shot right through the heart. If it's any comfort te yu he didn't suffer none."

"I know why he was murdered, Uncle John."

"Yu do?" McKenny said looking down his hawk nose at her.

"Yes. For the same reason Uncle Bob was murdered and . . . why he wants to kill me—"

McKenny suddenly looked uncomfortable. "I reckon I know lass. An' Jack an' me have shore been discussin' just thet fact. We're on te this MV's trail yu can bet."

"I know who he is."

"Yu don't say. Wal, tell me lass."

"Martin Vanhall."

"Vanhall? MV? Shore the name fits, an' I shore never considered him. But are yu shore, lass?"

"It has to be. Tell him Eula Mae."

"Well, Mr. Vanhall has been hanging around the ranch; spent a lot of time talking to Ted Stoes. And, he was here this morning spying on our room."

"Wal, thet ain't a lot te go on—"

"But, Uncle John, don't you see," Hannah insisted. "What do you know about him?"

"Wal, not all thet much."

"Eula Mae . . ."

"Mr. Vanhall came to the valley about two months ago, just about the time Uncle Bob was murdered. And dad says he doesn't talk or act, like a cattleman."

"Any idea where he hails from?"

"Well, he let drop to dad once that he was from Kansas City."

"Hmm. I'll send a telegram te Kansas City; see what I can find out about him," McKenny mused. "Yu girls keep the door locked."

"We will," Hannah assured him.

"Good. I'll check on yu later," he said turning to the door.

"Uncle John, have you heard from Jack?"

"Wal, lass," he replied scratching his chin. "I wish I could tell yu somethin', but I ain't heard from Jack in three days. An' nothin' from Abe Johnson either. Thet's shore worryin' me some."

"Oh," she sighed.

There was a loud pounding on the door. "Cap, yu in there?" someone called.

McKenny jerked open the door. One of his rangers stood there.

"Cap," he said lowering his voice, "One of Sheriff Talbert's deputies just found him."

"Yeah?"

"He's daid, sir. They're askin' fer yu."

McKenny turned to Eula Mae. "Lock the door," he ordered closing it behind him.

Hannah laid her head against the back of the chair, closed her eyes. Her cousin Edward was dead, and now Sheriff Talbert. And, she would bet, shot by the same person. Why? Her eyes suddenly flashed open. Of course! The rangers were closing in on the rustlers. Vanhall had to silence anyone who might identify him. And he believed she knew! That's why he was lurking in the hallway; waiting for a chance to catch her alone!

A knock sounded on the door. Eula Mae leaped to her feet and hurried to the door.

"Captain McKenny must have forgotten something," she said.

"Eula Mae—don't!" Hannah cried, but too late, the bolt had already been thrown. The handle turned and the door opened a few inches, enough for Eula Mae to see the caller. With a horrified cry she tried to shove the door closed, but Martin Vanhall was too strong forcing her back into the room and stepping inside.

"What are you doing?! Get out!" Eula Mae shouted.

Vanhall made no response, his eyes on Hannah. "Hurry, you're coming with me," he said.

"Why?" Hannah demanded.

"There's no time to argue! Come on," Vanhall insisted. He cast a nervous glance back out into the hall.

Hannah caught Eula Mae's eye, then glanced at the closet. Eula Mae blinked, nodded.

"I can't go out in public," Hannah said. "I—I'm not dressed."

"Put on a robe, hurry," Vanhall ordered. "You have one don't you?"

"It's in the closet."

He turned to Eula Mae. "Get it," he said.

She shook her head. "No."

Vanhall darted another nervous glance into the hallway. Then he quickly crossed to the closet and flung open the door, stared at the row of gowns. "I don't see a robe," he challenged.

"It's in the back," Hannah said.

Vanhall shoved the dresses aside leaned forward. Gritting her teeth Hannah got to her feet. Swallowing, Eula Mae rushed Vanhall and pushed him hard. Caught completely off balance he tumbled into the closet. Both girls slammed the door shut.

"What are you doing?" Vanhall cried, his angry voice muffled by the heavy door and his weight pushed against the door. It creaked inching outward. Hannah's wound felt on fire as she strained hard against the door. Vanhall was strong, forcing the door open a crack. Three fingers of his hand grasped the doorframe.

"Eula Mae, shove the . . . chest of draws . . . against the door," Hannah panted.

The chest slammed against the door hard and Vanhall let out howl of agony as his fingers were trapped between door and frame.

"We've got him," Hannah cried.

"Yes, we do," said a man's voice.

Hannah whirled about to see Mark Webb. It had been his weight that had provided the muscle to move the chest of drawers.

"Mr. Webb! Thank God!" she cried in utter relief.

★

CHAPTER TWENTY-SEVEN

Abe Johnson followed Jack Lintell into the cabin. The haze of gun smoke, pungent to the nose, still hung heavy in the air. The other rangers gathered at the door and peered inside their eyes taking in the sprawled bodies. Lintell's gaze fastened on Barlett's still form. There was much he had wanted to ask the man; much the man would carry with him to the grave.

"Gol-dang!" Johnson ejaculated as he surveyed the bullet splintered walls and table. "That must have been some shoot-out!"

"Some of you boys go through their pockets," Lintell said. "Bag everything you find. We'll strap their carcasses to their horses and pack them back to town."

While the men went to work Lintell walked back outside where he took a deep breath of fresh air. The impact of the shoot-out was slowly dawning on him and that familiar icy mood settled over him. He sat down under a tree and took off his sombrero. For a long moment he sat with eyes closed letting the incident replay in his mind until he finally came to grips with having to again take a life. When he returned to the cabin some time later he found that the men had the dead bodies loaded on their horses and were ready to head into town. Lintell walked up the slope to where he left his horse recovering his rifle from where he left it as he went.

It was mid afternoon when Lintell and the others arrived at the coroner's office on Soledad Street where the bodies of the three rustlers were unloaded. Word spread rapidly of the breakup of the rustler gang and people gathered to gawk at the dead rustlers laid out in their bloody and gruesome condition.

Leaving Abe Johnson to complete the paper work Lintell rode over to the old County jail on the northwest corner of Military Plaza where Ted Stoes and the remaining rustlers had been locked up; the same jail that had once held Hannah. There Lintell took Captain McKenny aside and made his report.

"Maximilian Vanderbelt . . . who the hell is he?" McKenny demanded. "The initials MV shore fit but who is he?"

"I reckon only a few know him by that name, Cap. Before he cashed Barlett laid it all out. Ed Harlan met this Maximilian Vanderbelt in Kansas City a few years ago. They came up with this rustling scheme. When Vanderbelt got here he changed his name and started a business using the alias Mark Webb—"

"Webb!" McKenny ejaculated fiercely. "Wal, I'll be a monkey's uncle!"

"Yeah, with a name change and an honest upstanding profession Vanderbelt's clandestine activity was safe. No one would suspect a respected businessman and lawyer. Hank Barlett was Vanderbelt's hired gun. He killed Robert Harlan to recover that book, and when we were closing in on the gang, he shot Ed Harlan and Sheriff Talbert on Vanderbelt's orders. And Vanderbelt has seen to it that anyone who could identify him was silenced . . . except—Hannah!"

“Wal, I just left her an’ Miss Casey about an hour ago. She was shore that this Vanhall was the rustler boss. I’ll have te tell her she was shore off track.”

“Cap, I want Vanderbelt.”

“So do I, son. I reckon we ought te find him at his office. Let’s go lock the bastard up!”

Mark Webb’s face swam before Hannah’s eyes. She had never been so glad to see another human being in her life.

“Mr. Vanhall is the murderer.”

“I think you are right,” Webb said.

“Miss Gibson,” Vanhall yelled. “No, please, listen to me!” With his free hand he pounded on the door. “Please, Miss Gibson—Miss Casey.” Then he muttered, “My fingers.”

Hannah didn’t want to feel compassion, but she was helpless not to.

“His fingers are caught. We’ve got to—”

“No, we don’t,” Webb said.

“He’s hurt,” Eula Mae cried.

She reached and tried to shove the chest, but Webb grabbed her shoulder and swung her around.

“No!” he shouted, and flung her against the wall where she uttered a groan and slumped to the floor breath knocked from her.

“Mr. Webb!” Hannah gasped.

Webb whirled upon Hannah his look cold and sinister.

"Mr. Webb?" she croaked stumbling backward.

"Leave her alone!" Vanhall battered the door with his body. "If you touch her you'll have to kill me, too!"

"That's the plan," Webb sneered fiendishly. "You ladies have done half my work for me. I wondered how I was going to make it look like an accident doing away with you," he said advancing on Hannah. "And then to find Miss Casey here—but now, I have the perfect solution dropped right into my lap. I dispose of you ladies, kill Vanhall with the same gun and place it in his hand. It will look like a case of murder and suicide. I, of course, will even give my legal opinion of the tragedy," he mocked as he drew a gun from inside his coat.

Hannah stared at the gun in Webb's hand. She couldn't have made such an appalling mistake! She couldn't! But, Oh, God, she had! Webb was the rustler chief! But the name—the initials, MV! She didn't understand.

"Confused are you, my dear?" Webb smiled seeing the bewildered expression on her face. "Well, I suppose you have a right to know, since no harm can come from it now. Your cousin and I came up with this rustling scheme four years ago. Ed was deep in debt and your uncle had cut off his purse strings, refused to pay his gambling debts. He was hurting for cash. And, of course, I never turn down easy money. It was such a simple plan. He did the rustling while I provided the front and the means to funnel the monies. So, under the alias Mark Webb, I established a business—"

"Your law firm! Mr. Bodkins is in on this too, I suppose," Hannah interjected.

"No, neither Bodkins nor Bower were a party to our scheme. And it was a good scheme. Except that your cousin got greedy, and wanted more. He came up with this book he used to record all his dealings, intending to double cross me eventually. So, you see, he had to be eliminated. He knew my true identity—Maximilian Vanderbelt, hence the initials M.V.—incidentally where is the book?

You've obviously hidden it well. No matter. With you dead it becomes irrelevant."

"Why did you have to kill Uncle Bob?"

"I didn't. Hank Barlett took care of that matter for me. But I'm afraid Hank got himself shot dead, and by that ranger of yours—"

"Jack!" she cried hope surging.

"Yes. So I have to complete this messy chore myself."

Three blocks from Vanderbelt's office Lintell and Captain McKenny happened to run into David Bodkins standing on the sidewalk. He spotted them at the same time they saw him. He waited watching them close the distance. Lintell surveyed the man closely as he approached. Bodkins was Vanderbelt's, alias Webb's, junior partner. Was he a partner in the rustling scheme too? If not, how much did this man know?

"Mr. Bodkins," Lintell said, "We're looking for Mr. Webb, is he in his office?"

"No," Bodkins replied. He appeared uneasy.

"Do you know where we can find him?"

"He's involved in something illegal isn't he?" Bodkins asked.

"Why do you ask," Lintell queried.

"Oh, I knew it!" he exclaimed, shaking his head in obvious distress. "I've been suspicious for some time, and this afternoon, when they brought in those dead men . . . he was beside himself, pacing in his office. When he left suddenly I decided to follow him. But I lost him in all the traffic."

"Where did you lose him?"

“The last I saw him it was on Crockett Street near the Menger Hotel—”

“How long ago was that?” Lintell demanded his whole body rigid.

“Half an hour, maybe forty minutes—”

“Oh—my—God!” Lintell cried and whirling about set off in a run.

Reaching the hotel he sprinted through the lobby and bound up the stairs two at a time racing down the hall to the room in which Hannah was staying. He rattled the door handle. It was locked.

“Hannah!” he yelled.

Moments later he heard the bolt slide and the door opened. Hannah, pale of face but eyes bright and a dazzling smile on her lips stood gazing up at him. He peered past her and saw Vanderbelt huddled on the floor bloody head in his hands. Eula Mae stood back from him, a pistol in her hands pointed at him. Standing off to the side was Martin Vanhall. He was holding one hand stiffly against his chest.

“We captured the real murderer,” Hannah said cheerfully.

“I see that,” Lintell grunted heart still racing. “How in the hell did you manage that?”

“Well, it’s kind of a long story,” Hannah replied, color filling her cheeks.

“I’m listening,” Lintell said pulling out his handcuffs and snapping them on Vanderbelt, who uttered a curse under his breath.

“I thought for sure Mr. Vanhall was the rustler boss; you know, Martin Vanhall . . . MV. So when he forced his way into our room demanding that I come with him I just knew for certain. Of course if he would have told me why he wanted me to come with him; that the real murderer was on his way up the stairs, I—"

"Would you have believed me?" Vanhall interrupted.

Hannah looked sheepish. "No. I was so sure you were the rustler boss," she replied giving him a remorseful look. "How is your hand?"

"Nothing broken," he said.

"We locked Mr. Vanhall in the closet," Hannah explained guiltily. "Mr. Webb—or should I say—Vanderbelt came in at that moment and . . . well, that's when we discovered he was the real rustler boss. He planned to shoot both Eula Mae and me, and then Mr. Vanhall and put the gun in his hand so it would look like Mr. Vanhall killed us and committed suicide."

"Hmm," Lintell muttered.

"Oh, he bragged about what he was going to do, how he and my cousin Edward had come up with the rustling scheme, but how Edward was cheating him. That's why Edward was keeping that little book—"

"Yeah, and when we started closing in on the gang, he had Hank Barlett silence anyone who might know his true identity," Lintell interjected.

"Exactly. But while he was doing all his bragging he forgot about Eula Mae," Hannah said looking at her friend who still held a gun pointed at Vanderbelt. "She struck him over the head with that little table," she beamed. "So, aren't you proud of us?"

"Yeah, I have to admit, I am." Lintell said grudgingly looking from one girl to the other. "But you better let me handle this Colt, though, Miss Casey," he said, reaching and taking the gun from Eula Mae's trembling hands.

"Thank you," she whispered.

"Vanhall, what's your part in all this?" Lintell asked.

With his uninjured hand Vanhall reached into his vest pocket and produced a leather wallet which he handed to Lintell.

"I'm a United States Marshall. We've been after Vanderbelt for six years for bribery of a U. S. Congressman. But he's been a slippery cuss with more alias than a dog has fleas, skipping from one dishonest scheme to another."

"How was he able to establish a law practice? He shore fooled everybody."

"That wasn't difficult. He has a law degree, or I should say, he once had a license to practice."

"So, who has jurisdiction here?"

"Well, it certainly would seem you do. The crime of murder carries a much stronger sentence than anything we have against him."

"I reckon you've got a point," Lintell nodded.

As he said this Captain McKenny, with Abe Johnson at his heels, burst into the room.

"Wal, Jack, I see yu got everythin' under control," McKenny said halting just inside and taking in the situation in one rapid glance.

"Not me, cap, but it was these two ladies. Shore they're the heroes," Lintell said.

At that moment Eula Mae uttered a sigh and collapsed in a faint—right into Abe Johnson's arms.

"Wal, I'll be dog-gone!" McKenny ejaculated.

★

CHAPTER TWENTY-EIGHT

Hannah Lea Gibson stepped up on the porch of the Bar H, her home since she was six years old and one that she had visited only once in the last four months. But now it belonged to her. She turned and gazed out over the broad acres, where the afternoon shadows were creeping. The wide green pastures were dotted with horses, and far beyond, in a larger pasture cattle grazed. What a strange and tragic path that had brought her back to this place she had run away from those months ago. So much had happened. She was truly an orphan now.

She turned and with an almost reluctant step opened the door and entered the house. She stood for a long moment as her eyes became accustomed to the dimness then gazed about the empty room. In the corner where it always stood was her uncle's rifle. The furniture was still arranged as she remembered it, yet it was different; strangely still, disturbing in its silence. There was no familiar footstep or hardy voice to greet her.

With aimless step she wandered into the hall and into her uncle's office. She stared at the big desk and blinked back tears. After a moment she walked back out in the hall and on to the spotless kitchen.

Everything was in its place, just as Anita had left it. She stared at the door to the storeroom. Then as though waking from a trance she opened the door and kneeling pulled back the panel that concealed her old secret hiding place. Reaching inside she pulled out the canvass bag. Carrying it out into the light she untied the leather strings and opened it. There staring up at her was a stack of greenbacks. The seventy-five thousand dollars! She turned and placed it back where she found it and re-secured the panel. It would stay safe there until she could take it to the bank. She started back up the hall when the sound of horse's hoofs reached her ears. She hurried to the front door and uttered a glad cry when she saw the rider. She stepped out on the porch and crossed to the edge watching as Jack Lintell swung easily from the saddle.

"Jack," she called smiling brightly. "Welcome to the Bar H."

"I reckoned maybe you'd change the name," he said advancing up the porch steps until his eyes were on a level with hers.

"No, why should I?"

"I just thought, you know, with all that has happened . . ." he shrugged.

"Yes. Sometimes I have to pinch myself so I know I'm not dreaming."

"Are you going to be all right staying here alone?"

"Of course," she replied. "Sunset and Santone's still with me, and Laigs and Brazos have hit me up for a job—"

"I reckon that's good, then I won't feel so bad about moseying on—"

"Mosey—on!" she faltered.

"Shore, the murder case is closed, and the rustler gang's busted . . . and you're a big rancher now. So there's no need for me to hang around," he said easily.

A tremor went through Hannah. She stared, eyes searching his. His expression remained unchanged and slowly a flush spread across her cheeks. After a long moment she lifted her chin defiantly.

"No, I guess not," she said coldly.

"Well, I reckon this is so long then, Sprite," he said looking everywhere but at her.

"Yes, I guess it is. Goodbye Jack Lintell!"

She suddenly couldn't see through the film over her pupils and she turned away. She heard the clatter of hoofs as he spurred the big roan into a gallop. When the sound had faded into the distance Hannah sank upon the porch steps as tears streamed down her cheeks. It seemed she was disposed to momentary lapses of judgment. But this one was the cruelest of all. Oh, how could she have thought he cared for her! It had been only a job to him; only another case to be solved. She felt sick and old and unhappy.

Jack Lintell rode away from the ranch as the westerly sun sank low in the sky. He felt sick and old and unhappy. He was oblivious to the fragrant breeze soft in his face, the smell of dust that rose from the clip-clop of Colonel's tireless hoofs as he followed the road toward San Antonio. He was relieved at last to ride into town and shortly to see the hotel. He desperately needed companionship, and he would find it among his fellow rangers.

"Wal, Jack," McKenny said when he answered the door at Lintell's knock. "I didn't expect yu back so soon."

"Yeah, well, I reckon a feller shouldn't drag out goodbyes," Lintell replied gruffly, flopping into the stuffed chair and staring moodily at the wall.

"Haw," the old ranger captain exclaimed. "Yu rode out there te say goodbye?!"

"What else should I have done?" Lintell growled. "She's a rancher now; something she's always wanted. I don't reckon she wants to be tied down to me what with the poor wages we Texas Ranger's get."

"Sit down, son. I got something te say te yu!" McKenny said.

For long minutes Hannah sat on the porch steps crying her heart out. The sun had set when finally she stood and made her way back into the house. It was dark inside but she never lit a lamp but sought one of the over-stuffed chairs and sank into it. It was there that the morning sun struck her tear-stained cheeks through the open window. She sat unmoving for a moment as the sound of an approaching horse reached her ears. She suddenly leaped to her feet wiping frantically at her puffy cheeks staring at the door. She heard the clink of spurs crossing the porch then the door opened and Captain McKenny stepped into the room. He halted upon spying her.

"Oh," she sighed unhappily. "It's you."

"Wal, lass, I reckon yu look like hell."

"Don't, Uncle John," she snapped.

"I reckon Jack don't look much better," he said shrewdly. "It seems he didn't get much sleep last night either."

"Uncle John!" she cried.

"Wal, I had a long talk with that boy last evenin', but I don't reckon I got through te him thet yu might care fer him—"

"Care! Oh, it's him that doesn't care!"

"Wrong, lass. When I cussed him fer not carin' fer yu—he liked te tore my head off. His eyes were terrible. An' it all come out in a flood. Care fer yu? Thet's nothin' atall. He so deep in love with yu—aw, it's all there in his white face an' burnin' eyes. But I reckon he thinks now thet yu're rich, anythin' thet yu feel fer him is just plain gratitude—"

"Oh, Uncle John!" she sobbed throwing herself into his arms, hiding her scarlet face in his vest, crying incoherently. "Oh—Uncle John—if you're lying—it'll kill me!"

"True as gospel, lass. He made me swear not te tell yu, but I reckon I had te break thet oath. Now, what are yu goin' te do?"

The door to Lintell's hotel room swung open and Lintell looked up to see his friend Abe Johnson.

"Gol-dang but yu look like yu been run over an' drug by a freight wagon," declared Johnson. "Maybe I best tell Cap that yu ain't up fer no new assignment."

"I reckon action is what I need, Abe. What is it?"

"Wal, the victim is waitin' fer yu in the room down the hall. I reckon yu can get the real lowdown from her—"

"Her! Look Abe, I'm not in the mood to take another case involving a woman!"

"Look, Jack, Cap told me te have yu take care of it, so if yu ain't up te it yu'll have te explain it te the victim. An' I think yu ought te do it at once. She shore seems under a strain. Besides, I got a date with that little red head, Miss Eula Mae."

"Humph! Well, I'll damn shore take care of the matter," Lintell said getting to his feet. "What room is she in?"

"Two-seventeen right down the hall."

Lintell was tense when he knocked on the door to room two-seventeen. He didn't relish this confrontation but he didn't want to get involved in another case where a woman was concerned.

He heard a faint "Come in" and opened the door. Sunlight streamed in the one window giving a touch of warmth to the room. He saw no one at first, not until he heard a gasp and wheeled to see Hannah. She had been standing behind the door, waiting, her face white, her lips parted, her eyes wide and dark.

"Jack," she whispered.

She wore a white dress. Her face was lovely despite the havoc he read there. That mark of grief drew him as subtly as the love that welled up upon seeing her. But he stood unmoving as she took a hesitant step toward him. He could only watch stupefied.

"Jack," she whispered again. "I've decided to sell the ranch—"

"Sell it? Why would you do that?' he demanded.

"Because—because I—Oh, Jack Lintell, because I love you!" she said tremulously tears welling in her eyes.

"Hannah," he cried huskily holding out his arms. She flew to him, swaying the last step to his arms. She hid her face and clung to him.

"Jack—darling. I—I had to come," she said in smothered tone. "I had to tell you."

He held her close and tight to his breast his head bent against her golden curls. At the moment he couldn't see well. He seemed to float in the dim room.

"Jack, don't—hug me—so," she whispered almost inaudibly. "My wound—is still—pretty tender."

"Oh, I'm sorry!" he cried and moved to step back but she clung to him.

"Don't leave me—just not so tightly."

He held on to her, yet drew back so he could study her face.

"You can't sell the ranch!"

"Why not—?"

"You grew up on a ranch. It's in your blood—"

"Not anymore."

"How you figure that?"

"I don't reckon I'll need it—what with you and me together off chasing rustlers and such. But before we do, we'll have to get married. Then we'll take a long vacation. After all, I'm seventy-five thousand dollars richer, not counting the money from when I sell the ranch.

He stared down at her. "You're not gonna have money from the sale of the ranch."

"I'm not?"

"No, cause you're not selling it. And you're not going off chasing crooks with me!"

"No?"

"No, you're not!"

"You shore are being bossy . . . now that you found out that . . . well, you know," she said sulking prettily.

"That you love me? Shore, it makes me feel wonderful!"

She gave him a dazzling smile.

"But it don't give me much confidence that you'd ever see fit to obey me in anything—"

"Jack Lintell!" she gasped clearly affronted.

"Well, you never saw fit to pay attention to my orders before."

"I did too! Well, most of the time . . ."

He frowned.

"Some of the time . . . ?"

His frown deepened.

"All right," she amended sheepishly. "Maybe . . . once . . . ?" she sighed hopefully.

"Glad you finally admitted it," he grinned.

"But why can't I go with you—?"

"Because, I'm turning in my badge—"

"Oh! But you—"

"Hush and pay attention," he said. "I got a big reward from the ranchers, and shore a nice bonus from the rangers for breaking up the rustler gang, so I reckon I'm not penniless—"

"Oh," she blinked.

"What I'm trying to say is . . . well, I reckon we could pool our money and—aw heck, Sprite, I need you beside me—"

"You . . . need me . . . ?" she sighed.

"You bet I do! You've got to show me how to run this ranch," he said huskily.

She stared up at him, eyes shining. He grinned down at her.

"I love you, Sprite," he whispered. "We'll do it together, you and me. And it'll be the best dang ranch in the whole State of Texas."

"I know," she whispered just before his lips closed over hers.

THE END